DESTROYER

LEGEND OF THE IR'INDICTI SERIES, BOOK FIVE

CONNIE SUTTLE

Print Second Edition (2018)
Print ISBN: 1-63478-068-X
Print ISBN-13: 978-1-63478-068-1
eBook ISBN: 1-939759-14-5
eBook ISBN-13: 978-1-939759-14-6

Published by:
SubtleDemon Publishing, LLC
PO Box 95696
Oklahoma City, OK 73143

Cover art by Renee Barratt @ The Cover Counts

To Walter, Joe, Larry, Lee, Dianne, Sarah and Mark.
Thank you.

ACKNOWLEDGMENTS

As always, this book is the result of collaboration. If it weren't for the support of my editor, my cover artist and my beta readers, it would be less than it is. All mistakes, as usual, are mine and no other's.

About the Author:
Connie Suttle lives in Oklahoma with her husband and a conglomerate of cats. They have finally banded together to make their demands, which has proven disconcerting to all humans involved.

You may find Connie in the following ways:
Facebook: Connie Suttle Author
Twitter: @subtledemon
Website and Blog: subtledemon.com

Demon Lost

Demon Revealed

Demon's King

Demon's Quest

Demon's Revenge

Demon's Dream

God Wars Series:

Blood Double

Blood Trouble

Blood Revolution

Blood Love

Blood Finale

Saa Thalarr Series:

Hope and Vengeance

Wyvern and Company

Observe and Protect*

First Ordinance Series:

Finder

Keeper

BlackWing

SpellBreaker

WhiteWing

Black Rose Queen

Queen of Thorns and Roses*

Other Titles from SubtleDemon Publishing:

Malefactor

Transgressor

by Joe Scholes

*Forthcoming

FOREWORD

A note about the locations in this series:

Cloud Chief, Oklahoma is a real ghost town, located near Cordell, Oklahoma. All of the land is now privately owned and the Cloud Chief community portrayed in this book is fictitious in nature.

CHAPTER 1

"An earthquake measuring eight point six on the Richter scale has been reported from a very localized area of Quebec," the newscaster announced as Winkler spoke on his cell with Matt Michaels.

The television was merely noise in the background as Matt reported that more than twenty Elemaiya had been killed in the old Chicago sewers; mostly by vampires. The Elemaiya had a reason to be afraid of vampires; they could move faster than most Elemaiya could think to relocate or defend themselves.

"Only minor injuries," Matt said. "I am more than happy with the results."

"I've got bad news on this end," Winkler said, "the kid has disappeared again and this time he took Salidar DeLuca with him. We can't find either boy. I was hoping you'd seen him, even though I'd ground him if he showed up there."

"He wasn't here—not that we saw, anyway. There's no evidence."

"I've got all of mine out looking in the likely places, and Andy is checking to see if he's using his debit card anywhere. That's how we found him the last time."

"Wait, what am I thinking? Hold on a minute," Matt yelled at someone to get a trace on Ashe's watch. "He was wearing the watch, wasn't he?" Matt asked.

"Yeah. Last time we saw him, he had it on," Winkler confirmed.

"Got it, sir," Winkler heard the voice from somewhere near Matt. "Mr. Michaels, that signal is coming from Quebec. Right where the earthquake happened."

"Earthquake?" Winkler and Matt Michaels chorused.

"Young one, do not fret, he isn't dead." Griffin, the tall, mysterious stranger knelt beside Ashe's limp body as Sali shivered and attempted to locate a number on his cell. The phone wasn't getting reception.

"Are you sure? I can't wake him up," Sali moaned, dropping onto the grass again. He'd been trying to wake Ashe for what seemed a very long time.

"He used up every bit of energy he had to force the Elemaiya to leave," Griffin said gently. "Here, help me get him up. Providing transportation usually doesn't count as interference. Usually." A comforting smile played about Griffin's mouth.

"But," Sali said before he disappeared from Quebec and reappeared inside Winkler's kitchen, causing Winkler to jump and curse loudly.

"Calm down, he's just unconscious. You might be, too, if you'd just caused an earthquake and kept it from spreading past a half-mile radius," Griffin laid Ashe's body on the large kitchen island. "He'll be hungry when he wakes." Griffin disappeared.

"Get that nurse on the phone," Winkler barked at Trace, who skidded into the kitchen. Trace made the call while Sali went to a cabinet in Winkler's kitchen, pulled out a glass, filled it with cold water and dumped it in Ashe's face. Ashe woke, sputtering and coughing, water dripping from his face and hair as he attempted to sit up.

"Whoa, kid," Winkler helped Ashe sit up when he saw how shaky Ashe actually was. "Come on, I have it on good authority that you're starving or something. Salidar, call your father and tell him you're safe and sound. Then I want you to tell me exactly what you two have been doing."

~

Ashe finished two protein drinks on the way to the restaurant. Trajan and Ace met Winkler, Trace and both boys in the parking lot of Pasquale's, a steak and seafood restaurant on the south end of Port Aransas. They'd decided to give Victoria's a wide berth since Adele was working.

"Kid, I never thought I'd see anybody who could eat more than a werewolf," Winkler spoke quietly as Ashe devoured a prime rib with a plate of spaghetti.

"Mr. Winkler, I thought I was going to pass out before all of them left."

"Who?"

"The Elemaiya," Sali answered for Ashe, who'd stuffed a bite of prime rib in his mouth. "They were all dressed for battle, Mr. Winkler. You should have seen it. The Roman army couldn't come close to that."

"Going to war," Ashe mumbled around a mouth filled with food. "Only way I could stop them."

"Why did you stop them, Ashe? I don't understand this." Winkler leaned back in his seat, confused by the entire incident. "We'd be better off if they killed each other."

"Can't happen. Chain reaction," Ashe muttered, twirling spaghetti around his fork and raising it to his mouth.

"Chain reaction?" Winkler was more confused than ever. "You're going to have to explain yourself, son."

"Salidar," Marcus walked in with Marco close behind him. "I hear you went missing for a little while, and now I hear you had something to do with that earthquake in Canada." Marcus' voice held anger and his dark eyes narrowed as he frowned at Sali.

"Dad, I didn't have anything to do with that," Sali tapped his chest with an index finger. "You'll have to ask Ashe about it."

"Not telling you anything," Ashe mumbled and refused to talk. Marcus growled.

"Marcus, take Sali and go, if that's why you're here," Winkler growled back. The full moon was too near for two Alpha werewolves to be at odds and in such close proximity. Trajan and Trace stood; ready to take on the Star Cove Packmaster. Marco pulled Marcus away and Sali slunk along behind them.

"Awkward," Ashe said as Trace and Trajan sat down again. "Should have left Sali at home."

"And perhaps you should have stayed home as well," Winkler snapped.

Ashe looked up from his food and stared at the Dallas Packmaster. Winkler acted as the hidden Second for the Grand Master, but few knew it. Ashe was one of those few. "Mr. Winkler, you'll have to trust me on this. I had to go. I would have stopped Mr. Michaels if I could have. Neither of you know exactly what you're dealing with."

"Do *you* know what we're dealing with?" Winkler tossed up a hand in disbelief.

"A little better than I did," Ashe said, buttering a dinner roll and biting into it. "Mr. Michaels will likely be sorry he did what he did. He killed the Dark King's brother."

"Ashe, you're not proving Marcus right, are you? You're not sympathizing with the—well, those people?" Winkler recalled at the last moment that he was in public and the waiter was on his way to refill iced tea glasses.

"No, Mr. Winkler. I sympathize with innocents. The Earth is filled with them, remember?"

"Kid, I have a headache and you're talking in riddles. I'm not sure you know what you're saying right now," Winkler said, pinching the bridge of his nose. "Finish your dinner and let's get out of here. I'll have the nurse check you over."

"Suit yourself." Ashe shrugged and went back to his food.

～

"Could be a little anemic," the werewolf nurse looked Ashe over after they arrived in Star Cove. "But a few good meals should take care of that," he added. "With lots of protein and iron."

"Mr. Winkler, I felt almost the same after the thing with the water," Ashe remarked while slipping on his shirt. The nurse had him take it off for the brief examination.

"So what did you do, then?"

"Well, it wasn't quite this bad, and I cleaned Betsy's out on chicken and dumplings." Ashe referred to the best diner in Cordell, Oklahoma. Winkler paid the nurse with a wad of cash and sent him out the door. He grinned and told Winkler to call anytime. Winkler just waved and shut the door behind the werewolf.

"Now, young man, I want to ground you, but I'll trust you this time and accept that you somehow needed to be where you were. A little heads-up next time so we won't run around like scared rabbits?" Winkler lifted an eyebrow at Ashe.

"I know. I'll try not to worry you next time."

"Sounds good. This isn't the best thing, so close to the full moon," Trajan patted Ashe's back. "Man, I thought we'd lost you and Sali both."

"Trajan, I'll do my best to send mindspeech next time," Ashe climbed off the barstool at the island. "I'm really tired and I'd like to go to bed, now."

"Yeah, get some rest, kid. They're holding Hayes' service in the morning. Did you want to go?" Winkler asked.

"I don't know. What do Hayes' parents want?"

"I think they want all his classmates there, to see him off," Winkler sighed. "This is hitting them terribly hard."

"Yeah. I know," Ashe muttered.

"Don't dwell on that—we understand that you can't be in two places at once."

"I wish I could," Ashe said. "Goodnight, Mr. Winkler. Trajan. Trace." Ashe walked toward his bedroom that doubled as an office. If things went as planned, the move to the beach house would happen

Friday after the service for Hayes, which would be held deep in Shirley Walker's groves.

～

"Salidar, tell me exactly what you saw," Marcus demanded. Denise stood with Marco inside the DeLuca kitchen, watching as Marcus grilled his youngest son. Sali squirmed uncomfortably. Finally, deciding that Winkler had likely gotten the same information from Ashe, Sali described everything he'd witnessed in Canada.

"Ashe can't have caused an earthquake. That's just not plausible," Marcus raked fingers through his dark hair. "It was just a coincidence."

"Even the authorities are saying they don't know why it didn't affect any other area—something that big would have," Denise ventured to say.

"Denise, don't interrupt," Marcus growled. Denise kept quiet after that.

～

"You're saying the boy did this?" Wlodek spoke with Edmond over the phone. Edmond and Hector had listened outside the DeLuca home while Marcus questioned Sali. Eavesdropping was the best way to get information that might have stayed with the werewolves, otherwise.

"That's what the young werewolf says. He insists that Ashe Evans transported him to Quebec, kept him shielded—that was his term— shielded, walked through an entire camp of Elemaiya without raising a stir and then appeared between two armies. The werewolf boy says Ashe lowered the shields of those armies and talked with the leaders from both sides before an attack was precipitated by one side. Ashe then caused the earthquake to stop the battle and send all of them on their way."

"Quite fascinating," Wlodek murmured. "You're sure of what you heard?"

"I have an excellent memory, Honored One. Those words are verbatim."

"Why is he still so young?" Wlodek whispered. "We have so many uses for him."

"As you say, Honored One," Edmond said respectfully. "Casimir can make the turn immediately if you ask it. We will take the boy while he sleeps. According to the young werewolf, Ashe is quite exhausted after the episode in Canada."

"No doubt," Wlodek observed dryly. "Nevertheless, he is still underage and the risks of turning at this point are too great. Perhaps if we have need of him, we can use his father to bring him to us. If strong vampires supervise him, he should do as he is bid. Especially under compulsion."

"I imagine that Hancock and his sire might keep him in line."

"Just as I was thinking," Wlodek agreed. "But we are speaking in hypotheticals at the moment, are we not? Keep a watch on the boy. He will be more than useful to us in the future."

"We will do as you say, Honored One." Wlodek hung up first. Edmond hit the end call on his cell more slowly.

Ashe had used up what little energy he had to become mist and hover over Edmond's head. Mentally sighing, he misted back to his bedroom where an illusion of him lay as if sleeping on his cot. "Messed up, messed up, messed up," he pounded his pillow before flopping down on it with a frustrated sigh.

Rabis watched as the Queen paced. She muttered profanities under her breath as she trod the same ground repeatedly. Rabis wisely kept quiet. He knew, if she didn't, what might have happened had Parlethis taken the Dark King's crown and handed it to Friesianna. The two could never be used together. Never.

The Queen refused to heed the H'Morr's warnings and lusted after Baltis' crown anyway, just as Baltis coveted hers. Long ago, Rabis and his father, Saldis, had foreseen what might happen if both crowns were used together. It would be disastrous.

Saldis had given his life for his son Rabis, so Friesianna would never know the true author of the H'Morr. Rabis kept his head bowed as if in deference to his Queen while she continued her rant. Parlethis, too, kept quiet. Rabis knew it was the only thing keeping Parlethis' head and body connected at the moment.

"Contact our spies," Friesianna snapped after stopping in mid-pace. "See if they have discovered Baltis' new hiding place."

"Yes, my Queen." Parlethis was happy to escape her presence intact.

~

Baltis was more than displeased and three of his captains lay dead at his feet. They'd ran like frightened hares when the ground began to shake. Baltis punished them as they deserved.

His brother was dead. Baltis had no idea where the humans had taken his brother's body—Wildrif was still weeping over the ordeal at the lake and could tell him nothing. Laridael had brought the quarter-blood along, although he was also mourning his lost brother. Laridael's twin, Liridael, had died beside the Prince.

"Come, Laridael, we must plot revenge against the humans for our brothers' deaths," Baltis said. Laridael nodded and obediently followed his King through the sands toward the King's tent.

~

"Kid, you may have to slow down a little," Winkler grinned as Ashe finished off his second ham steak for breakfast.

"I'm good now," Ashe sighed, leaning back in his seat. The breakfast restaurant in Star Cove served up good, plain fare seven days a week. Ashe's cell rang as he watched Winkler finish a cup of coffee. "Sal, what is it?" Ashe said without looking at the phone before answering.

"Just wondering if you're coming to the service, dude," Sali replied.

"I'm coming," Ashe replied.

"We'll bring him," Trajan offered, knowing Sali would hear.

"Good. See you there," Sali said and hung up. Ashe's cell rang again before he could return it to his pocket.

"Randy?" Ashe said when he answered the call—again without looking.

"Ashe, are you available for dinner tonight? I'd like you to meet Sara." Ashe looked up at Winkler who nodded slightly.

"Yeah. What time?"

"Around seven?" Randy asked. "Her plane gets in at five, so that will give us enough time to check her into the hotel and meet somewhere. I'll let you know where, later."

"Sounds good," Ashe said and hung up. This time the cell did go into his pocket.

∾

"Just wear something comfortable," Winkler said later. "No shorts," he called out as Ashe went to dress for Hayes' service. Winkler drove to Shirley Walker's groves, something he normally let someone else do for him. Ace had come along and went to stand immediately with Wynn the moment they arrived at the designated spot.

Ashe, his light-brown hair blown by the breeze rustling through groves of grapefruit trees, followed Winkler, Trace and Trajan to a grassy clearing lying near the center of Shirley's extensive orchards. The carved, wooden coffin was already there, with several werewolves standing vigil.

"It's tradition if you die a hero," Trace whispered to Ashe. "Six werewolves stand guard through the night."

"Then James Johnson should have had the same," Ashe said quietly.

"Ashe, what do you know?" Winkler dropped back to walk beside his ward.

"I can't explain it right now," Ashe replied. "Maybe later."

~

Mr. Dodd, the history teacher, delivered the eulogy. He spoke about sacrifice and lives taken too soon. Ashe watched Buck and his mother, who stood next to Hayes' parents. Not once did Adele glance in his direction.

~

"I'm sorry I didn't get here sooner," Ashe informed the prisoner. Somehow, Chad and Jeremy had imprisoned the man in an old, abandoned bunker left over from the early nineteen-sixties nuclear war scare. Ashe didn't expect the man to be forthcoming about his true nature. Not immediately, anyway.

Lifting his eyes, Lewis Sharpe shivered inside his six-by-six foot prison. The young werewolf and shapeshifter had dumped his drugged body in the cage two weeks earlier. Their visits had been sporadic to provide food and water, and he'd been without for three days. He still couldn't understand how a shifter had collaborated with a werewolf against one of their own.

"Come on," Ashe was somehow inside the cage, helping Lewis up without opening the door. Lewis, thinking he was hallucinating—people didn't walk through barred cages, after all—allowed the tall youth to pull him off the concrete floor. Ashe slipped a shoulder beneath Lewis' arm and disappeared with his burden.

"You have to be quiet here," Ashe told Lewis as he set a glass of water on the kitchen island for the former prisoner. Lewis blinked dark eyes at Ashe before gulping the water thirstily, his hand shaking as he held the glass.

"Slow down, you don't need to choke, there's plenty more," Ashe did his best to calm Lewis. "I'm Ashe, by the way. Ashe Evans. I have canned and packaged food in the pantry, here," Ashe pointed to the small pantry in question. He'd taken Lewis to the hidden room beneath Winkler's new beach house. "So, what will it be? Canned soup, spaghetti or chili?"

"Kid, who are you?" Lewis rasped, coming to his senses. His reddish-brown hair was shaggy and needed washing, as did the rest of him. Ashe was glad he didn't have a werewolf's sensitive nose; Lewis needed a shower in the worst way.

He required food and water first, however, and Ashe wasn't about to call the man to task about his hygiene. It wasn't his fault, after all. When Winkler and the others questioned Chad and Jeremy, they hadn't asked about potential prisoners. Ashe had picked up remnants of extreme sadness emanating from Lewis, who'd determined that he'd been left to die in his cage.

"I'm just a not so average kid," Ashe replied. "Tell me who you are. I promise to get you home by Monday."

"What day is it?" Lewis asked. "And I'm Lewis. Lewis Sharpe, from Russellville, Arkansas."

"It's Friday, August eighth," Ashe replied. "Full moon is," Lewis finished Ashe's sentence for him.

"Sunday," Lewis muttered hopelessly.

"It's all right," Ashe reassured the shapeshifter. "My mom shifts into a peregrine falcon on full moons."

"Your mother's a shifter?" Lewis asked, blinking at Ashe in confusion. Ashe emptied a can of spaghetti into a bowl and shoved it into the microwave while the man continued to stare at Ashe.

"Yeah. But things are a little strained at the moment. Don't worry, you're as safe as you can be for now, and as soon as you finish eating, there's a washer and dryer behind those doors in the center of the room, a bathroom and shower past that plus that bed over there so you can rest. I'm sorry there's no door in or out of this place, but if you're quiet, nobody else will know you're here until I come back."

"If there's no door," Lewis lifted the fork Ashe placed before him and dipped into the bowl of microwaved spaghetti, "How did you get in here to begin with?"

"The same way I'm getting out," Ashe replied. "You'll hear noise above your head all day—people will be moving in. There's nothing to worry about as long as you stay quiet, all right? At least until I can explain things to the owner."

"Kid, you just hauled me away from certain death. I think I can stay quiet for a little while. Especially since that cabinet is filled with food and there's plenty of water." Lewis nodded toward the kitchen sink where Ashe stood.

"There's probably soda and juice in the fridge, but you needed water first," Ashe said. "I have to go before people start looking for me." Lewis' fork dropped from numb fingers when Ashe disappeared before his eyes.

CHAPTER 2

"$\mathcal{I}$'m getting my computer unhooked," Ashe called out when Winkler half-shouted his name.

"Son," Winkler stood in the doorway to Ashe's room that doubled as an office and bedroom, "as soon as you get that stuff carried out to the van, we'll go on. I've got movers coming for the rest."

"All right, Mr. Winkler. It'll only take a few more minutes." Ashe knew Winkler was feeling the approaching full moon, just like the other wolves. Andy had growled at somebody earlier, and that wasn't like Winkler's trusted assistant. Ashe placed the computer and monitor in a box, the power cords, battery backup and surge protectors in another.

The files he was working went into a third box. Andy wanted those to go with them on the first trip. Ashe knew now he was working on investigations Matt Michaels had turned over to Winkler. Ashe misted the first box out, followed quickly by the second and third while Winkler watched from the doorway, a cup of coffee in his hand.

"Does this mean you're done now?" Winkler asked dryly when Ashe showed up again after the last box.

"Yeah. Let's get the hell out of Dodge," Ashe quipped, walking toward the door this time. Winkler grinned and tousled Ashe's hair before following him out.

"The Grand Master and Thomas Williams will be here tomorrow afternoon," Winkler said as they walked to the van parked in the driveway. "Kids will fly down from Dallas tonight," he added.

"The Grand Master wants to talk to the prisoners?" Ashe asked.

"Yep. Thomas will likely come with him. He's a good friend of Weldon's, as was his dad. Thomas, Sr. gave his life to protect the Grand Master around thirty years ago. Weldon won't ever forget that."

"Mr. Winkler, how much control do you have right now?" Ashe asked. They stood inside Winkler's suite of rooms, watching while new furniture was delivered and placed. Winkler's new cook and house staff had arrived already to supervise.

"As good as can be expected," Winkler said softly.

"How good would you be around, let's say, a shapeshifter who becomes a deer?" Winkler, who'd been watching while a massive bed frame was put together, jerked around to face Ashe.

"Kid, is this gonna give me a headache?" Winkler asked.

"Probably." Ashe hunched his shoulders uncomfortably. "He says his name is Lewis Sharpe, from Russellville, Arkansas. Chad and Jeremy kidnapped him to throw a wrench into the works come Sunday night. He's down in the hidden room in the basement."

"Things can't help but happen around you, can they?" Winkler pulled out his cell and called Alvin "Bear" Wright.

"Principal Wright here," Bear answered.

"Bear, we have one of yours over here; perhaps you should intercede on his behalf since he was kidnapped by a werewolf and a shapeshifter."

"I'll come get you, Mr. Wright," Ashe offered, knowing the shapeshifting Principal would hear.

"Good," Bear said and hung up.

"I'll go out in the hall," Ashe said. "Meet me downstairs?"

"I'll bring Trajan," Winkler nodded.

"No more than that—I'm not sure a deer feels that comfortable around wolves," Ashe muttered.

"Not sure I would, either," Winkler acknowledged dryly. "We'll be there waiting." Ashe made sure nobody was there to see before he relocated to Bear Wright's front door and rang the doorbell.

"What have you been up to, young one?" Bear asked when he answered the door, hauling a freshly laundered knit shirt over his head. Ashe found himself liking the bear shapeshifter more and more as time went by. There wasn't anything formal or stiff about Bear Wright.

"Mr. Wright, Chad and Jeremy kidnapped a shapeshifter from Russellville, Arkansas," Ashe explained when Bear's head popped into the neck of the shirt and the fabric settled over his muscled torso. "And I may need your help come Sunday night."

"Kid, I'll do what I can," Bear nodded. "Let's go talk to this shifter."

"Ready?" Ashe asked the moment he landed Bear in Winkler's basement.

"Waitin' on you—what took so long?" Trajan teased.

"I'll remember you said that the next time you want to go somewhere," Ashe said. "We'll try not to freak out Mr. Sharpe."

Mr. Sharpe did freak anyway, jumping when Ashe reappeared with three others. Lewis had a bath towel wrapped around himself while the dryer hummed in the background. He was sipping a soda and watching television when he was startled by visitors.

"Son, these are friends," Bear Wright said immediately, nodding toward Winkler and Trajan. "We've got those two miscreants who took you locked up; we just didn't think to ask them if there was any other criminal activity committed beyond the murder of a young werewolf here in Texas."

"They killed somebody? I'm not surprised," Lewis reached out a hand to shake with Bear. He could tell by scent that the Star Cove Principal was a shapeshifter, just as he knew that Winkler and Trajan were werewolves.

"This is William Winkler and his Second, Trajan Gibson," Bear finished the introductions.

"As in *Winkler Security* William Winkler?" Lewis held out his hand. "Damn. Never figured you were a wolf. I'm a deputy for the Russellville Sheriff's department. At least I was, till those two shot me with a tranquilizer gun and locked me in a cage, somewhere."

"About six miles from here, in Shirley Walker's cotton fields," Ashe nodded in the proper direction. "I figure they hauled him here on one of their trips and left him in that bomb shelter. He was about to starve when I found him."

"What were they planning to do with you?" Bear asked.

"They said a distraction on the full moon. That's all I know," Lewis replied with a shrug. "Is there any chance I can borrow a phone? I have people to call."

"Hold on a little," Winkler raised a hand while he pulled his cell out of a pocket with the other. In seconds, he had Matt Michaels on the line. "Matt, we need to run a little interference for a missing deputy from Russellville, Arkansas," Winkler said when Matt answered.

"I heard about that," Matt said, tapping on his laptop. "You have him?"

"We do, now. The kid found him in an old bunker not far from here. Tranquilized and kidnapped by those two we have locked up."

"I'll call the Arkansas Bureau. We'll take care of it," Matt said. "He'll have his job back and no questions asked."

"Tell them he'll be in touch come Monday," Winkler said. "Trajan, get Trace on the phone and have him pick up some clothes for Deputy Sharpe."

"Dude, isn't Arkansas one of the worst places to be a deer shapeshifter?" Ashe asked softly. Lewis Sharpe barked a laugh.

~

"Mr. Tanner, we have to do it on the full moon. Our target is moving into the fortress today—two weeks ahead of schedule, according to my informant."

"Then I hope your informant is prepared to help," Zeke Tanner growled. Josiah hadn't wanted to make the call; he knew Zeke would be more out of sorts than usual this close to the full moon. He just didn't want his head snapped off by the rogue werewolf.

"My informant will most certainly be ready to go," Josiah did a bit of growling himself.

"Good. I want a call, first thing Monday," Zeke said and hung up. Josiah ended the call with a sigh; he had last minute plans to make.

Ashe eyed his new bedroom furniture critically, trying to decide if he liked everything where it was. "I want the bed here," he said, gesturing with his hands. "So I can see the water when I wake up in the morning."

The set was moved before the mattress and box spring were placed. Ashe gave a thumbs-up to the furniture delivery crew. The mattress was settled on the bed and Ashe pulled the new comforter and sheets from his closet to make it up; his clothes and other belongings had arrived an hour earlier.

Lewis had gone home with Bear Wright to talk about his kidnapping with the Star Cove Principal. Ashe knew Bear also wanted to discuss organizing the shapeshifter community with the Arkansas deputy.

Ashe pulled his cell out the moment it rang. "Randy?"

"Ashe, meet us at Pasquale's," Randy said. "About fifteen minutes. Can you make that?"

"Sure," Ashe replied.

"Mr. Winkler, Trajan, I'm meeting Randy at Pasquale's," Ashe announced as he walked into the spacious kitchen. Winkler's new cook, a werewolf named Craig, was busy preparing a meal for the others while familiarizing himself with the new kitchen. He looked up from his work when Ashe entered.

"Be home by eleven," Winkler said, sipping a mixed drink Craig handed to the Dallas Packmaster.

"Will do, boss," Ashe nodded and walked out, disappearing before he reached the front door.

∿

"What's up with the kid?" Craig asked as he handed a plate of appetizers to Trajan and Winkler.

"Don't upset him; his parents have pretty much abandoned him," Winkler said. "I'm his legal guardian, so treat him just like one of my kids."

"He's a talented shapeshifter," Trajan added, pulling two crab cakes onto a plate. "I wouldn't get on his bad side, if I were you."

"Why? What can a shapeshifter do to a werewolf?" Craig asked, snorting derisively.

"Fry you, to start with," Trajan said.

"You're such a kidder," Craig said and went back to his cooking.

∿

"Ashe, this is Sara." Randy couldn't stop the helpless grin from spreading across his face. Sara, perky and smiling, with short, red hair curling riotously due to the beach humidity, took Ashe's hand when he held it out. Ashe stiffened and went completely still.

"Ashe? Ashe, what's wrong?" It took Randy nearly a minute to get Ashe's attention again. Sara had stared at Ashe, her smile disappearing the moment Ashe had taken her hand. Ashe blinked and let Sara's hand go.

"I'm sorry about your dad," Ashe said. "Really sorry. Please, sit down. I'll be all right in a minute." Randy watched, concerned, as both Sara and Ashe sat at the table, Ashe rubbing his forehead as if he had a headache. Sara appeared frightened.

"Sara, it's nothing to worry about," Ashe's blue eyes studied her face. "I just see things, now and then. It's what I am. Randy, if you take her to your mother after this, you need to tell Sara that she's a werewolf first."

"Ashe," Randy hissed. That was information he wasn't prepared to give. Sara need never know.

"Dude, Sara's a shifter. A small one. I've already dealt with one shifter today who might make a meal for the Pack. Sara's another one of those."

Sara was now staring at Randy in shock. "Your mother's a *werewolf?*" she squeaked. "You're not a wolf, Randy, your scent is human. How did you know about my dad?" She turned to Ashe, her eyes troubled. "And we shouldn't be talking about this in a public place!"

"I have us shielded, nobody will hear," Ashe muttered, knowing Sara was upset and Randy angry.

"Ashe, how in the name of hell?" Randy stared at Ashe.

"Dude, we'll have a talk soon. You don't remember a lot of things because the vampires don't want it."

"There are vampires?" Sara hissed.

"My dad is a vampire," Ashe sighed. "At least the one I think of as my dad. I really don't know who my real father is. Or my mother. The waiter's coming," he added. Randy drew in a breath—the waiter was approaching from behind Ashe. How could he know?

"But," Sara began. She couldn't decide whether to stay or get up and walk out. How did this sixteen-year-old know anything about her? How?

"Baby, don't," Randy reached out a hand and covered hers with his. Sara sat back with a sigh, still trying to get her heart to beat normally again.

Don't worry, I'm just different, Ashe sent mindspeech to Sara, who jerked in her seat while the waiter poured water into glasses and prepared to take drink orders.

~

"I've got eight coming in next weekend," Bear informed Lewis, passing a soft drink to the shifter. They sat in Bear's makeshift office inside his Star Cove home. "Some of them are Old Ones."

"You managed to get them to agree to a meeting?" Lewis popped the tab on the soda can to drink.

"I know a couple of them really well. They convinced a third one to come with them," Bear nodded. "I'd like a representative from every faction, if I can get it."

"How old are the two that you know?" Lewis asked.

"One is nearly four hundred," Bear said. "The other is around three hundred, I think."

"My dad told me stories about the Old Ones when I was little," Lewis said. "He told me that a shapeshifter married a wizard and that's where the Old Ones came from."

"I don't know what happened, truthfully, and they won't talk about it," Bear said. "But something happened to give them longer lives. What I do know in each case was they had shifters for mothers. No information at all on the fathers."

"And no way to find out," Lewis muttered. "I wish I could make it back for that meeting, though, but I've been away from work too long as it is. If Mr. Winkler hadn't gotten Matt Michaels on the phone, I might have some tall explaining to do over this without letting anything slip."

"Those two boys are scheduled for termination and rightly so," Bear nodded. "And there's something else going on, I just don't know what it is."

"That Ashe kid is something else."

"To put it mildly. I'll get you back to Winkler's tonight; you don't need to be anywhere near Star Cove when the vampires rise." Lewis stared in shock at Bear's words.

~

"Sara, you're safe, I promise," Randy had dragged Ashe along to his mother's home, just in case. Ashe made no comment as Randy reassured his girlfriend. He'd watched Sali as he drove past with Dori in his car as Ashe had ridden into Star Cove in Randy's back seat. Sali was likely taking Dori to a movie, with pizza planned afterward. Ashe sighed. Those things didn't seem to be in the cards for him. Marco, too, was out on a date with Cori.

Randy used a key to get in the front door of Dawn Smith's Star Cove home, calling out to her as he walked inside, followed by Sara, who walked timidly as if she were stepping on eggshells. Ashe patted her shoulder reassuringly as she looked around, sniffing the werewolf scent, most likely.

"So," Dawn met them in the media room, her eyes going straight to Sara while her nostrils flared at Sara's scent. "What's your animal, girl?"

⁓

"Wildrif, you will stop this incessant weeping and inform me as to which installation will be easiest to breach? And you will also use your contacts to find human explosives. I have no care what kind. My soldiers will relocate inside this *base* thing, plant the explosives and then leave immediately. We will see how they accept retaliation from the Dark Elemaiya."

Baltis hissed the last words while Wildrif sniffled and wiped his nose on a sleeve. Baltis exercised his last bit of patience as the quarter-blood then wiped his mismatched eyes and stared up at the Dark King.

"I must consider this," Wildrif dropped his gaze, staring at his shoes instead. The Dark King had not taken thought for Wildrif's comfort or mode of dress—Wildrif's shoes were nearly worn out, as was his clothing.

The quarter-blood seer could only think of his time with Obediah Tanner, who was now deceased. Obediah hadn't treated him respectfully either, but at least Wildrif had been dressed better and had gotten regular meals. Now he was forced to beg for his dinner from the cooks in the Dark King's camp.

The deserts of Arizona could be just as unforgiving as anything Wildrif had ever seen, and it made him wish for the relocation talent that the half and full Elemaiya possessed. He cursed his half-blood mother for birthing him as a quarter-blood and thanked the day she'd died in battle against the Bright ones.

"Think quickly, Wildrif; I wish for the human authorities to know my justice is swift. They shall pay for my brother's life," Baltis flipped his dark-red robe and stalked away from the filthy seer.

"Yes, but my justice runs long and deep," Wildrif muttered when no one could hear. "*Long and deep.*"

⁓

"Ashe, find an excuse to get us out of here," Randy muttered softly as his mother puttered about the kitchen, talking over Sara at every opportunity. Sara had sunk into quiet misery as Dawn spoke of this or that.

Randy was shocked when Sara didn't want to give her animal away to his mother, but Dawn kept chipping away at the pretty veterinarian until Sara admitted she was a rabbit. Ashe knew that feeling—as the bumblebee bat, he recognized the ridicule when your animal didn't stack up to larger, stronger predators.

"Look, I promised Mr. Winkler I'd be home soon," Ashe said, looking pointedly at the watch Matt Michaels had given him. "Randy, I really need to go. Don't need to get Mr. Winkler or Trace all riled up," he added.

"We'll go, then. Mom, thanks for the sodas," Randy leaned over to peck his mother on the cheek. Sara waited until they were out the door to breathe a relieved sigh.

"Baby, I didn't know it was gonna be like that, I promise," Randy placed an arm about Sara's shoulders and led her to his small Chevy.

"Look, I can get myself home," Ashe said as Randy and Sara climbed into the car. "Sara, really, don't let this bother you. If it'll help, I'll show you my animal. Trust me, yours is nothing to be ashamed of," Ashe said.

"You don't have to," Sara said, but Ashe was already flapping before her face, his clothing dropping onto the concrete drive in a heap.

"Oh, my gosh, it's a bumblebee bat," Sara laughed and clapped her hands. Ashe, smiling mentally, knew that as a veterinarian, Sara would know exactly what he was. "They're endangered," she added. Ashe knew that, too.

Go with Randy, Ashe sent mindspeech to her. *Things will work out. I promise.* Ashe flapped away on the ocean breeze, leaving Randy, Sara and his clothing behind.

"I'll get it," Randy sighed. Lifting Ashe's clothes from the driveway, he tossed them into the back seat of his car. "Let's go, sweetheart. I owe you a drink, and it'll be something a little stiffer than soda."

"Kid, I don't think I've ever seen you come home nekkid before," Trace grinned as Ashe walked out of his closet, dressed only in cargo shorts.

Pulling his watch and cell to him from the back of Randy's vehicle, Ashe tossed both on the bed and then summoned a shirt from the closet. Ashe was dressed again quickly, shoving the cell in his pocket and buckling the watchband around his wrist.

"I wish I knew how you do that," Trace sighed, surprised again when a pair of shoes sailed out of Ashe's closet and landed in the young man's hand.

"It's easy—a few Elemaiya can do it—it's called summoning," Ashe explained. "And that reminds me, I have to pay Sali's speeding ticket online and send a gift to a friend."

"Sal got a speeding ticket? Does his father know?" Trace made himself comfortable on the new chair inside Ashe's bedroom.

"I don't know. It'll be classic Sali to tell Marcus DeLuca everything he can about me and leave a little matter like a speeding ticket out of the narration," Ashe flopped onto the side of his new bed and ran fingers through slightly curly brown hair.

"He was your friend—a good one, once upon a time," Trace pointed out.

"Yeah. I wish I could get the old Sali back. Now, all I have is the new Sali, no parents and strange vampires who report every move they see me make to the Head of the Council."

"How do you know that?" Trace asked, watching Ashe closely.

"I can mist, remember? They can't see, hear or smell me while I'm like that. I can hover right over their heads while they spill everything they know right to Wlodek. The old bastard."

Ashe bounced off the bed and went to stare out his bedroom window. The moon, nearly full, hung low over the gulf water. Ashe could see the waves piling up on the shore below. With his acute hearing, he could hear them as well.

"Kid, I'd take you to my parents in a heartbeat if I had my way," Trace said softly and walked out of Ashe's bedroom.

"Yeah." Ashe wiped away a bit of wetness from his cheeks.

"We will wait until after the full moon and demand that he be brought to us," Wlodek informed Aedan Evans, who sat before his desk, next to Anthony Hancock. Gavin Montegue, Anthony's surrogate sire and also an Assassin for the Council, stood nearby, examining a few titles written in Latin on Wlodek's bookshelves.

"These rogues are multiplying, and we must deal with them swiftly before they recruit others to their cause. It cannot be helped that they lost most of their holdings in this financial crisis. Instead of working to regain their wealth, they are looking to take it, instead."

Wlodek sighed at the financial state of affairs across the globe. He and many others had sunk a large portion of their holdings into gold bullion and had not suffered. Others had chosen to invest their wealth in other things. Fortunes had been lost—Wlodek knew this. Old vampires, being proud, would not ask for assistance. Instead, a few had decided to go rogue and take what they could from humans.

"What do you believe Ashe might be able to do for you?" Aedan asked coldly. His face betrayed no emotion, but inside he was terrified. Terrified that Wlodek would take his child and break the rules, making him a vampire at age sixteen. That age was much too early, and Aedan had no desire for his child to be turned without his fully informed consent. Charles, Wlodek's assistant, sat quietly in a corner, typing the details of the meeting into his laptop.

"Perhaps you have not been privy to recent events," Wlodek said, just as coldly. "You have separated yourself from your family. While I fail to understand your motives, I have my contacts inside the community now and have heard much. Perhaps it is time for you to renew your acquaintance with your child. In fact, I instruct you to contact him. Tell him that the Council's jet will be in Corpus Christi in four night's time to bring him to London. He will help us capture these elusive rogues."

"It will be as you say, Honored One."

"Of course it will. Go now. Contact him at your earliest convenience. Anthony, Gavin, stay. I wish to speak with both of you."

Aedan walked out of Wlodek's office. Wlodek waited patiently until Aedan was out of hearing before informing Tony Hancock and Gavin Montegue that they would be working soon with Ashe Evans.

CHAPTER 3

"Hey, Wayne. Wynter," Ashe nodded when Winkler's twins walked into the media room.

The largest flat-screen money could buy hung on a wall, with theater seating in front of it. A bar and barstools were off to the side, with another wall built with floor-to-ceiling plate glass to view the gulf.

Heavy curtains could be pulled if necessary to block the light. Ashe was sipping a soda and watching a baseball game with Trajan and Trace when Winkler arrived from the airport with his children and Ace, who'd gone along as bodyguard.

"Heard you were a member of the family," Wayne slapped Ashe on the back when he stood.

"Just a step-member," Ashe replied. "Inadvertently, since I'm an orphan and all." Being snubbed by his mother earlier still stung. Surely there was something left of him in her memory. Surely. Ashe was angry with his father as well—how could Aedan do that? It wasn't that long ago he'd said that Ashe was his boy and to never forget that. Aedan and his mother had done the forgetting.

"Kid, don't dwell on that," Trajan said softly.

"Well, sometimes it's unavoidable. I'm going to bed, Mr. Winkler.

Nice to see you again, Wayne. Wynter." Ashe didn't bother walking out of the room—he relocated.

"That's just unsettling," Ace grumbled at Ashe's sudden disappearance.

～

"I've heard a few interesting things about you." Thomas Williams, Jr. was introduced to Ashe over lunch the following day. Weldon Harper, the Grand Master, had flown into Corpus Christi with Thomas, and Winkler had gathered everyone at his favorite sushi restaurant afterward.

"All exaggerated," Ashe smiled and shook hands with the Sacramento Packmaster. Ashe liked Thomas Williams immediately.

"Doubt it," the Grand Master broke his chopsticks apart and set about eating his appetizer. "Kid, we're among friends, here. You say we'll catch one of Zeke Tanner's minions tomorrow night?"

"I hope so, but things are wavering a little," Ashe breathed a sigh and stared at his empty plate. Just the thought of what might go wrong had his stomach tied in knots.

"Ashe, I'm not sure I want to hear about things wavering," Winkler was already dipping into tempura shrimp.

"No, that's not really it, Mr. Winkler. I mean, there's still somebody out there who's feeding him information, and now we might not get them, too."

Winkler was worried, he knew. Ashe had informed the Dallas Packmaster that Tanner was targeting him, through a third party. Tanner wanted Winkler dead and Ashe knew that. Winkler didn't even question—he'd had rumblings to that effect himself, being in the security business.

The Grand Master didn't doubt it, either. Winkler had been instrumental in the capturing and killing of Zeke's brother, Obediah. It was logical that Zeke would come after Winkler in some way.

"The good news is that the Assassin doesn't know the Grand Master and I are here," Thomas used a fork to spear shrimp. "We can help. All we need is to coordinate with the shapeshifter. I hope we can come from behind and downwind, so he won't know until we're on him."

"He won't know; I'll have you shielded," Ashe grumbled.

"Kid, eat," Trajan jerked his head toward one of the heaping plates of appetizers. Sighing softly, Ashe picked up his chopsticks.

~

Ashe couldn't help but slyly watch as Thomas and Wynter were talking on Winkler's huge deck later. Dressed in shorts and a halter-top, Wynter was sitting in the sun, a pair of designer shades hiding her eyes as she talked and laughed with the Sacramento Packmaster.

She had no suspicions—she believed Thomas had come to help her father and the Grand Master take down a rogue werewolf. Thomas was smiling and laughing with Winkler's daughter. Wayne, too, was sitting nearby and talking easily with the newcomer. Ashe lifted himself off the deck chair he'd occupied and walked into the beach house.

More spacious and secure than the last one, Winkler had hired more help to keep this beach house up and running. Ashe knew they were werewolves, from the Dallas Pack. One of the two doubled as Andy's assistant. Loren Bennett was short for a werewolf—only slightly taller than Jimmy, Winkler's former cook who'd died earlier in the summer. Loren was an omega wolf. Ashe liked him. Loren offered Ashe another soda as he closed the French doors leading into the house.

"No, thanks, I still have a little left," Ashe held up his glass. "I really shouldn't be drinking too much of this stuff. It's all sugar."

"Werewolf metabolism burns right through that," Loren grinned. "Shifters, too, or so I've heard."

"I have to expend energy in a different way," Ashe said.

"How?" Craig, the new cook, walked in on his way toward the deck.

"I just do," Ashe shrugged and brushed past Craig on his way toward the stairs.

"That kid is as strange as they come," Craig muttered, believing Ashe out of hearing range. Ashe heard Craig's comment clearly as he ran lightly up the stairs to his room.

"Aedan, our marriage is over. You said so yourself. When you pulled financial assistance away from me for that *boy*, and wrote the letter stating you weren't his father and wouldn't support him, well, I had little choice. I'm not his real mother. Someone here in the community told me that. I passed your letter to Mr. Winkler and granted legal guardianship to him. I have copies of the paperwork if you want them," Adele snapped at Aedan over the phone. Honestly, he'd walked away, why was he calling now? "Mr. Winkler seems more than wealthy enough to support the boy."

"Adele," Aedan sighed over his cell. "The boy has a name. We raised him. He's just as much yours as anyone else's."

"Not anymore—the courts here say so. If you think you're going to get him back now, well, you'll have to show up in court. During the *day*." Adele terminated the call angrily.

"Honored One, we have a problem," Aedan Evans looked across Wlodek's wide expanse of antique desk.

"I heard," Wlodek growled. He'd listened to the entire conversation. "Had you consulted with me, I would have warned against removing support for the child. Were you overzealous with compulsion as well?" Wlodek lifted an eyebrow the slightest bit.

"I was emotional at the time," Aedan admitted. "I did not think my words through. Nathan tells me that Adele has taken her newly found single status to a logical conclusion and is now in another relationship."

That shocked Wlodek, although he used the vampire mask to show no reaction to the news. He'd promised his second child, after all, that things would go back to normal for Aedan in two years, right after Ashe's eighteenth birthday. This could seriously impact that promise.

Wlodek wanted to sigh but held it back. Perhaps Flavio was correct and Wlodek had erred after all. Now, Ashe might be out of his reach if Weldon Harper chose to side with Winkler over the boy. Wlodek knew that all-out war could resume between the werewolf and vampire races if this weren't handled diplomatically.

"Charles!" Wlodek shouted. Charles was standing in Wlodek's office in seconds.

"Honored One?" Charles asked softly.

"Charles, how many rogues are currently in the Unites States?"

"At least twenty, perhaps more," Charles replied immediately. He had an exceptional memory, even for a vampire, and most vampires had amazing recall.

"Contact Gavin and Anthony. Have them ready to fly to the U.S. at a moment's notice. I will attempt to get the Grand Master's permission for Ashe Evans to help them clear out our rogues there, first."

"Of course, Honored One. Would you like for me to call the Grand Master as well?"

"No, I'll do it myself."

"As you say, Honored One." Charles whisked out of Wlodek's office.

"Aedan, go home. Pick up your next assignment from Charles before you leave."

"I will, Honored One." Aedan dipped his head to the Vampire Council's highest-ranking member and walked out of the spacious office swiftly. Wlodek released the sigh he'd been holding before lifting the phone and punching in the Grand Master's number.

"Honored One, the child has school to consider," Weldon spoke as diplomatically as he could to the Head of the Vampire Council. "He is sixteen, as you recall. If you wish to utilize him in tracking your rogues, then I demand equal time. I have rogues as well, and not enough trackers to hunt them. Have you truly thought this through? He's still a child. We could exhaust him at best, kill him at worst. He has no experience or training in this area, while those he goes against are, in most cases, much older, more devious and certainly more experienced."

"I intended to send two of mine to guide him," Wlodek had been neatly backed into a corner.

"And I could provide some training, but honestly, how much free time will he have? His guardian is demanding he pass the GED and then take nine hours of college courses, in addition to working part-time to cover the cost of his educational expenses." Weldon had chosen to fabricate that part, but he didn't want Wlodek to know that Winkler had volunteered to pay for everything as long as Ashe kept his part of their bargain.

"I can help with expenses, if he assists in taking down rogues," Wlodek almost growled. Once again, Wlodek wanted to curse over Aedan's refusal to support his son. The subject of support was a glitch —a hole in the agreement Aedan had signed with the Vampire Council in order to have a child. Nowhere did it say that he was obligated to provide for the child.

At the time, it had been understood. Aedan had obviously read the agreement and discovered the flaw. Now, Wlodek had little legal ground to stand on and potential enmity and possible war with the werewolves if he didn't cooperate. He considered punishment for Aedan, and then recalled that Ashe had shown up immediately when Aedan had been in danger before. Wlodek heaved a mental sigh.

"I will speak with Winkler. I think perhaps one or two weekends per month might be utilized for your purposes, Honored One, as long as it does not interfere with full moons or other important activities."

Weldon winked at Winkler, who sat across from him in Winkler's private study. Thomas Williams was also listening from a seat nearby. Wlodek believed that Weldon was at his home in North Dakota.

"If that is what I can get, then it will have to be enough. I will speak with you soon regarding this arrangement." Wlodek's voice was even, displaying no emotion.

"Absolutely, Honored One. Soon—after the full moon."

"Of course." Wlodek hung up.

Winkler burst out laughing. Thomas Williams grinned. It wasn't often that Weldon had such a strong upper hand against Wlodek of the vampires.

Ashe, who'd hovered overhead as mist, was satisfied with what he'd heard and relocated to his old house in Star Cove. Someone had told his mother he wasn't hers—Wlodek had mentioned it when he'd first spoken with Weldon.

Someday, that person might regret that they'd interfered. Meanwhile, Ashe materialized inside his old bedroom in Star Cove and studied the shelves of books. He still had clothing and a few other belongings there. If he gathered all of it into his mist, he could get it in one trip.

∽

"Kid?" Winkler knocked lightly on the door before letting himself inside Ashe's new bedroom. What greeted his eyes had the Dallas Packmaster raising both eyebrows. Piles of books were everywhere on Ashe's floor while clothing and other belongings were scattered across his bed. Ashe was busy shelving books inside his small library.

"Got everything out of the old house," Ashe said without turning toward Winkler. "Hope you don't mind."

"Kid, this is your home. Of course you can bring your stuff."

"I was wondering, too, Mr. Winkler, if you'd ask my mom for the paperwork from when I was born. You know, the birth certificates, the donated egg thing, the vampire scientist thing—all of that? It's in my dad's old safe. I doubt she remembers it's there, but we ought to ask. I think I want it," Ashe turned blue eyes toward Winkler's nearly black ones.

"I'll ask," Winkler raked fingers through black hair. "But I can't promise anything. I think she's, well," Winkler didn't have to finish.

"Unstable, you mean, where I'm concerned?" Ashe asked softly. "Yeah. I got that already."

"Ashe, you're a good kid. One of the best I've ever met. You didn't deserve any of this," Winkler said, just as softly. "And I know we haven't been the best where you're concerned, either, but Trajan, Trace and I, well, you're part of us, now."

"I know. Someday, I think I'd like to see Trajan and Trace's parents. They sound nice."

"They are. Maybe we can invite them down, or send you home with Trace some weekend. I can't have both Trace and Trajan gone at the same time, but one of them can go with you."

"I think I'd like that, Mr. Winkler. Just to be someplace normal for a little while."

"Yeah. Kid, you haven't forgotten that your GED exam is Tuesday, have you?"

"No, Mr. Winkler. I think I can pass it, but I'll study a little more on Monday, when things aren't so unsettled."

"Still ready to go tomorrow night?"

"Yeah. But be prepared to only get one. Things are solidifying against the other one. For now. But don't worry, we'll get the leak eventually. I can promise you that." Ashe shoved books onto the shelf harder than warranted.

"Kid, I trust you. I just hope we get them before they do any major damage."

"Yep. Mr. Winkler," Ashe gazed steadily at his guardian.

"What, Ashe?"

"Be ready for the shock when it comes." Ashe's eyes had darkened and filled with stars.

"Kid, get some sleep, okay?" Winkler could only stare at those star-filled eyes for a few moments before looking away. It was as if they laid anything bare they looked upon, and Winkler wasn't sure he was prepared for his soul to be stripped and exposed.

"I will," Ashe replied and went back to shelving books.

～

"Ashe?" Marco watched as Ashe settled himself at the huge breakfast bar Sunday morning. Trace, Trajan and Winkler had already eaten and taken themselves to the new weight room to work off a little steam before the full moon.

"Marco," Ashe replied, accepting a plate of food from Craig, the werewolf cook.

"Cori says your mom got upset last night when she came home from work. Thought somebody had robbed the house until she realized it was only your stuff missing. Mr. Winkler explained when she called that he'd let you in to get your things. That wasn't how it happened, was it?"

"I owe Mr. Winkler an apology. I didn't think she remembered that somebody else had that room. I figured she was ignoring it."

"I think it was Buck who sniffed your scent," Marco admitted glumly.

"You had to ruin breakfast, didn't you?" Ashe lifted his plate and dumped it in the sink, turning on the garbage disposal. He stalked out of the kitchen immediately after, leaving a contrite Marco behind.

~

"Marco already spilled the beans. I thought Buck worked for you. Isn't he smart enough to add two and two? Or is it his personal mission to make me miserable?" Ashe muttered when Winkler jogged up beside him. Ashe had taken off at a run down the beach.

"I talked to Buck afterward," Winkler said, keeping pace with Ashe. Ashe knew Trajan and Trace were running at a distance behind him and Winkler, guarding both of them. "He realized he should have kept his mouth shut the moment the words came out of it, but Adele was already walking into the empty bedroom and having a fit. It's the full moon, remember? Everybody's tempers are flaring."

"Why should she care? I'm not her kid anymore. She didn't need any of that stuff. I just got it out of her house for her." Ashe was weeping and trying to run ahead of Winkler.

"Let him go." Winkler stopped, allowing Trajan and Trace to catch up with him. "If I could get my hands on Aedan Evans right now," Winkler growled.

"Boss, you'd have to stand in line. I think you're third, right now," Trajan slapped Winkler's shoulder. "Trace and I have a few things to say first, and none of 'em are nice."

~

"Cori, I screwed up." Marco spoke with Cori later as he walked the perimeter of the new beach house. He was on guard with Ace at the moment.

"What did you do, Marco?"

"I told Ashe that his mom thought the house was burglarized after his stuff came up missing. I should have kept quiet and let Winkler tell him."

"Marco, what would you do if your mother didn't recognize you anymore?" Cori asked. "Ashe has enough trouble, and you probably said it all wrong."

"I did," Marco winced. "Ashe dumped his breakfast in the sink and walked out. Craig was cussing about ruining good food and wasting his time."

"Did Ashe hear that?"

"Ashe hears everything."

"Yeah. Maybe you should tell Mr. Winkler what Craig said."

"Maybe."

"Marco, just do it. We don't need somebody else persecuting Ashe. At least he cleans up after himself, instead of making the cook do it for him."

"I get the idea that Craig just likes to complain. Plus, it could be the full moon. I'll give it a day or two and see if he calms down."

"Fine. But don't let this go too far if he really doesn't like Ashe for some reason. Not every werewolf likes shifters."

"Cori, I know that. That doesn't have a thing to do with me and you."

"I know that, too. Marco, I love you. I do. I just ask you to remember that Ashe was my friend before we ever went out. He's kept secrets—my secrets—for a long time. I owe him. He's never made a big deal out of keeping the community alive. Do you think we'd have lived through that attack by Tanner and his Elemaiya? If Ashe hadn't been with us, they'd have taken Dori and the others straight to Mexico, after killing just about everybody here. That doesn't include what he did for me when Jeremy, well, you know."

"I know. Cori, look. I'll watch out for Ashe as much as I can, but I'm not always the most tactful person or the best person in this sort of thing. Dad and I aren't speaking much and Ashe is in the middle of that."

"I think we need to wait a few days before we start that conversation. Dad had a fit when he found out your dad doesn't trust Ashe anymore. He went off somewhere, probably to call Aedan. Aedan made him, you know. Aedan is my dad's sire. We didn't know until Aedan told Adele and Ashe just before he left. Daddy told us right after, since Aedan had already let the information out. Marco, Daddy owes Ashe, too. I don't know what that might mean now or in the future, but he does."

"I hope it means he might stand with Ashe if any of those other three get any ideas," Marco growled.

"Marco, that's scary."

"Yeah, but if he stands with Ashe, don't you think that they can take down just about anybody?"

"I didn't think about that. Ashe called me back from death. I was almost gone and he changed that. He neutralized the poison and made it so I could come back. If he can do that, what else might he be able to do?"

"You know I love you. I owe Ashe in ways I can't begin to explain. And yes, somebody who can do that might be able to do almost anything."

"I wish you were here right now," Cori moaned.

"If I hadn't upset Ashe this morning, I could be there in a blink. I'll see you tomorrow, Cori. I have to get back to work." Marco said good-bye and hung up.

~

"Ace is worried about me. We'll be out in different places tonight," Wynn said. She and Dori had settled on the deck behind the O'Neill's house. Both had swimsuits on, but neither thought to get in the pool. The last time they'd gotten in, Hayes had played volleyball with them.

"What are we gonna do without Hayes?" Dori brought up the subject. "Larry and Jeff won't talk to anybody, they're so depressed. Hayes' parents haven't come out of the house since the funeral. I don't know what they'll do for the full moon."

"Stupid Chump and Wormy." Wynn used Ashe's derogatory nicknames for both boys.

"We could be dead too. Cori almost was," Dori muttered. "If Ashe hadn't come."

"We haven't treated Ashe very well, have we?" Wynn stared at her best friend.

"Sali needs a good kick," Dori agreed. "Just because Marcus decides to get prejudiced, all of a sudden."

"Sali's still alive because of Hayes and Ashe," Wynn said. "Marcus can stuff it."

"Don't say that too loud," Dori rose and looked around, making sure no one else was in the adjoining yards. "Wynn, Marcus is still the Packmaster and he's officially in charge. We don't need him having somebody spy on us, too."

"You don't think Sali would do that, do you?" Wynn stared at Dori.

"I'm thinking about breaking up with him," Dori whispered. "I'm afraid to say anything around him now, and that's not good. You're supposed to be able to share stuff with your steady, don't you think? I'm afraid he'll take anything I say about Mom and Dad to his parents, and I sure don't want that."

"You think?" Wynn's eyes widened.

"Yeah. When we started dating, I said a few things. Now I'm worried."

"Then if you're thinking about it, do it quick. But not today. Full moon," Wynn pointed out.

"Yeah. Maybe tomorrow. Definitely before Wednesday; we're supposed to start school, then."

"Yeah. Without Ashe and without Hayes. Dori, you dumped Ashe. Will he still be friends with us, you think?"

"He'll always be friends with Cori. So maybe he'll put all that in the past. Didn't we have a good time that day we went out to eat and to the beach?"

"Yeah. I nearly forgot about that since, well, the other stuff happened." Wynn traced her finger down the arm of her deck chair.

"I know."

"Maybe we could ask him to go out with us sometime, after I break up with Sal."

"Ace may want to come."

"Then I'll ask Cori to go. Come on, let's go inside and get something to drink."

"I expect you to be in place and waiting," Josiah Dunnigan informed his accomplice over the phone. He kept in contact with his spy by cell phone, because there was a chance someone might be watching if they were to meet in person.

Josiah was getting odd rumblings in the area. Rumblings of things that were impossible or nearly so. Nevertheless, those rumors existed. His accomplice had even informed him of some of those rumors, shortly before they seemed to be forgotten completely.

Josiah knew there were vampires in Star Cove. Worried about that, actually, until his accomplice stated that they were charged with guarding the shifters. Josiah breathed a relieved sigh and made his plans. "Just be there, all right," he demanded and hung up before there was a reply.

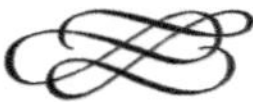

CHAPTER 4

She had gone over the map of the terrain around the run area twice with Winkler, Trajan, Bear Wright, the Grand Master and Thomas Williams. "He'll be here," he pointed to a small stand of trees and mesquite. The thicket lay near a clearing, where the Pack would race past. "He thinks his accomplice will cause a distraction, but that won't be the case," Ashe sighed.

If Chad and Jeremy had succeeded with their plan, then there truly would have been a distraction—in the form of a deer shapeshifter, thrust into the midst of a Pack on a moonlit night.

Poor Lewis Sharpe would have been torn apart in his weakened condition, and eaten before anyone realized he was a shapeshifter. That would have given Chad and Jeremy ample time to carry out their plan and shoot Winkler and Trajan with poisoned darts.

"Kid, are you up for the executions tonight? I don't know who Marcus has asked to do them." Winkler turned dark eyes on Ashe, who lifted his eyes to stare at his guardian.

"I can relocate for a minute if I need to."

"Is that what you call it?"

"It's what it's called on that paper Hancock gave me," Ashe pointed out.

"I forgot about that," Winkler sighed. "I still have my copy in the safe." Ashe shrugged at Winkler's comment.

"Anyway," Ashe went on, "I'll be there with Principal Wright behind me, and the Grand Master and Mr. Williams when the time comes. Don't worry, our culprit won't get far."

~

"Kid, you didn't eat breakfast and I never saw you at lunchtime," Winkler pointed out later when Craig set out a light meal two hours before sunset. Ashe felt queasy as he stared at the roast beef subs Craig had laid out buffet style, with chips and baked beans.

"Yeah. I ought to eat something, I guess," Ashe agreed and took the smallest sandwich he could find. He wasn't touching the beans; his stomach was tied in knots as it was.

He felt something stirring, altering the conditions once more, but he didn't want to upset Winkler or deviate from the plan. Things would go as they would, one way or another. He had one other he might call on, and if he hurried, then he might have things in place before everything fell apart.

~

"I heard you were planning the takedown, and I know Zeke is hunting us. You have to include Eudora and me so he'll call off his trackers. Otherwise, we're as good as dead."

"I'm not sharing the money with you," Josiah growled at Fergus Haskell over the phone. "You can help if you want, but Zeke will decide for himself if that's enough to keep his trackers away. He said they were tailing you."

"Look, all we want to do is try to make this right with Zeke. He won't stop hunting us until we're dead if we don't make this right with him," Fergus begged. "We're pulling into Corpus now. Where can we meet and coordinate?"

"I was about to have dinner so I can focus on what needs to be done later," Josiah pointed out. "Meet me at Darrin's Steak House—it's on Padre Island Drive on the south side. You can't miss it."

"We'll be there in less than half an hour," Fergus said and hung up.

"Yeah, you can be the bait," Josiah muttered and pocketed his cell.

~

"You don't sound surprised that I called," Ashe was the one who sounded surprised.

"Let's just say that I had a visit—from a tall, brown-haired man," Kyle Williams, Corpus Christi's only resident vampire, informed Ashe after answering his cell.

"You know Griffin?" Ashe almost squeaked the name.

"Yes. Actually, my sire knows Griffin better than anyone I know. I've only seen him a few times over the past eighty-six years, but I do know him. He said to help out if I could. What do you need, young one?"

"I need backup, because things have just gotten a little more complicated than I originally thought. I'll come get you. Did Griffin tell you that was all right?"

"He said you had unusual methods, and that I could trust you."

"I can keep you hidden until the time is right, but you'll have to work fast; we've got three areas to cover now, instead of the original one. At least your two will be closer together."

"I'll do what I can," Kyle replied. "When are you coming?"

"I'm here, now." Ashe stood inside Kyle's underground bunker, his cell phone in his hand. "Don't worry, I'll get you back home afterward and your location is safe with me." Ashe explained with mindspeech what was needed while he ferried Kyle to the werewolf running area outside Star Cove.

~

"Ashe flies. He has no need to come to Star Cove for the change," Nathan pointed out to Hector, Edmond and Casimir. Hector was the one asking, as the Honored One might expect an account of the boy.

"Where is he, then?" Edmond demanded.

"No idea. I'm sure Winkler is making arrangements for him to be safe. After all, Ashe is so tiny when he turns that he could fly about in Winkler's cavernous home without any harm or threat," Nathan replied stiffly. "It is too late to contact the werewolf—you see the others here have already gone." Nathan jerked his head toward the twinkling lights of the small community.

He and the other vampires stood on the small strip of sand east of the Star Cove paranormal neighborhood, waiting for the shifters to make the change. They would watch and make sure the community was safe, but they would not interfere.

"I do not like this," Hector pointed out.

"Then perhaps you should tell Wlodek when you speak to him next," Nathan said. "Perhaps he will give you another assignment."

"I will suggest no such thing. We have already informed him of the location of the child. We had no idea the boy would not return for the full moon."

"Why should he? There's nothing here for him now," Nathan sighed. He wanted to shake his head over the turn of events that left Ashe without parents, but his sire had not consulted him before doing as he did.

"We will make sure the boy is safe before we retire for the day," Casimir finally spoke up. Of those there, he was eldest and Wlodek had left him in charge. Casimir, too, had no idea what Aedan Evans had been thinking, leaving the child in the hands of werewolves and vulnerable to the others who hunted him. Nevertheless, he had to work with what he had. At the moment, he had no information on Ashe's whereabouts.

"Fine with me." Nathan turned to walk back to the community and take up his normal position on a rooftop so he could see the shapeshifters as they wandered, prowled and hunted through the subdivision. Casimir and the others soon followed.

~

Ashe could see Sali standing at the outer edge of the Pack—they were all still in human form, waiting for the two scheduled for execution to arrive. Only the executioners and those scheduled to die would make the change for the planned execution. Afterward, the Pack would turn and hunt.

Ashe wanted to shiver, even though he was mist. Weldon Harper, Thomas Williams and Bear Wright were with him. Winkler stood near Trace and Trajan at the inside of the werewolf circle, not far from Marcus DeLuca and Micah Rocklin.

Marco, Wayne, Wynter and Winkler's other wolves stood in a knot behind Winkler. Ashe spotted several others in the crowd. Mr. Dodd. Greta Rocklin. Denise DeLuca, standing next to Randy's mother, Dawn. Even Hayes' parents were there.

Ashe truly did want to sigh, then. Larry and Jeff were standing with them. Six more wolves walked into the moonlit circle, pulling Chad and Jeremy with them. Their chains had been removed somewhere and now both struggled against their captors.

"I hate you," Chad attempted to spit at Marcus as he was hauled before the Star Cove Packmaster. "You killed my dad," he added with a snarl. The two werewolves who held him hauled him back as he lunged toward Marcus. Jeremy, held securely by other werewolves nearby, just looked terrified. He'd never been this close to the entire Pack on a full moon.

"Your father challenged me fairly, and was taken down fairly," Marcus said evenly as Chad glared at him. "You were too young to see that I tried to convince him to back off. He refused. You know the laws, just as I do. You will be punished for breaking those laws. Who offers to take the execution of Chad Everett Daniels?"

"I take it," Micah pulled his shirt off and unbuckled his belt.

Ashe wanted to moan. He'd always liked Marcus' Second. Now, Chad would be ripped apart according to werewolf justice and Ashe would have to listen. He could close his mental eyes, but his hearing he could not mute.

Both Micah and Chad had turned in a matter of moments and Micah charged. The growls, yelps and carnage were just as bad as Ashe imagined it might be. Micah was swift, at least. Less than ten minutes it took, for the execution to be completed.

Micah remained wolf, his muzzle bloodied while Chad's dismembered torso lay on the grass inside the werewolf circle.

"Who will take Jeremy Paul Booth's execution?" Marcus asked. Before Trajan could step forward, Ashe made up his mind. *This is a secret you'll have to keep*, Ashe informed his passengers as a seemingly solid replica of him appeared inside the werewolf circle.

"I will," Ashe's projection announced.

"I will not allow it," Marcus hissed. Ashe's doppelganger turned to the Star Cove Packmaster.

"Why not?" Ashe appeared to ask. "I was instrumental in his capture. Aren't there allowances for something of this nature?"

"There are," Winkler spoke up, earning a frown from Marcus. "The Pack may vote to allow it, if the shifter or one responsible for the capture is capable of taking the execution. And as this is another shifter," Winkler shrugged.

"Then vote," Ashe was sending his voice and coordinating the image of himself so the words would fit mouth movements.

"Pack, the vote has been requested. What say you?" Marcus growled. The Pack voted and Ashe won, by a margin of two votes. Ashe saw from afar that Sali had abstained. Jeff and Larry voted in his favor, as did Hayes' parents.

"Kid, if you fail," Marcus was ready to turn.

"I won't," Ashe replied. Turning his double around, Ashe stared at Jeremy, who lifted terrified eyes to Ashe.

"What are you gonna do, empty?" Jeremy's voice quavered on the insult but he still managed to say it.

"It will be painless, Jeremy Paul Booth," Ashe said. "I do this for your parents, who have always tried to treat you well. They deserve a better memory of your passing."

Ashe's image lifted his hands and Jeremy, beginning with his feet and legs, seemed to separate into tiny, sparkling particles, like a fire at night throwing off sparks. Each spark glowed brightly as it flew away, until it burned out and vanished. Jeremy's head was the last to disintegrate, eliciting a collective sigh from the crowd. Ashe's image turned to Marcus. "You doubt me," he said and disappeared.

"Turn and hunt!" Marcus shouted. Ashe recognized the anger in the command. He felt Weldon Harper's discomfort inside his mist. *We'll be down in a minute,* Ashe reassured his living cargo. When the last wolf had turned and raced away, Ashe sped after them to set his cargo down at the appointed spot.

⸾

"Just stay there. If I can't cause a little havoc, then you'll have to," Fergus hissed at Eudora.

Eudora regretted the day she'd let this pompous male into her life. Regretted that she hadn't stayed behind with her husband, Jarrett. She could have accused Fergus of overpaying her and then blackmailing her afterward. Anything would be better than this—out to create a distraction in the middle of more than fifty werewolves and risking her life to do it.

"Turn, you stupid bitch," Fergus wasn't done. He was already wolf when Eudora removed her clothing.

⸾

See? Ashe sent mindspeech to Bear, Weldon and Thomas. They did—Josiah Dunnigan was unaware as they approached, shaking from his refusal to turn as he lay in the grass, a rifle pointed at the Pack racing past, waiting for Winkler to run by.

Ashe knew Winkler was running near the back of the Pack; it was expected if you were a guest of the local Packmaster. The local Pack would be first to take down the quarry and share in the meal.

⸾

Fergus smelled vampire. Only it was already too late—his throat had been cut and he was bleeding out on the grass before he heard Eudora's wheezing—the vampire had surprised her as well. His last thought, as he lay dying, was that at least this was a swifter death than what Ezekiel Tanner had planned.

~

Ashe knew Josiah would die, he just hadn't expected him to be torn apart so quickly. Winkler and Trajan's wolves flanked Ashe as he watched Weldon Harper's werewolf savage Josiah's throat. Weldon growled angrily one last time before decapitating the rogue and flinging his head aside.

"I figure you guys can't change back now," Ashe sighed as he surveyed the bloody scene before him. "So I'll leave you to your hunt. There are two more bodies a quarter of a mile back, but I had a little help with those two. Recognize the names Fergus Haskell and Eudora Long?"

Ashe turned to Winkler's wolf, who whined his acknowledgment. "Yeah, I figured you would. Well, happy hunting. I've had enough blood for a while, I think. I'll be at the house when you come in, Mr. Winkler." Ashe misted toward Kyle, to return the vampire to his Corpus Christi home.

~

"Randy?" Ashe slipped into the hotel room Randy had reserved for Sara. It was the full moon—Sara had to turn. Ashe wondered briefly about Lewis Sharpe, but the deer shifter had gone to the dunes on the beach to turn. Ashe figured Lewis had plenty of experience hiding from humans and other predators, so he forced thoughts of the Arkansas deputy from his mind.

"Ashe, look. It's Sara." Randy held a pretty, reddish-brown, flop-eared rabbit in his arms.

"Sara?" Ashe walked over to where Randy sat on the side of the hotel bed and stroked Sara's left ear. "You're so pretty," Ashe soothed.

"Ashe, why aren't you changed?" That thought had just occurred to Randy.

"Don't have to unless I want to," Ashe whispered. "It's who I am, Randy. What I am. Different. I'll always be different."

"Mom said she heard that from somebody in the community, but she wouldn't tell me who. Says that's why Adele thinks you're not hers."

"That's complicated, Randy. And a touchy subject," Ashe pulled his hand away.

"Sorry, man. Should have realized," Randy apologized.

"No. I'm glad to have the information. Take care of Sara." Ashe misted away.

~

Ashe had never been to Paris. Had only seen it on television or in magazine photographs. He sat on the roof of Notre Dame du Paris and watched boats travel the waters surrounding the small isle the cathedral occupied.

The sun was shining and people were moving about. He knew he'd end up in many photographs if he didn't shield himself, so he did. He watched tourists and locals, all on their way here and there. Heard the native language that somehow he could understand. He shook his head at the wonder of all of it.

"Gotta go," he sighed and relocated.

~

"Kid, I thought you were going to be here when I got back," Winkler's words were growled low. He'd showered and dressed, although sunrise had not yet arrived.

"Mr. Winkler, I had some thinking to do. So I did it. On top of Notre Dame."

"The one in Paris?"

"Yeah."

"Kid, sit down." Winkler pointed to a barstool in the kitchen. He'd already chased Craig out and Trajan and Trace were keeping the others away, too. Ashe sat heavily on the indicated barstool. "Kid, what was that I saw earlier—what you did to Jeremy? Where is he now?"

"It's called separating particles," Ashe blew out a labored sigh. "I pretty much caused Jeremy's atoms to fly away. He's with the universe, now."

"Kid, you have to be joking." Winkler stared at Ashe.

"Nope. See that?" Ashe pointed to the toaster oven sitting on the kitchen counter. Lifting his hands, Ashe caused it to separate, the metallic fragments popping softly as they winked out of existence.

Winkler raked a hand through his hair and cursed. "Kid, I'm not sure I want to see that again," he said, worry in his voice.

"I'll try to keep it for emergencies," Ashe muttered, his head down. "I wouldn't have done it except for the reason I told Jeremy. His mother needs to know he didn't suffer. The dead don't care. The living have to deal with the horror left behind."

"Yeah. I get that," Winkler whispered. "Go to bed, Ashe. We'll talk later."

"Okay." Ashe stood and walked out of the kitchen.

"It was painless, Diane. I promise. Chad's wasn't, but Jeremy's was. Ashe told him, there at the last, that he was making it painless because you and Neil didn't need terrible memories." Greta Rocklin held Diane Booth's fingers in her own. "He never suffered."

"Here." Marco held out his cell phone—he'd recorded it. Diane Booth wept as she watched her son's sparks separate peacefully and fly away.

"Honored One, I fear that we should just kill the child and be done. I hear of a frightening power he holds," Hector left the message for Wlodek, since Wlodek would be sleeping. "I will explain later, when I receive better details." Hector terminated the call.

"Say those words again, and I'll kill you where you stand," Nathan Anderson had Hector lifted up one-handed, his throat in a crushing grip. "I am older, and therefore command you to never say that to anyone again, or contemplate it, do you hear me?"

Hector barely nodded before Nathan dropped him. Hector sagged to the ground. "And you will not retaliate," compulsion was thick in Nathan's voice. Aedan had trained him well. "Go. It is nearly dawn." Hector ran.

~

"Who did we take down last night?" Weldon Harper settled on a deck chair next to Ashe, a cup of coffee in his hand. Craig was preparing a late lunch in the kitchen. Ashe hadn't slept well so he'd gotten up shortly after noon. Now the werewolves were up as well. Lewis Sharpe was still asleep in a guest bedroom on the third floor.

"Josiah Dunnigan. Know who he is?" Ashe turned to the Grand Master.

"Yeah. From the Amarillo Pack. And that fool Nick Robbins swore none of his had any connections to Obediah Tanner. Looks like Josiah was connected to Obediah and Ezekiel."

"Not anymore," Ashe pointed out, watching the waves slosh over the sand on the beach. The day was bright and sunny, and the tide was higher than normal. Tourists were forced to walk through the loose sand farther up unless they wanted to wade in the surf.

"I may pay Nick a visit on the way home," Weldon grumped. "Stupid fool."

"Take Thomas with you," Ashe said.

"You think I need backup?"

"You might. Ask Nick how he paid his mortgage off early."

"Kid, you're just downright scary, sometimes. What was that I saw last night? I'm still having a hard time coming to terms with it."

"That reminds me, I need to replace Winkler's toaster oven," Ashe said. "It's called separating particles. Not many can do it, but there are a few races that can."

"Are you telling me that other Elemaiya?" Weldon sounded shocked.

"No, I'm the only one of the Elemaiya who can do it," Ashe said. "There are other, more powerful races than the Elemaiya. Want to make a quick trip to Corpus and pick out a toaster oven?"

"I wondered what happened to that," Craig snapped when Ashe set the box containing the new toaster oven on the kitchen island.

"Here's a new one, better than what you lost," Ashe said. "Now, you will not remember anything that happened last night concerning Jeremy's execution." Ashe placed compulsion while Craig's eyes went blank.

"And you can be more civil to the kid, here," Weldon held out his coffee cup for a refill.

"Yes, Grand Master," Craig almost bowed before reaching for the coffeepot.

"It's good to be the king," Ashe whispered as he and Weldon walked onto the deck again.

"Sometimes. Until you take all the phone messages and listen to the multitude of complaints," Weldon said.

"There's that," Ashe agreed. "Sali always said that about Marcus."

"I was a Packmaster once, too. Sacramento," Weldon sighed. "Thomas' father was my Second. He took over when I challenged old George. I think George expected it. Put up a hell of a fight, though."

"Can't hold your spot if people think you're weak," Ashe said.

"Kid, where is this coming from? That's written in the first Grand Master's memoirs."

"Grand Master, I'm the Ir'Indicti. If I didn't know, then people would question the title." Weldon pressed but Ashe wouldn't explain what Ir'Indicti meant.

❧

"He admitted it. Came right out and said it," Weldon told Winkler later in a private meeting. "But he wouldn't tell me what the word meant."

"I'll work on that," Winkler said. "And I'll keep you posted if I learn anything. If I didn't trust the kid, I'd have been terrified after what I saw last night. I called Nathan and explained things to him—there'll be compulsion placed tonight."

"Good. We don't want that to get out."

"Nope. But I have to tell you, I wouldn't hunt him for any amount of money, Weldon."

"I'm just glad he's on our side."

CHAPTER 5

"Randy, tell me what Ashe really is," Sara packed the last of her clothing and zipped the bag. Her flight was scheduled at seven, but she wanted everything ready to go so she and Randy could have time on the beach together. "He doesn't smell like any shifter I've encountered. And he doesn't smell human, either."

"I don't really know what he is. It makes me think there's something that I've forgotten, or been made to forget," Randy stared out the hotel window. The small hotel wasn't on the beach—those rooms were too expensive. He could see the other side of the U-shaped hotel from Sara's room.

"Those vampires would do that? I'm glad I've never lived near any of them," Sara shivered as she came to stand next to Randy. He placed an arm around her shoulders.

"What I do know, I think, is that Ashe would defend us with his last breath." Randy nodded at his conviction. "Come on, let's wade in the water before I have to let you go."

"Thomas, are you, well, engaged or anything?" Wynter had gone shy for a moment as she hooked her arm in Thomas'. He'd asked her to walk down the beach with him.

"No—not at all," Thomas replied, offering a genuine smile. Both wore dark glasses to keep the glare of the afternoon sun away. Werewolf eyes were sensitive the day after a full-moon run.

"Thomas, I really like you," Wynter admitted, hooking long, black hair behind her ear with her free hand—it insisted on blowing in her face while she attempted to voice her thoughts to the Sacramento Packmaster. "Maybe more than a little," she added. "I don't know what Dad has planned for me, but if I can convince him to maybe change his mind or something, would you be interested—well," Wynter felt uncomfortable at being so forward with Thomas, "what I mean, is, would you consider a possible relationship? Maybe date a few times and see if we might," Wynter floundered and stopped, blinking hesitantly at the tall, dark-haired werewolf.

"I'd love to," Thomas leaned in and kissed Wynter nicely, stealing her breath and making her heart thump faster.

~

"Wynn, are you all right?" Ace kneaded Wynn's shoulders gently, searching for any bruises or other harm that might have befallen during the full moon.

"Ace, I'm fine, stop worrying," Wynn patted the white werewolf's cheek and smiled at him. She'd pulled her white hair back and tied it with a blue ribbon. Ace found himself wanting to pull the ribbon away, allowing Wynn's hair to fall loosely about her shoulders.

"Baby, I don't know if I can last two years," Ace muttered, giving Wynn a quick peck instead.

"Ace, I know it'll be tough, but we promised Mom and Dad," Wynn pointed out, pulling away from him.

"Yeah. But I have to tell you, I worry about you most of the time."

"I know. We're pretty safe here inside the community. I don't go out much anymore unless you're with me."

"True. We just need to keep it that way."

"My resources have decreased," Wildrif whined to Baltis. "But I was still able to select a target." He held out a paper map to the Dark Elemaiyan King.

"Fort Arland, in the state of Georgia?" Baltis lifted an eyebrow at Wildrif's suggestion.

"Yes, my King. I was able to locate sources of explosives not far away, so it should be simple for your warriors to relocate inside the base, leave these explosives behind and then relocate far enough away as to be beyond suspicion."

"Very nice, Wildrif. What may I give you as a reward?" Baltis smiled at the quarter-blood seer.

"New shoes, my King?" Wildrif nodded hopefully to Baltis. "These are worn through the soles." Wildrif moaned pitifully, staring down at the offending boots.

"Very well. Raze," Baltis called out to one of his newly appointed Destroyers, "Get the seer shoes and clothing." Baltis waved both away with a flick of his wrist and went back to studying the map Wildrif had given him, the army base circled in red upon it.

"I dislike the heat in Texas this time of year." Gavin seldom complained about anything, but he didn't like this assignment. Nevertheless, the Honored One had instructed him and Anthony to go.

Gavin also had a list of rogue vampires, with their last known location in the U.S. on his tablet. He used to take a laptop on his travels, but the tablet replaced it and was much easier to carry.

"Anthony, are you ready?" Gavin called out. They were to fly to New York first, spend the day sleeping there in a safe house and go on to Texas the following evening.

"I'm ready." Tony peered around Gavin Montegue's bedroom door.

Both lived in a manor house decorated in Louis XIV style. Many of the furnishings were antiques from that era.

It wasn't Gavin's favorite era by any means, but his cousin René, who was Anthony's sire, had loved the period. René had died not long after Tony's turning, leaving the manor to his cousin and his only remaining vampire child.

"Who should we go after first?" Tony walked in and lifted Gavin's tablet, scrolling through the information.

"I thought Rydley Huntington," Gavin muttered. Rydley was a mere three hundred years old and had always been reckless, in Gavin's opinion. Rydley was now bilking humans out of millions, posing as a wealthy investor. He'd killed a few humans, too, who'd attempted to pull away from his schemes. "He's currently in Georgia, if those records are correct."

"How recent is this information?" Tony asked.

"Last sighting two days ago, according to Charles. Charles also says that there is a rumor that Rydley may be dealing arms and ammunition—to the right buyers, of course."

"That's frightening. Do you think he has contacts with terrorists?" Tony tossed the tablet onto Gavin's bed with a sigh.

Before his turning, Tony had been Director of the Joint NSA and Homeland Security Department. He was well aware of the implications, should vampires become involved in terrorist activities. "I don't know what to think about working with that kid." Tony voiced one of his concerns aloud.

"Anthony, we have been instructed to do so. Therefore, we will work with him. Should he refuse to obey, compulsion will be placed. It will be a simple remedy." Gavin's dark eyes narrowed as he stowed the tablet in an outside pocket of his leather carry-on.

"We'll have to place compulsion for daylight hours anyway."

"Very true. I have no desire to have him turn to mist or get away in some other fashion. I had hopes that Wlodek would send Aedan with us, but that was not to be. I have no desire to work with a young one, Anthony," Gavin's whisper was almost a growl. "I have no patience for this."

~

"Hey, Ashe. What's shakin'?" Marco pulled up a deck chair and sat beside Ashe on Winkler's deck.

"Last-minute studying for the GED." Ashe held up the large, paperback study guide. "Test is Tuesday. Just in time for the vampires to arrive."

"The two the Council is sending?"

"Yeah."

"Know who they are?"

"Tony Hancock and his surrogate sire, Gavin Montegue."

"Did Winkler tell you who they were?"

"Nope. He knows both of 'em, though."

"What do you think they'll be doing—besides hauling you around on weekends and telling you what to do?" Marco blinked dark eyes at Ashe, who'd gone back to reading the study guide.

"That's pretty much it. They won't trust me, that's for sure. Just like I won't trust them. Maybe we can meet somewhere in the middle." Ashe shut the study guide and dropped it on the deck beside his lounge chair. "Marco, so many things are happening, right now. So many things I need to take care of, and all of it is a big, fat headache." Ashe rubbed the space between his eyebrows to prove the point.

"Anything you can talk about?" Marco leaned back in his chair and stared at the gulf waters.

"No. It's best if you don't know."

"Want to talk about last night?"

"I did what I could, so Jeremy's parents wouldn't suffer. I'm sorry if you and the others are scared witless, now."

"I hear Josiah Dunnigan won't be a problem anymore. Or Eudora and Fergus."

"That doesn't mean Zeke Tanner won't send somebody else—and we still didn't get the leak from Star Cove."

"Take down one problem and two more appear, huh?"

"Marco, did you actually read some Greek mythology? You

continuously surprise me." Ashe turned his head and grinned at Marco, handing the werewolf his first real smile in days.

"I may have read a little," Marco shrugged with an answering grin.

"Marco," Ashe was serious again, "why did Sali abstain last night? Is this the way it'll be from now on? He'll refuse to support me in any way?"

"I don't know why he did that, unless he was worried about what Dad might say afterward. Dad voted against you taking the execution, too."

"Yeah, I guess that could be a problem. For those folks who still have a dad."

"Ashe, you still have people who care about you."

"I know. It's just not the same."

"Yeah. Understood."

"How's Cori?"

"Cori's good. Talked to her this morning after I hauled my ass out of bed. Star Cove was pretty quiet, last night."

"I'd have settled for quiet."

"Yep. Look, executions, they're never fun. They're necessary, though. If it hadn't been for stupid Chump and Wormy, Hayes would still be here."

"I know. They were aiming for Winkler, just like those others who were killed last night."

"Zeke Tanner has a lot to answer for."

"Yeah."

~

"Buck, I don't know." Adele blinked at Buck, then dropped her eyes to the small velvet box he held. The box was open and a large diamond winked in the afternoon light. "It's just so sudden. I don't know what to say." Adele turned away.

"Adele, you know how I feel about you. Worried about you last night, too." Buck didn't say what else worried him. He'd seen what Ashe had done, and it frightened him. Buck wondered how many Star

Cove residents might remember what happened after night fell and the vampires walked through the community.

"I want to, Buck. I do. Will you give me a little time? Maybe another month? I might be ready then."

"I'll save this, then." Buck closed the small box with a quiet snap and pocketed it. "If you change your mind and want it sooner," he didn't finish.

"I'll let you know."

I paid your speeding ticket. Here's the receipt, the email read. Sali stared at the email before clicking the attachment, showing that the ticket had been paid by credit card. Sighing, Sali toggled back to the email. Ashe hadn't written anything except the terse notice that the ticket had been taken care of. Sali went to the next email in his inbox. It was from Dori.

Sali, it's just not working between us. I don't want to date anymore, Dori's message read. Sali wanted to fling his monitor through the bedroom window. Growling, he rose and paced like a restless wolf through his bedroom for several minutes before sitting down and sending a reply.

Thanks for breaking up with me on the Internet, his fingers tapped out a quick message. *That's so classy, Dorilou. What did your Ocelot do last night? Play with a ball of string?* Sali went to the first insult he could think of, knowing it would make Dori spittingly angry.

Hitting send before he could change his mind, Sali rose and paced again. His first reaction after sending the email was to text Ashe and discuss the breakup. Sali reminded himself that he couldn't—he'd ruined things with Ashe. Told too many of Ashe's secrets to those who probably didn't need to know them. Realized after a bit that he might have placed Ashe in danger by doing so. And then he'd abstained on the vote to allow Ashe to take Jeremy's execution. He hadn't supported his friend.

"Damn," Sali muttered, raking fingers through thick, black hair.

He'd not only managed to lose his best friend, he'd alienated him, too. School would start in two days and he no longer had a best friend or a girlfriend. Things had certainly taken a turn for the increasingly bad and appeared to be speeding downhill at an accelerated rate. Kicking his desk chair angrily, Sali snatched up his car keys, rushed out of his bedroom and headed for the front door.

~

"Any problems during your full-moon change last night?" Bear Wright asked as he drove Lewis Sharpe to the Corpus Christi Airport.

"You've got a real problem with coyotes on the island," Lewis muttered. "I spent half the night getting chased by those suckers."

"I'll let Winkler know—maybe his wolves will help solve that problem," Bear grinned.

"That would be outstanding," Lewis muttered. "If there are any smaller shifters, they could end up getting hurt," he added. "Just drop me off at the gate; I can handle things from there. I wish I could stay for that meeting you're having, though."

"Maybe you can make it back if we can convince the shifters to come together. I'd appreciate your vote on the matter." Bear pulled a card from his shirt pocket and passed it to Lewis. "We need to band together. A lot of us can't make a stand against the vamps and wolves if they decide to hunt us again."

"Yeah. Understood." Lewis turned his gaze to the passenger-side window and the rest of the trip was made in silence.

~

"Here's a backpack. Make sure you strap it on tight enough when you turn, or you'll lose your clothes, the gun and the fake ID I just paid for," Zeke Tanner glared at the youngest werewolf assassin who worked for him. "Fail me, and you'll join the others, here." Zeke jerked his head toward the taxidermic animals crowding his private study.

Peyton Miller swallowed hard. The white buffalo in particular seemed to be glaring at him with a glassy, accusing stare. Zeke had tracked the stuffed buffalo down through his contacts.

The animal had been confiscated in New Mexico with the rest of Obediah Tanner's belongings. Zeke had arranged to have the buffalo stolen back and shipped to him. Peyton knew a lot of money had surrounded that transaction, and the Amarillo Packmaster had been involved.

Peyton shifted uncomfortably at Zeke's words and the turn his thoughts had taken. Killing in Mexico was one thing, where drug wars abounded and police protection and intervention was light. Killing in the U.S. was another thing, especially if one of the Grand Master's closest friends was the intended target.

"Make sure you travel light—I want this done as quickly and as discreetly as possible." Zeke breathed a half growl. "I wish I could bring Josiah back to life, just to watch him die again."

Peyton hid the shudder that threatened to become visible, and struggled to keep his heartbeat at a regular rhythm. It wouldn't do to show his increasing fear to Zeke, and it certainly wouldn't do to allow Zeke to hear his thumping heart.

Peyton couldn't wait to make his run as wolf across the border, to get away from Zeke Tanner and everything he represented. In his heart, Peyton wanted to leave Mexico behind—for good. His main worry was how quickly Tanner might send someone after him, once he learned Peyton had abandoned his assignment.

"Gavin, what is this?" Tony stared at the bag from a popular electronics store that Gavin tossed onto the safe house's kitchen table.

"The latest in technology—a miniature tablet," Gavin grumped. "The salesclerk assured me that this will keep any young one occupied for hours."

"You're mollifying him through daylight hours? That's so unlike you." Tony wanted to smirk but held it back. One never smirked in Gavin's presence. One might roll his eyes while Gavin's back was turned, but even that was a risky proposition, as Gavin could move faster than the eye could blink and Tony was too afraid of his surrogate sire to offer excuses.

~

"Ready for the GED?" Winkler settled his tall frame on the opposite end of the sofa Ashe occupied.

"Yeah." Ashe was toying with a side-pocket flap on his cargo shorts. "Mr. Winkler?" he turned his gaze to Winkler, whose dark eyes were watching him. Ashe figured it was curiosity mixed with genuine concern.

"What is it, Ashe?"

"What happened to that rifle and the poisoned darts that Chump and Wormy had?"

"They're locked away in my gun cabinet."

"Good. I don't want anybody else to have access," Ashe sighed.

"Agreed," Winkler nodded. "We don't need another death like that. If Marcus had any sense, he'd be thanking you that there weren't more deaths."

"Marcus doesn't trust where he should," Ashe's eyes filled with stars before clearing abruptly. "Randy's girlfriend is a shapeshifter. She turns into a flop-eared rabbit. She's pretty, too. Both ways. I think it might be dangerous if she comes back to Star Cove."

"I heard she was a veterinarian. A good one."

"Yeah. Randy's in love."

"If she shouldn't come back to Star Cove, what do you expect Randy to do, kid?"

"I don't know. I can always lend him money to fly to Chicago, I guess. Or she can meet him in San Antonio when she flies down. I just don't know how to tell him that."

"I have a condo in San Antonio," Winkler said. "Three bedrooms. Plenty big enough and in a good neighborhood. Trace uses it sometimes, when his partner visits. Randy could borrow it if he wanted. I'll let him know." Winkler raked fingers through his hair before pulling out his cell and tapping in a reminder.

"Heard from the vamps?"

"I got a text from Tony—Anthony Hancock." Winkler offered Ashe a wry grin. "I know he says his last name is Rockland, now, but that name is for humans. He said they landed in New York to spend the day. They'll be here tomorrow night, around midnight."

"I called him a hero in a paper I wrote for a school assignment," Ashe went back to worrying his pocket flap. "I didn't know much, back then."

"Will it make you treat him differently—to know that he didn't do all those things the history books say he did?"

"I figure he didn't have much control over that part, and at the time, he was probably protecting somebody else."

"He was. He was protecting Lissa. Sort of. I wanted to protect her, too. You see how that turned out."

"I can't figure out how they don't remember her."

"Kid, I can't figure out why they don't and the wolves do. You have to leave around seven in the morning to get to the testing location on time. Breakfast is at six. Trace will take you to Beeville, and see you get lunch at the break."

"I'll be ready, Mr. Winkler."

"Good. There's still time for a run on the beach or a workout in the exercise room before dinner."

"I think I'd like a run," Ashe rose and stretched.

"I'll get Trace or Trajan to go with you."

"I'll get my shoes on."

"The kid was asking about that dart gun," Winkler jerked his head toward the locked gun cabinet inside his study. Ashe had already gone to bed and Winkler was having a last-minute meeting with Trajan before heading for his bedroom.

"That worries me, then," Trajan sighed, shaking his head. "Not much gets past Ashe. You think somebody might try to break in?"

"The house is alarmed and the cabinet is locked. I'm not sure what else to do with it."

"How about letting the kid take it into the hidden room in the basement?"

"There's a thought." Winkler nodded, considering the idea. "How about this—you arrange to have a smaller gun cabinet delivered tomorrow, and I'll put the dart gun and darts inside it, then ask Ashe to do his thing and leave it inside the closet in the hidden room. Nobody but you, Trace and I have to know anything about it."

"Sounds like a plan. If you don't have anything else for me, I'll head toward bed." Trajan stood and stretched. With his arms held up, Trajan filled a lot of space. "We have to get to that board meeting in Dallas by ten," Winkler said before covering a yawn. "Jet will be ready at six-thirty."

"Don't remind me." Trajan walked out of Winkler's study.

∼

"Salidar, please explain where you've been most of the day, and why you're coming home at midnight. I left three messages on your cell and you failed to reply." Marcus' voice was a low growl. Sali sat at the kitchen table, a rebellious expression on his face. "Are you going to answer me?" Marcus went on when Sali failed to reply.

"Dad, I was out. My cell ran down. I'm sorry." Sali's tone indicated he was far from sorry.

"Grounded," Marcus announced flatly. "Give me your keys and go to bed, Salidar. You are not to leave the house outside school hours for two weeks."

"Fine." Sali slapped his car keys on the table. "Car was out of gas, anyway," he muttered, rising and stalking away.

"Three weeks," Marcus called out. Sali kept walking.

∼

Wildrif's cell battery was almost drained, and there were few options in the Arizona desert to recharge it. He had calls to make, and hoped the battery would last at least that long.

"Don't stray too far," Rumble, the last of Baltis' new Destroyers growled at Wildrif as he walked past the guards posted on the eastern edge of the Dark King's encampment.

"Just getting a bit of exercise," Wildrif replied meekly, his head down. Rumble snorted and let the quarter-blood seer go. There wasn't anything for miles, Rumble knew, and the seer would find nothing but death should he stray too far. Rumble felt it might be a fitting end for the unwelcome misfit, but Baltis did seem to find him useful at times.

Wildrif walked for perhaps a quarter mile before pulling the precious cell from his pocket and making his first call—the most important one. The call was answered on the second ring.

"Master Tanner?" Wildrif spoke after Zeke's gruff "hello."

"Wildrif? What do you have for me?"

"A suggestion, Master Tanner. And a request."

"What's the suggestion?"

"Do you still have your contact in the U.S. capital?"

"I do."

"I will send a message containing vital information. You should forward it to him. He will take appropriate action."

"I'll do that. What's the request?"

"Might I be removed from the Dark King's loving embrace? He has become more than tiresome."

"I can have somebody at your current location in two days."

"I will be waiting."

"Good. Here's what I want you to do."

CHAPTER 6

Curtis Roberts, Director of the U.S. Intelligence and Foreign Communications Division, toyed with a printout of information he'd received from his source in Mexico.

The title of Curt's division sounded completely benign. It wasn't. He had authority even the CIA couldn't claim. He'd held his position for nine years, after the division had been created by an outgoing President during a lame-duck session. As yet, the current President, still in the first year of his term, hadn't been notified of the IFC's actual role in national security.

"This is more than interesting," Curt handed the printout back to his personal assistant, Calhoun. "With this information, we can make arrests before the day's over."

"Who should I notify?"

"Matt Michaels. His people can move the fastest."

"What about the last paragraph here?" Calhoun dangled the paper by a corner. "It says there may be more coming, to prove we can trust the source."

"I'll wait to see what more coming actually means. These three names are good, but I'd need something better than that to make the source unimpeachable, in my opinion. Get with Matt Michaels, hand him the names and see if he can make arrests. If this information is wrong, well," Curt shrugged.

"We let Matt Michaels take the fall for it," Calhoun grinned.

"He's just too squeaky clean," Curt agreed. "Keep me posted with texts—the meeting I have on the hill may take all day."

"Of course, sir."

⁓

"Nervous?" Trace glanced at Ashe as they drove toward Beeville. Coastal Bend College was their destination for the test, and they'd left Port Aransas in plenty of time.

"Yes and no," Ashe sighed. "I know," he held up a hand as Trace started to reply. "That's not much of an answer. I have mixed feelings about this, Trace. I can't explain why, right now, but I do."

"You think you won't pass?"

"I can pass." Ashe hunched his shoulders. "No worries about passing."

"Winkler already pulled strings to get you enrolled at the University of Texas. He knows the College President."

"Yeah." Ashe looked out the passenger window.

"Kid, what's wrong?"

"Trace, ask me that question in a few weeks. Okay?"

"You're starting to scare me, Ashe."

"You think I'm not already there?" Ashe turned and blinked at Trace.

"Let's get through today, and we'll let tomorrow take care of itself," Trace muttered, turning onto Charco Road. Ashe saw the college sign near a parking lot, which was already filling up.

"Good thing we left early," Ashe sighed.

⁓

"What are you wearing tomorrow?" Wynn flopped onto Dori's bed. Dori had been restless and out of sorts all morning, calling Wynn right after breakfast and asking if she wanted to do anything on their last day of summer vacation.

"No idea. Maybe I should have waited to break up with Sali. At least he has a car and could take us somewhere," Dori grumped, dropping onto the floor in a cross-legged position. "I still have enough money to buy new shoes."

"Ace is out of town," Wynn nodded. "I miss him when he's gone. I know not to be a pest," she held up a hand at Dori's lifted eyebrow. "I don't call or text. We agreed that he'd let me know when he wasn't working. We talk, then."

"At least he's a mature werewolf." Dori frowned. "Unlike Sali, who resorts to childish insults at the first opportunity." Dori still hadn't shown Sali's last message to Wynn. The insult was too embarrassing.

"What do you think tomorrow will be like? Ashe won't be there. Hayes is gone. Larry and Jeff are still not talking to anybody, and Sali's back to being a jerk." Wynn examined her blue toenail polish with a critical eye. She'd have to redo it before classes started in the morning. "I'd really like to get my bangs trimmed," she added. "I wonder if Mom will let me borrow the car."

"We can ask, but if we don't have somebody with us," Dori said. "Marcus laid down the law after Hayes got killed. I still don't understand what happened to Jeremy. Sali told me that Micah took Chad's execution," her voice dropped to a whisper. "But he wouldn't talk about Jeremy."

"Well," Wynn scraped off blue toenail polish with a fingernail, "Ace told me. He said Marco told Cori, too, so I'm surprised she didn't tell you."

"Tell me what? I haven't really seen Cori lately; she's been busy moving into her dorm room."

"Ashe did it. Ace wouldn't explain how."

"It was that scary?" Dori blinked at Wynn in confusion.

"No. He said it was—unusual. That's all."

"That describes Ashe. Completely. He's unusual." Dori got up and wandered to her bedroom window. "I still want to go out today, but

Mom's with Cori, hauling a load of stuff for her dorm room in the car. Dad's asleep and nobody else we know is available to ask."

"Yeah. Ace wouldn't like it if we're not guarded. I hate being cooped up here."

"Cori says Ashe is taking the GED today. You know he'll pass it."

"He'll pass it," Wynn agreed. "Do you ever get the feeling that Ashe not only passed us by, but he did it at warp speed?"

"It's scary. I remember when he was a laughingstock, because he couldn't turn. Now, he's working for Mr. Winkler and about to start college. Two years ahead of us."

"I can't believe Sali and Ashe aren't friends anymore. I thought they'd stick together always."

"Things change," Dori nodded. "Let's go outside. Maybe we can find somebody to give us a ride." Wynn slid off the bed and followed Dori out the door.

"Amos, how are you?" Bear Wright shook Amos Thompson's hand and then stood aside to allow the buffalo shapeshifter inside his home.

"Bear, we haven't talked in a while," Amos nodded.

"You're right. Not since your brother Alex disappeared all those years ago." Bear led the way to his kitchen, where he offered Amos Thompson a seat at his kitchen island. "Want coffee?"

"Sure. Thanks."

"I still miss Alex," Bear said, dumping coffee in the coffeemaker. "He and I, we put up a hell of a fight for the Marines in Dubya Dubya Two. You went off and joined the army, so you missed it."

"Our parents said they couldn't face losing both of us, so we went in separate directions. Thought it gave us a better chance."

"Yeah. Not easy to deal with, knowing Alex survived the war, only to fall into somebody's trap later on. I always suspected the Tanner bunch, but there was never any proof."

"I'd just like a body to bury, if there is one," Amos sighed. Bear set a fresh cup of coffee in front of his old friend. "I was hoping somebody coming to your meeting might know what happened to Alex. He was in Arizona when he disappeared."

"Hard to believe it's been thirty years," Bear agreed, pouring a cup of coffee for himself. "That gives me an idea, though. If we set up a network so shifters can put up names of missing friends or family members and allow the rest of the shifter community to take a look, then some of them may know what happened."

"I was hoping we could ask, at least," Amos sipped his coffee.

"I think it's a good idea. As soon as we can set a date, we may have more shifters together in one place than we've ever had before. I have copies of the werewolf and the vamp rules—don't ask how I got the vamp part, but I think we can cobble something together to protect the community using those as guidelines."

"We need it," Amos said. "Have, for a long time. We needed leverage back in the day, when we were nothing but target practice for werewolves and vamps. That prejudice still exists. More than most think."

"I know. The Grand Master and I are friends and have been for a long time. He understands, but that doesn't go for all the wolves."

"That prejudice may not go away in our lifetimes," Amos sagely agreed.

~

"Jasper, call out the dogs," Matt said. "We may have leads on those three who blew up the courthouse in South Carolina."

"Are you kidding me?" Jasper, a werewolf and Matt's assistant, grinned at his boss. "Nobody had anything on those guys."

"I have names," Matt waved a printed page at Jasper. "All three of them have petty crimes in their background, and now we have addresses, thanks to an unnamed source. It's enough to make arrests, and if we can pull confessions out of them, well, so much the better."

"Gonna get one of the vamps on this if we can make the collar?"

"You bet." Matt flashed Jasper a wide grin. "Why are you still standing there? Get going."

~

Ashe deliberately got a few questions wrong. Things were going well, too, until he got to the essay question. "Describe the qualities of a good parent," stared back at him. Ashe sighed. He dithered. Finally, steeling himself, he began to write.

~

"How did it go?" Trace asked as he and Ashe walked toward the SUV.

"Fine," Ashe mumbled. "I passed."

"Kid, you worry me at times." Trace hit the fob button to unlock the van and slid onto the driver's seat. Ashe climbed in slowly on the passenger side.

"I'm worried about the vamps coming in tonight."

"Mr. Winkler will be back by then. He knows both of them."

"I know."

"Classes start at UTA next week. Homework," Trace grinned, attempting to lighten the mood.

"Yeah."

"Want new school clothes?"

"To go with the ton of stuff Mr. Winkler bought for me at Banana Republic?"

"Shoes?"

"Maybe." Ashe smiled.

"Dinner out?"

"Maybe."

"Steak, seafood or something else?"

"Mexican?"

"Kid, you just said the magic word." Trace steered away from the college and headed toward Corpus Christi.

~

"Thanks for giving us a ride, Mrs. Smith." Dori sat in the front seat of

Dawn Smith's late-model sedan. Wynn climbed into the back seat after letting her mother know that she and Dori were riding to Corpus Christi with Randy's mother.

"It's no trouble, girls. I was going to the mall anyway—Randy needs new shirts for work."

"He's such a good writer," Wynn offered. "I read some of his articles online that he wrote for the Chicago paper."

"I can't believe he's falling for that worthless girl," Dawn said. "Did you meet her?"

"No. I think she had a hotel room in Port A," Dori said. "We didn't see her."

"Ashe met her," Dawn huffed. "She's supposed to be so smart, getting through college and going to veterinarian school. Seemed too timid to me. Fitting, I guess, since she's a bunny when she turns."

"I didn't know that," Dori blinked at Dawn in confusion. "She's a shapeshifter? Did Randy know about that?"

"Not until she got here."

"Wow. I don't know what to say," Dori muttered.

"He'd be better off with a werewolf or a larger shifter. Somebody who can protect him, if necessary. That rabbit is dinner."

"Well, maybe somebody else will come along," Dori offered. Dawn seemed angry and Dori didn't know how to deal with that. Dawn pulled into the mall parking lot and located a space not far from the entrance.

"Where can we meet, in case we get separated?" Dawn asked as they walked in the mall.

"We can be back here—whenever you're ready," Wynn offered, tossing long, white hair over a shoulder.

"Two hours? I should be done by then," Dawn said.

"Sounds fine," Dori shrugged.

"Great. See you later." Dawn started to walk away when her phone rang. "Hello?" she answered the call. "What do you want, now?" she asked, anger evident in her voice again.

"Let's go that way," Dori steered Wynn in the opposite direction.

"That was weird," Wynn whispered as they walked away quickly.

She cast a quick glance over her shoulder. Dawn had her back turned to them, still talking on the phone. "Come on. There's a shoe store this way."

~

"There's a Mexican restaurant here at the mall, and we can find shoes at the same time," Trace steered the SUV into a parking space.

"Sounds good," Ashe opened his door and climbed out. "If we're lucky, we may not be going home alone." Ashe stuffed the tail of his shirt into his jeans and began walking toward the entrance. Trace had to trot to keep up with him.

~

"Dori—look! There's Ashe and Trace." Wynn pulled Dori away from a rack of shoes and pointed.

"Let's go. Maybe we can get a ride home with them. It makes me uncomfortable when Mrs. Smith talks about shifters like they're scum."

"Yeah. Let's go."

"Ashe?" Dori called out. Ashe turned quickly, followed closely by Trace.

"Hey, Dori. Wynn." Ashe started walking toward them. "What are you guys doing here?"

"I could ask you the same," Dori grinned.

"We're here for Mexican food. Then Ashe wants new shoes," Trace grinned.

"We were looking at shoes, too, but Mexican food sounds awesome," Wynn said shyly.

"You can eat with us—I'll buy," Ashe offered.

"That's great. I'll call Mrs. Smith and let her know we're with you, if that's okay," Dori said. "We rode in with her, but she wants to leave in about half an hour."

"We'll take you home, no problem," Trace agreed. "Call your parents, too, and let them know."

"Great," Dori bounced on her toes. Wynn pulled the cell from her purse and placed a call to Dawn Smith.

~

"Why do they always bring flour tortillas when these corn tortillas are so much better?" Dori dropped a spoonful of salsa on a buttered corn tortilla, covered that with a little queso and rolled it up before biting into it with a happy smile.

"No idea. I have to ask for these every time." Trace had introduced them to the tasty goodness of warm corn tortillas as an appetizer. "The old Mexican restaurant we went to in Denton always served these."

"This is pretty darn good," Ashe agreed, helping himself to another tortilla.

"Says the bottomless pit," Trace grinned.

"I'm a growing boy," Ashe laughed.

"You'll be as tall as Trajan and Trace if you keep that up," Dori snickered.

"Close, maybe," Ashe agreed.

"Mrs. Smith said you met Randy's girlfriend," Wynn said, taking a chip from the complimentary basket and dipping it in the bowl of salsa.

"What did Mrs. Smith say?" Ashe turned to Wynn.

"That his girlfriend seemed too timid."

"She said Randy's girlfriend was dinner," Dori snorted. "It made me mad."

"It should make you angry," Trace muttered. "There's no excuse for that."

"I need to talk to Randy," Ashe grumbled before hauling out his cell and punching in a number.

~

"Ashe? What's going on, man?" Randy answered Ashe's call.

"Hey, Randy. I had a talk with Mr. Winkler yesterday. He said you're welcome to invite Sara down next time and meet her in San Antonio. The plane tickets will be cheaper and he has a three-bedroom condo there you can borrow."

"Really? That's great. I gotta tell you, I was worried that Sara might not want to come back—I think Mom scared her. You know why."

"Yeah. I know why," Ashe agreed. "Look, I'm having dinner with Trace, Dori and Wynn, so I need to let you go. I just wanted to tell you what Mr. Winkler said."

"Thanks, man, that's really good news. See ya." Randy ended the call.

"That was quick," Trace grinned at Ashe as their waitress placed plates of food on the table. "Randy will like the condo. It's really nice and not far from downtown San Antonio."

"I'd love to see San Antonio. We passed through on our way here, but didn't stop," Dori said. "Ashe, Sali and I broke up."

"I know," Ashe said. "You don't have to go into details. Sali and I are on the outs, too."

"Yeah. I hear that," Dori cut into her enchiladas. "Sali needs a hard kick in the pants."

"I don't know about that," Ashe said, lifting a taco and crunching into it. "He's done a pretty good job beating himself up."

"I got a text from Cori. She says Marco told her that Sali got grounded for disappearing for hours yesterday and not answering Marcus' calls." Dori sipped her soda and blinked innocently at Ashe.

"So, the rumor mill is as strong as it ever was, huh?" Ashe went back to his taco.

"Obviously," Wynn replied. Her phone rang. "It's Ace." She was almost breathless as she answered the call.

"Hi, baby," Ace's voice was clear to Ashe's enhanced hearing. "We just hit the ground in Corpus."

"Tell him we're at the Mexican restaurant in the mall, if he wants to join us," Trace said. He was listening to the conversation, just as Ashe was.

"Mexican? Baby, we'll be there in a few minutes," Ace chuckled and hung up.

"We'll need more space," Ashe informed the waitress when she came to refill glasses. "We've got three more coming."

"Three?" Dori lifted an eyebrow.

"Ace is driving Winkler and Trajan," Trace explained. "Had to go to Dallas for a board meeting this morning. They probably left right after the meeting was done and didn't take time for dinner."

Two restaurant employees pulled up an extra table and laid out a new basket of chips with salsa.

"We'll need another basket of chips, more corn tortillas and two orders of queso," Trace grinned at the waitress.

❧

"Mom, Mr. Winkler, Trajan and Ace got back and they joined us at the restaurant. Trace is bringing us back when we're done," Dori assured Lavonna Anderson over her cell.

"That's fine, as long as I know where you are, honey," Lavonna said.

"We're fine, Mrs. Anderson," Winkler said, knowing Lavonna would hear.

"Thank you, Mr. Winkler."

"This is so nice," Wynn leaned her cheek against Ace's shoulder. The white werewolf leaned in and kissed the top of Wynn's head.

"I have an announcement to make," Winkler grinned as soon as Dori ended the call with her mother.

"What's that?" Trace asked.

"Wayne and Wynter flew back to Dallas with me this morning. Wynter came and asked me a question. I made a phone call. She and Thomas Williams, Jr. are officially engaged."

"Really?" Wynn clapped her hands and laughed. "That is awesome, Mr. Winkler."

"Yeah. It really is awesome," Winkler grinned.

~

"Kid, do you want to go back to the airport with us tonight to pick up the vamps?" Winkler asked on the way home. Trace and Ace had offered to drive Wynn and Dori home; Ashe chose to ride with Winkler and Trajan.

"I can," Ashe nodded. "That way, Mr. Montegue can get a good look at the kid."

"Kid, that vamp is more than seventeen hundred years old. Almost everybody is a kid to him."

"Around midnight?" Ashe asked.

"Yeah. You can get a nap in, if you want, before we leave."

"Maybe."

~

"Curt, that information was pure gold. We have three in custody and they're answering questions now," Matt Michaels said. He was watching through one-way glass as one of his vampire agents questioned a detainee his werewolves had arrested earlier in the day. Two had tried to run. They hadn't gotten far—not many could outrun a werewolf, even in human form. This one was admitting his part in the courthouse bombing, and naming the other two as his accomplices.

"That's great news. I'll look forward to seeing the newsfeeds tomorrow," Curt replied and hung up.

Matt pocketed his cell with a sigh. Six people had died in that courthouse bombing. Matt hoped Curtis Roberts' new informant kept supplying reliable information. He wondered, though, what Curtis might eventually ask in exchange.

A tenuous civility existed between Curtis and Matt, but Matt refused to trust Curtis. His distrust was one of the reasons he'd asked werewolves to go after the targets—he trusted them to do the job and not take unnecessary risks.

"This is my last communication until your wolves pick me up," Wildrif informed Zeke Tanner. "This side will be busy tomorrow when they hit the army base," he added. "Nobody will notice I'm gone for a while."

"Good. Make sure you're at the rendezvous point," Zeke managed to snap before Wildrif's cell went dead.

CHAPTER 7

"Gavin Montegue, this is Ashe Evans." Winkler made the introduction.

Ashe stared at Gavin Montegue while visions raced through his mind. He saw Gavin with Lissa. In many places. He saw them together, kissing at the base of the Guardian, the statue standing atop the dome of the Oklahoma Capitol. He saw images of Vampire Council meetings. Saw Lissa, nearly bald, as she stood before Gavin and argued with him.

"Kid, you in there?" Trajan jostled Ashe's arm, bringing him away from what he'd seen.

"Mr. Montegue," Ashe sighed and held out his hand to shake with the vampire. Surprisingly, Gavin took Ashe's hand.

"Ashe is one of the most respectful young men I've ever met," Winkler rattled ice cubes in his glass as he spoke with Gavin later in his study. "I'm asking that you give him the benefit of the doubt. I've learned that when the kid says something's important, then it's important."

"I hear he has unusual methods of getting from place to place. Have seen evidence of it, in fact."

"He's pretty broken up over his parents," Winkler changed the subject. "If you could, tread lightly in that area. I have no idea what his father thought he was doing, but Ashe is suffering as a result. That's not all, either. Adele, his mother, is already in another relationship, and I can only imagine it's because Aedan placed compulsion. This new guy has offered her a ring and a marriage proposal."

"Moving rather quickly, don't you think?" Gavin rumbled.

"I think so, but I can't control everything."

"Understood. I hear that college classes commence next week. We'd like to make use of the young man's talents through the weekend."

"I thought you might. Gavin, he's not vampire. I think I know how Wlodek feels. I hope that's not the case with you. We've worked together before, you and I, and I'm hoping that I can trust you now as I have in the past."

"I hope that remains true, although you know I can't circumvent a direct order from Wlodek."

"Yeah. I know that. Look at Aedan."

"Aedan is a shell. I fear he may be contemplating a trip into the sun, my friend. Should he learn of this marriage proposal you speak of, it may come sooner than anyone might expect. I am nearly a thousand years older than Aedan. I have seen this, many times."

"That will kill the kid," Winkler growled.

"I know not how to prevent it, should Aedan choose that path."

"This is impossible." Winkler rose to pace behind his desk. "Gavin, this kid, well, he's more than special. I don't know how else to explain it. If things continue to go wrong for him, I don't know what he might do."

"What has happened? That I do not yet know?" Gavin's face held no emotion, but Winkler knew this vampire. Probably better than any other vampire. Their friendship was based on mutual respect. Wlodek had no idea that Winkler and Gavin knew one another as well as they did.

"Have you ever heard the phrase, separating particles? I've seen it, and I still can't explain it. Hell, it's incomprehensible." Winkler raked fingers through his hair in frustration. "I trust the kid, but if his father walks into the sun, I just don't know what he might do."

"I am unfamiliar with this term. Can you describe it?"

"The kid took an execution the night of the full moon," Winkler began. "And I watched as the condemned just turned to sparks that floated away and winked out. The kid said that the condemned was with the universe, now."

"You're sure of this?" Gavin lifted an eyebrow.

"Yes. I'm sure of it. At this point, I don't know what might work against the kid, if you get on his bad side. Get my drift?"

"I worry about placing compulsion, then," Gavin muttered. "The Honored One did not tell me I was bound to report that sort of thing to him, but Anthony—I think Anthony may be required to do so."

"Then you'll have to keep that secret if it turns out that the kid isn't susceptible."

"I can control Anthony."

"I sure hope you're right. Out of curiosity, why are you being sympathetic to Ashe?"

"I realize this is seemingly out of character," Gavin muttered. "But before I left London, I had a visit from Merrill. You remember him, don't you?"

"Oh, yes. I remember him, all right."

"Merrill says this is important. If he says it's important, then it's important."

"I believe you."

"You will study these instructions and follow them precisely," Baltis paced before his chosen troops. "This explains how they are to be placed and set to explode. The moment they are set, relocate. I do not wish for you to be anywhere near there when the explosives detonate."

Six handpicked Dark Elemaiya examined the paper instructions they'd been given. The previous evening, Baltis' four new Destroyers, Raze, Ruin, Ravage and Rumble, approached the dealer Wildrif had contacted and purchased explosives from him. Baltis had spent a great deal of gold to procure them, after a demonstration was given in a remote location.

"Shall I go with them tomorrow?" Laridael asked quietly as Baltis stopped pacing to stand beside his personal guard. He and Baltis watched carefully as the six Elemaiyan soldiers studied their information.

"No need," Baltis waved away Laridael's concern. "This is quite simple, actually, and we will have our revenge. Soon."

~

"I don't like vamps in the house," Craig muttered as he dropped a plate of food in front of Winkler.

"They're asleep in the basement and their doors are locked," Winkler snapped, making Craig flinch. "You will leave them alone, do you hear?"

"Gavin won't waste time on your ass, he'll remove your head if you're too disrespectful," Trajan sat down at the kitchen island opposite Winkler.

"Disobey me, and I'll look the other way while he removes your head," Winkler muttered before pulling out his phone and tapping in a message.

"Kid, you ought to be sleeping late, since those vamps want to keep you up most of the night," Trajan remarked as Ashe shuffled into the kitchen, dressed in a T-shirt and shorts. "But since you're up, eat breakfast and I'll meet you in the weight room."

"Good morning to you, too," Ashe mumbled as he settled beside Trajan. "Is it torture the kid day, today?"

"Sure is." Trajan offered Ashe a wide grin. "And after that, we can run on the beach. Can't have you getting slow and sloppy." Trajan ruffled Ashe's hair. Ashe ducked his head and smiled.

~

"Did you get a reply from those vampires last night?" Thomas Williams settled at a table inside their hotel coffee shop. Like Weldon, he gripped a cup of coffee in his hands as he studied the Grand Master's face.

"Yep," Weldon grinned. "Dalroy said he and Rhett would be happy to provide some backup for us when we meet with Nick tonight. Ever since the kid said we might need help, I've been a little spooked. Dalroy can place compulsion and we'll get the truth, one way or another."

"What time?" Thomas asked.

"Nine-thirty, at Nick's place. It'll make it easier when I ask how he paid off his mortgage in less than five years."

~

"There it is." Trajan pointed out the new gun cabinet to Ashe. He, Ashe and Winkler stood inside Winkler's study, examining the gun cabinet that had been delivered half an hour earlier. "I put the dart gun and darts inside it already. You just have to carry it inside the hidden room downstairs."

"With pleasure," Ashe nodded, sizing up the cabinet and discreetly examining the lock. "Want to come with me?"

"Sure do," Trajan's teeth flashed white as he grinned broadly at Ashe. "Somebody will have a hell of a time gettin' to it after that."

"That's just what I was hoping for," Ashe agreed.

"I'll come, too," Winkler said. Ashe gathered Trajan, Winkler and the gun cabinet in his mist and dropped three floors to the basement.

~

Sali paid no attention as Mr. Dodd talked about the Berlin Wall and how it was torn down in 1989. Ashe had always sat beside him in the classes they shared. Now, the seat Ashe would have chosen was vacant, and Wynn and Dori occupied desks near the front. Larry and Jeff sat near the girls, leaving Sali surrounded by an island of empty chairs.

There was no large book to hide behind, either—textbooks were on tablets this year—Mr. Winkler had seen to that. The tablet was much easier to carry, but it couldn't connect to the school's Wi-Fi; the password hadn't been provided. Students could use their Wi-Fi at home to do research if they wanted.

Sali snorted softly. If Ashe were there with him, he probably would have hacked into the school's system already. Sali considered slipping the cell phone out of his pocket and sending a text to Ashe, telling him he was sorry. About everything. Sali winced uncomfortably. He'd give it a few days. Maybe Ashe would forgive him, then.

Peyton hadn't been inside a supermarket on U.S. soil in years. Zeke had always kept him in Mexico, sending him after rival cartels. The human competition never stood a chance. Zeke usually sent his older wolves after rival werewolves, although those were few in number. Peyton wondered, and not for the first time, just why Zeke thought him competent enough to go after William Winkler.

"Man, I haven't had these in years." Peyton pulled a large bag of his favorite cheese puffs off a shelf. They went into his grocery cart. Sodas came next, followed by snack cakes and other items he hadn't gotten in a long time.

He'd rented a motel room in Laredo, Texas, intending to spend a night or two before selecting a city to lose himself in. He'd have to outthink Zeke Tanner if he expected to stay alive, and that was no easy prospect.

"You go at sundown," Raze instructed the six Dark Elemaiya Baltis had selected for the mission. "The state of Georgia is one hour later than it is here, and the building we've selected will be unoccupied at that time. It will take one relocation from here, and you will return to this location as soon as the explosives are placed and set. Do you understand?"

Raze had traveled to the Kansas City area the night before with his six companions. He watched carefully as each of the six nodded at his words. These were Baltis' best troops, and half of them were captains in Baltis' army. "We are ready," Baltis' senior captain bumped a fist against his chest and nodded respectfully to Raze. "We await your command."

~

"All will be well," Wildrif bowed respectfully to Baltis. "You will see."

"Good. Leave me." Baltis waved a hand in dismissal. Wildrif bowed again and walked away from Baltis' lavish tent, reminding himself not to hurry or draw attention from the others. By the time the night was over, the human government would be angrier than an anthill under attack and he would be on his way to Mexico.

He'd made arrangements with Tanner, too—Baltis would think him dead when he disappeared. A body, dressed in his clothing and mangled beyond recognition, would be left behind in the desert. He hadn't considered it, but Zeke Tanner had. Obediah had been crafty, but his older brother Ezekiel eclipsed him. Zeke had sent Wildrif to New Mexico years earlier to keep an eye on his younger brother.

Wildrif sighed heavily. The Ir'Indicti had prevented him from seeing Obediah's capture and the destruction of Obediah's empire. Wildrif hadn't seen the Ir'Indicti's arrival either, but that was an unpredictable event. Even the best Miriasu couldn't have seen it; it wasn't for them to see. If the Ir'Indicti became involved in any event, Wildrif's visions wavered or failed altogether.

He'd seen Beldris' death easily enough—the Ir'Indicti hadn't been involved in that. He had failed to see his appearance in Canada, and what happened as a result. Wildrif had come to rely on information on those surrounding the Ir'Indicti, and he was getting better at tracking his movements. Soon, things would fall into place and Wildrif would have his revenge.

"I'll be better off in Mexico for the moment," Wildrif muttered to himself as he walked past the camp's perimeter. The guard spared him a perfunctory glance and turned away.

∾

"Nick, seems your takeover bid didn't go so well."

"You didn't tell me you were bringing vamps," Nick, held easily by Rhett, cursed as he snapped at the Grand Master.

Weldon stood before Nick, arms crossed comfortably over his chest as he watched the Amarillo Packmaster. Nick, thinking only the Grand Master was coming for a visit, had six wolves waiting to bring Weldon down. He'd thought to take the Grand Master position and change the landscape for werewolves throughout the world.

"I don't tell a lot of people a lot of things. That's my business. Six good wolves died tonight, because they didn't want to cross their Packmaster. You're responsible for their deaths. What do you think I'm about to do with you?" Weldon's dark eyes bored into Nick's hazel gaze.

"Gonna have one of your pet vamps do it for you?" Nick hissed.

"If I were you, I'd shut up. One of those vamps is holding you, remember?" Weldon's voice was a growl. "I'll do this myself, with Thomas as a witness. It'll be more painful than a quick head removal by Rhett, there."

"Screw you," Nick struggled in Rhett's implacable grip.

"No, thanks. Now, are you gonna die honorably, or are you gonna make Rhett chase you when he lets you go? Remember, he'll have you again before you can blink if you try to run."

"I'll take you down, you flea-ridden mutt," Nick snarled.

"You can try," Weldon's growl was low and menacing. "Rhett, let him go." Rhett nodded to Weldon and released his hold on Nick Robbins. Weldon didn't bother to undress. His clothing ripped as he became werewolf and leapt at the Amarillo Packmaster.

～

"We'll fly to Atlanta tonight, to look for a vampire we suspect of theft, illegal arms dealing and the killing of humans," Tony explained to Ashe while Gavin silently looked on.

"You think we need that outmoded method of transportation?" Gavin stared as Ashe's eyes went a dark blue and stars swept through their depths. "I will take you to Atlanta. Before you deal with Rydley Huntington, we will make another stop—at Fort Arland. Your targeted vampire has managed to sell explosives to the Dark Elemaiya, and they are planning to destroy most of the base tonight if we don't stop them."

"What the hell?" Tony backed away from Ashe, whose eyes slowly cleared.

"I mean it," Ashe shrugged. "I know what I know."

"You know where our quarry is?"

"Yeah." Ashe shrugged again.

"This will make things a lot easier," Tony muttered. "A lot scarier, too."

"Anthony, you will keep this information to yourself," Gavin commanded.

"Yes, Anthony, you will keep this information to yourself," Ashe repeated, placing compulsion on Tony. Tony's eyes unfocused for a moment before clearing. He blinked. "Yeah. I guess I will," he nodded.

～

"Weldon?" Winkler answered the Grand Master's call on his cell.

"Just wanted to let you know that Amarillo is without a Packmaster right now," Weldon said. Winkler heard clearly the sounds of Weldon dressing while he spoke.

"Took down Robbins?" Winkler asked.

"He tried a coup, earlier. Thought I'd be alone when he set six of his wolves on me. If Thomas, Dalroy and Rhett hadn't been with me, things might not have gone so well. Tell the kid thanks for giving me the heads-up."

"I'll tell him, but he's in a meeting with the vamps here—upstairs in my study."

"They'd better take care of him. Do they even have a clue how valuable—and vulnerable—he is?"

"I think Gavin may have a clue. Jury's still out on Hancock."

"Keep an eye on that cook of yours. I don't think he has a high opinion of shifters."

"I'll fire his ass."

"Don't fire him. Send him to Amarillo and let him help clean up this mess."

"I'll send him in the morning."

"Thomas can pick him up at the airport."

"I'll let you know what time."

～

"Trajan, we'll need a new cook," Winkler turned to his Second after ending the call with Weldon.

"I heard," Trajan pulled two sodas from the fridge and handed one to Winkler. "I hear Florence Thompson is a good cook."

"Amos' wife? The swan shifter?"

"Yeah. She made those pies you ate half of at the potluck gathering not long ago."

"That apple pie was almost as good as Lissa's," Winkler sighed. "Can you call her tomorrow? See if she's interested? I know she and Amos had to sell their livestock before the move. If she's bored, she may consider cooking for wolves. Assure Amos she'll be as safe as we can make her, and she can go home every night. Offer her weekends off, too; we can go out."

"How much?" Trajan asked.

"Offer her four thousand a month, if she does three meals five days a week, and she can carry dinner home for Amos."

"Why don't you ask Amos if he'd like a job? He can help guard the perimeter and get a little exercise, too. That way he won't miss his wife's cooking during the week," Trajan grinned. "He used to guard Cloud Chief. All he can do at Star Cove is sit inside that dinky guard shack."

"Then offer both of them a job," Winkler nodded.

"I'll call first thing in the morning, and tell the wolves they have to behave."

"If they don't want the job, see if anybody else in Star Cove is interested."

"Will do, Boss."

~

"Peyton, you've been in the same place for too long." Zeke's growl worried Peyton. "Did you think I wouldn't have a locator on that cell I gave you?"

Peyton gulped. He hadn't considered that, and he knew he should have. "Just getting my bearings, Mr. Tanner," Peyton replied, attempting to keep his voice calm and even. Zeke could smell fear from a hundred miles away.

"I expect you to be in Corpus Christi by tomorrow," Zeke snapped. "If I see you haven't moved, I'll send somebody after you. Got it?"

"Yeah. I'll be in Corpus by nightfall tomorrow."

"Good. We'll discuss a game plan when you get there."

~

Kid, what are we waiting for? Tony sent mindspeech to Ashe. He, Gavin and Ashe were hidden behind a forklift inside a darkened warehouse. Surrounding them were crates, boxes and supports filled with grenades, bullets, shells, rocket launchers and all sorts of weapons.

Six Elemaiya. The dark kind. With explosives bought from Rydley Huntington, Ashe replied. *You take care of the Elemaiya. I'll handle the explosives.*

What do you plan to do with the bodies? Tony asked.

88

Send them back where they came from, Ashe's mental voice was grim. *It'll cause trouble down the road, but it could mean bigger trouble in the interim.*

That's very comforting, Tony's response was sarcastic.

You used to do this kind of crap for a living. Vampirism has definitely gone to your head.

Don't get smart with me.

Then get smart with yourself. Look around you. What will this do if we let it happen? The nation goes on lockdown, people start looking for terrorists under their beds and wars start. End of story.

Kid, the vamps generally stay out of human affairs.

Except for those who work for Matt Michaels. Or the ones Wlodek has stashed here and there around the globe, so he can keep his fingers in every pie. Except for those, you mean?

Kid, watch your mouth.

Get ready, Ashe warned, just as six Elemaiya appeared inside the warehouse.

∼

"What the hell?" Winkler and Trajan were drinking their sodas on the deck and watching the waves roll in under a waning moon when Winkler received the text from an unknown source.

Hello, Mr. Winkler, the message began. *My name is Peyton Miller. I've been working for Zeke Tanner in Mexico for more than twenty years. I've managed to get away from him, but he'll be hunting me, soon. He's hunting you, too. I'd like to meet with you and share information, in exchange for protection.* Trajan was beside Winkler's chair quickly and reading over Winkler's shoulder.

"What the hell?" Trajan repeated Winkler's confused statement.

∼

Peyton ground the cell Zeke Tanner had given him under his heel, destroying it as best he could. He'd just purchased another cell at a discount store and used it to contact William Winkler. He'd gotten Winkler's number from Zeke, who'd gotten it from another source.

It didn't matter now—Peyton's life hung in the balance, and he'd prefer a quicker death from the Grand Master than what he'd likely get from Zeke and his trackers. No matter what happened, Peyton would be traveling to Corpus Christi. If Winkler agreed to meet with him, whether to kill him or listen to what he had to say, he no longer cared. Peyton was tired of the drugs and the killings.

Gavin Montegue, ancient vampire that he was, had never seen anything like this. Ashe, holding out a hand, had caused knapsacks filled with explosives to disintegrate and float away as harmless sparks. Six headless bodies littered the concrete floor of the base warehouse—Gavin and Tony had seen to that. Ashe now contemplated the bodies while a wave of nausea hit him.

"Kid, don't get sick. I hate that smell," Tony whined.

"I'll be fine," Ashe rasped, drawing in a shaky breath. "I just have to get it out of my mind before I send them back to Baltis."

"Baltis?"

"King of the Dark Elemaiya. He was doing this in retaliation for his brother's death in Chicago."

"One of those Matt Michaels and a few vamps took out?"

"Yeah. Baltis doesn't have much recourse against the vamps—and he's scared witless of you guys anyway. You move too fast. Humans, though, he doesn't mind killing because he's gotten away with it too many times."

"Young one, might we move faster? Anthony, stop distracting him," Gavin muttered.

"Gotcha," Ashe mumbled, holding out a hand again. The six bodies, with their heads, disappeared. "Now, all we have to do is clean up the blood and any evidence that we were here and we're good."

"We have to move swiftly." Wildrif was pulling off his clothing while one of two werewolves dressed a mangled, unrecognizable shapeshifter in Wildrif's discarded outfit. Wildrif had more clothing brought by the werewolves, but he'd just had a vision of six headless bodies appearing at Baltis' feet back in the camp. Wildrif's life would be worthless if Baltis found him again.

It didn't matter; Wildrif still had his contacts with the Bright Queen, and she was more than willing to listen. Zeke Tanner, too, would be putty in his hands. Wildrif had spent years building trust with both, and they would willingly listen to anything he suggested. Things were falling into place surprisingly well. Who cared if the Earth was destroyed, as long as Wildrif's revenge could be served?

Baltis' rage could not be contained. Ruin had contacted Raze, who as yet didn't realize what had happened. Six bodies and their disconnected heads lay at Baltis' feet, and he had already destroyed the tent and most of his belongings. Dark Elemaiya fled from Baltis' wrath, as he pulled energy from his crown to blast the sands beneath his feet.

CHAPTER 8

"Hello, Rydley. Didn't expect us, did you?" Tony grinned at Rydley Huntington.

The house in Atlanta where Ashe had taken Gavin and Tony was quite large. Rydley had employed compulsion to convince the wealthy owner to allow him access to his home and his extensive bank account. Explosives filled the six-car garage, too, forcing the human occupant to leave his expensive automobiles parked in the driveway.

"What the?" Rydley didn't get to finish his question; Gavin held him by the throat. "You will be still and answer questions. No other words will pass your lips." Gavin's eyes were red and the tips of his fangs showed as he placed a mind-bending compulsion on three-hundred-year-old Rydley. Rydley could only nod his compliance; Gavin held his throat too tightly.

What about the human? Ashe asked.

The compulsion will die when Rydley does, Tony said.

That's not scary or anything, Ashe replied.

Kid, don't say scary to me. I have a whole new respect for you, now.

"Hmmph," Ashe responded aloud and crossed arms over his chest.

"Shhh," Tony whispered.

Ashe watched as Gavin questioned Rydley Huntington about his dealings in arms, who he'd sold to and what, which humans had died and which he still did business with. The list was long. Ashe listened with interest.

~

"You weren't gone as long as I thought you might be," Winkler remarked as Ashe wandered into the kitchen at noon the following day.

"Mr. Winkler, have you ever seen a vampire die?" Ashe opened the fridge and stared at its contents absently.

"Yeah. Several times. Killed a few of 'em myself. Why do you ask?"

"They just turn to ash. Dust. Whatever." Ashe shrugged.

"Yep. You can clean up an entire vamp with a hand vacuum." Winkler sipped the cup of coffee in front of him—he'd made a pot for himself.

"That's funny. And not funny. At the same time," Ashe hauled the milk jug from the fridge and pulled a tall glass from a cabinet. "Where's grumpy?"

"Grumpy?"

"Craig."

"Oh. Sent him to Amarillo this morning after breakfast. Grand Master needed help cleaning out the Amarillo Pack. Nick Robbins is no more."

"Too bad. He was involved in a lot of crime. Inadvertently sometimes, through Josiah Dunnigan. Didn't argue when he got paid, though."

"Weldon never did trust him. Nick tried to take down the Grand Master last night. Obviously that was a mistake."

"Yep."

"Kid?"

"What, Mr. Winkler?" Ashe gulped half a glass of milk quickly.

"Know anything about Peyton Miller?"

"He contact you?"

"Yeah."

"You should hire him."

"What?"

"He's mighty tired of Zeke Tanner. Might be willing to help fight off what Zeke sends our way."

"Kid, I've already talked with the Grand Master. He wants to question Peyton before executing him. This'll throw a wrench in the works." Winkler shook his head, his dark eyes focused on Ashe.

"I just saved the Grand Master's posterior. Maybe he'll cut me some slack on this." Ashe drained his glass of milk. "Who are you getting to replace Craig? Good move, by the way. He was prejudiced up to his eyeballs."

"I hired Amos and Florence Thompson this morning. She'll cook, and he'll help guard during the day."

"Another good choice. Mr. Thompson is cool."

"It's not every day you meet a white buffalo shapeshifter," Winkler flashed a grin. "They're even rarer as shifters. Almost as rare as unicorns and bumblebee bats."

"Don't dis the bat, man."

"Not dissing the bat," Winkler laughed.

"Who's dissing the bat?" Trace walked in and ruffled Ashe's hair with a large hand.

"Everybody," Ashe ducked his head to hide a half-grin.

"Heard you got into it last night," Trajan slouched into the kitchen and went straight to the coffeepot.

"Gavin and Tony, well," Ashe shook his head. He still found it difficult to believe how fast they'd moved. Six heads had been removed before Ashe could blink twice. And then there was so much blood—blood he'd had to destroy by turning it to sparks. If it hadn't been important to return the bodies to the Dark King, he'd have done the same with them. He found it nauseating to look at them afterward. Sighing, Ashe worked to get the visions out of his head.

"Kid, it's the nature of what we are. What the vamps are. The way I hear it, those six were prepared to destroy Fort Arland. How many others would have died if they'd succeeded in their plan?"

"I tried to send a message to the Dark King. Tried to tell him his revenge against the humans is useless. He may choose another target to go after," Ashe muttered, pulling out a barstool at the island and sitting down. "Displacement."

"You mean choosing someone else to vent your anger on?" Winkler lifted an eyebrow while he sipped coffee.

"Yeah. Guess you had a chat with Gavin and Tony after we got back last night."

"It wasn't even one o'clock when you got back. Tony said it was the fastest they'd ever gotten anybody."

"I hope he doesn't expect that every time," Ashe replied, rising and going back to the fridge. "Anybody else want scrambled eggs?"

"Why can't the teachers get together and stagger homework assignments?" Dori was already complaining about the assigned paper in English, the math homework and the research required for a history exam. She and Wynn sat at a table in the new school cafeteria. She could see Adele Evans behind the serving line, talking with the two shapeshifter women serving lunch to the students.

"Our school is getting smaller," Wynn remarked, ignoring Dori's complaint. "We only have sixty-two students this year."

"There isn't a first or second-grade class," Dori agreed, watching as students went through the line to get trays of food. "You don't think the shifters and werewolves are dying out, do you?"

"You know," Wynn pointed her unwrapped straw at Dori before dropping it into her milk carton, "that sounds like a good essay to research and write at the end of the year."

"You think we can find that out? You think there's information out there?"

"I think Principal Wright might know a lot."

"You think he'll talk to us?"

"He might."

"I didn't expect to get visitors this soon." Bear Wright smiled at Wynn and Dori. His empty lunch tray lay before him—he'd eaten at his desk in order to get paperwork done during the meal break.

"We just had a thought," Wynn began. "When we were at lunch, talking about how there's no first or second-graders this year."

"And we were wondering if this is a problem everywhere, and not just here, in Star Cove," Dori added. "And we thought it might be a good topic to research for the end of school essay."

"That's very insightful," Bear nodded. "And it's something that I've done research on, too."

"What did you find out?" Wynn asked breathlessly.

"I'm afraid numbers are dwindling," Bear sighed, leaning back in his chair. Unlike Principal Billings', Bear's office chair was more modern and cloth-covered. It didn't creak when he moved. "That's one of the topics I wanted to discuss with the shifters who are coming to visit this weekend. Just to see if they've noticed it, too, and have any ideas," the Principal sighed. "Do your research, girls. I'll accept a joint paper at the end of school if you work on it together."

"Really? You'll let us do that?" Wynn clapped her hands and bounced in her seat.

"Sure. It's a weighty topic and deserves as much work as you both can put into it."

"Thank you so much, Mr. Wright," Dori smiled. "This will be so awesome."

❦

"Ashe? This is Wynn."

"Wynnie, I'd know your voice anywhere." Ashe left his cell on the island while he ate scrambled eggs and bacon. "What do you need?"

"We might need help doing research. Dori and me."

Ashe grinned and didn't correct Wynn's English. "What's the project?" he asked instead.

"We noticed that there aren't any first or second-graders, and thought it might be a good topic to research for our end-of-year essay.

We asked Principal Wright about it, since he might know something. He said the numbers are dwindling, and he's willing to let Dori and me do a paper together."

"That's outstanding, Wynn. I warn you, though, if I give you information, a lot of it may not have concrete evidence to back it up."

"It won't be true?" Wynn sounded troubled.

"It'll be true, I just can't back it up with physical proof, that's all. Some people might question its veracity, because of that." Ashe wiped his hands on a napkin and lifted his second glass of milk to take a drink.

"Ashe?"

"What, Wynn?"

"Who uses words like veracity?" Wynn teased.

"Wynn, I haven't heard you tease in a while. It's kind of nice," Ashe grinned.

"Yeah. Ace likes it, too."

"I imagine he does. I also imagine he thinks he won the lottery—like every time he looks at you."

"Ashe, stop it." Ashe's grin widened—he knew Wynn was blushing.

"How's Sali?" Ashe asked, switching topics.

"He sits by himself in class. I'm not sure he talks to anybody. Larry and Jeff only talk with each other. Everybody misses Hayes."

"Hayes was an omega. He knew instinctively how to calm people and keep them happy."

"A brave omega."

"Yeah. Look, Wynn, keep an eye on Sal for me. Discreetly. If things look like they're not going so good, will you let me know?"

"Can I ask Dori to help?"

"If she can keep it to herself."

"I'll tell her that. I don't know what to do, Ashe. I know school just started and all, but it seems so different. Like we've set our feet on a path we can't change, and the destination may not be what anybody planned."

"You're a real unicorn, Wynnie."

"What does that mean?"

"It means you're special. In a very good way. You have insights that others don't, sometimes."

"Ashe, stop making me blush. It's embarrassing. I have to get back to class."

"I know. Have fun." Ashe ended the call with a sigh. Less than thirty seconds went by when he received mindspeech from Dori.

Ashe?

Dori?

Sali only ate half his lunch.

That's a problem.

Yeah. He's moping, too. Like the world ended and he didn't participate.

Interesting concept, Dori.

Well, it's like something big happened, and he wasn't a part of it. Because he's too dumb.

Dori, Sali isn't dumb. He's smarter than people think. He just makes bad choices now and then.

Then he needs to stop playing dumb. And he needs to wise up.

That's redundant, Dori.

I guess it is, huh?

Yeah. Did you talk to Wynn already?

Yeah. Ever since Sali and I broke up and you stopped talking to him and Marcus grounded him and took his keys away, he won't talk to anybody. Now he's not eating. Sali always eats.

Agreed. Does he go home right after school?

He has to. His mom is waiting at the door to make sure the grounding is enforced.

Good to know. Don't you think you ought to pay attention in English, instead of sending mindspeech? Ashe added a mental chuckle to his words.

Fine, Dori's reply was falsely grumpy.

~

Sali walked past his mother, who stood at the front door of the DeLuca home, waiting for her youngest to arrive.

"Straight from school, as commanded," Sali muttered as he headed for the hallway leading to his bedroom.

"Want a snack?" Denise DeLuca called out. Sali didn't reply.

Sali cursed softly as he turned the knob to enter his bedroom. His stomach growled, but he wasn't going to let his mother know it was also tied in knots. Everything was wrong with his life. *Everything.* How many times had Marco gotten away with stuff Sali always got grounded for? How many times had Marco flouted Marcus' commands and driven away from Cloud Chief in a huff? It was always Marco this and Marco that. Marco now worked for Mr. Winkler, probably the most wealthy and successful werewolf in the U.S. Nobody thought much of Salidar DeLuca. He'd just be a minion in a Pack someday.

Sali walked into his bedroom with a sigh, shut it behind him and leaned against it, his eyes closed.

"Dude, want a burger?" Sali's eyes popped open in shock. Ashe sat on his rumpled bed, waving a sack full of Dandee Burgers' food at him. The scent of hamburgers and fries hit his sensitive nose like a blow.

"He's reading in his bedroom, I peeked," Trajan informed Winkler, who'd asked where Ashe was.

"Andy has something Ashe needs to look at when he comes down for dinner. Loren caught a discrepancy and we need the kid's help."

"He ought to be sleeping, in case the vamps have other business tonight."

"I know. We'll have to be careful, Traje. He gets tired. Needs sleep. Just like anybody else. We can't expect him to work day and night."

"Yeah. The Thompson's will be here first thing tomorrow, at least."

"Thank goodness. We can order pizza tonight. Get extra. We can always put leftovers in the fridge."

Sali wolfed down the first burger and was halfway into the second before taking a long pull on the large soda Ashe brought for him.

"Dude, I'm sorry. Really sorry. I messed up," Sali bit into his burger again and chewed while he watched Ashe's face.

"Yeah. We all do, sometimes." Ashe leaned against Sali's headboard. Sali ate at his desk beside the bed, leaving the bed for Ashe. His mother hated it if he dropped food on the comforter.

Sali watched as Ashe raked fingers through his slightly curly, light-brown hair and closed his eyes. "Sal, I watched a vampire die last night. Six others, too. Those vamps don't mess around when they kill somebody."

"Dad said they were here." Sali took another bite of burger. "I really want to ask about the full moon incident, but I won't. I'm not giving Dad another thing. If he wants to know, he can ask you himself."

Ashe opened his eyes and turned toward Sali. "It's called releasing particles. Reducing something to its most basic level and letting the energy float away. Only a few can do it, Sal. None of the Elemaiya have ever been able to. Feel free to tell Marcus that, if he really wants to know."

"I heard something else, too. About your mom. And Buck."

"Don't bring that up. It's painful."

"Yeah. Understood."

"Sali, what would you do if you found out your dad, well, that your dad was really depressed? Thinking about ending it all."

"My dad isn't depressed. He's just an unbending tyrant," Sali muttered before stuffing the last bite of burger in his mouth.

"I'm not talking about your dad."

"Oh. You're talking about yours, aren't you?" Sali blinked dark eyes at Ashe. Aedan, depressed? That wasn't good. It was ridiculously easy for a vampire to end it all. Took minutes, at the most, if what he'd heard was true.

"Do you have us shielded?" Sali finally thought to ask.

"Since I showed up. Your bedroom is soundproofed, dude. You could scream your lungs out and your mom still won't hear," Ashe grinned wryly.

"That's kind of amazing," Sali observed. "What are you gonna do about your dad? I'd probably ask Marco to help, and then go tell dad he couldn't do that crap. People need him."

"That's an interesting idea," Ashe said, leaning against the headboard again. "I was out late last night, and Mr. Winkler thinks I'm reading a book in my bedroom. I'm gonna leave, Sal. Maybe I can sleep for an hour before Mr. Winkler orders pizza."

"Dang. Pizza for dinner sounds good. Mom's probably fixing meat loaf or something."

"Meat loaf sounds good to me. I guess the days are gone when I could invite myself to your house for dinner."

"Yeah. Life sucks, sometimes, doesn't it?" Sali shook his head at Ashe.

"It sure as hell does."

～

"Is it okay if I take a nap for an hour or so?" Ashe's hair looked a bit wild, as if he'd raked fingers through it several times before walking into Winkler's study. Winkler tapped figures into a spreadsheet on his computer as Ashe stopped beside his desk.

"Not a problem," Winkler looked up from his work. "I'll order pizza around that time, so you can get up and shower before we eat. The Thompsons will be here tomorrow, so you'll get decent meals during the week. We'll go out to eat on weekends if the vamps haven't hauled you to another state. Make sure they remember to feed you if you're gone overnight."

"I'll do that," Ashe replied dryly.

"I have something else, too." Winkler lifted a folder off his desk and offered it to Ashe. "An investigation into unusual expenditures. Not mine," Winkler added as Ashe took the folder and opened it. Ashe's eyes unfocused briefly while Winkler watched.

"Mr. Winkler, this one is playing with fire." Ashe handed the folder back to Winkler.

"What does that mean?" Winkler took the folder with a puzzled frown.

"It means he has known criminals on his payroll. From everywhere. The criminals get a big payday for information, because they know they'll be protected by the one paying them. That he won't reveal information on them to anyone else, and he'll let them know if other authorities are getting close. In other words, he's keeping them in business, for the few pieces of useful information they might be willing to hand over. People are still getting killed, kidnapped, drugged, raped and enslaved, and they're getting a bonus for doing it."

"You're joking?" Winkler was stunned by this revelation.

"Mr. Winkler, he's playing with fire." Ashe misted from Winkler's study, leaving a worried werewolf behind.

"Matt, that's what Ashe said. That he's playing with fire, and paying criminals big money for small amounts of information while protecting them. You didn't give me any pertinent information so I don't know who this is, but if the kid's right, it sure doesn't sound good." Winkler had shut his study door so his call to Matt wouldn't be overheard or disturbed.

"Damn. It's too bad my vamps can't work during the day. I really need my best investigators on this. I think I'm inclined to believe the kid—I just got good information from this source, after I'd exhausted all avenues. The incident in South Carolina was looking like an unsolvable crime when bingo, this guy hands me pure gold. This makes more sense than you might think. Damn, I need that kid."

"The vamps sort of have him for the moment," Winkler grumped.

"I heard. I also heard the Grand Master forced them to share. Wish I had that much clout."

"If you need him for only a day or so, we might be able to work that out. The kid doesn't need a jet to get around anymore."

"True. That boggles my mind. It makes me wonder if this guy knows anything about Ashe." Winkler easily heard Matt Michaels tapping a pen on his desk as he considered the thought. "I don't want him to know about this kid. If he has contacts with criminals, how much damage do you think he might do if he tells them?"

"That doesn't sound good at all," Winkler growled. "I'm concerned, now. How highly placed is this guy?"

"High. Too high. Has too much authority, without enough controls. I only got wind of this when our esteemed congressman let something slip in a vampire-assisted questioning session. It always pays to follow the money."

"Doesn't surprise me that Jack Howard was involved. This makes me think that Zeke Tanner is on the payroll," Winkler speculated.

"That's a frightening thought," Matt agreed. "We never could discover how all those drugs were funneled across the border from Juarez. The kid figured it out quick."

"Yeah. Just drive werewolves a few miles south, strap a backpack on their wolf and send 'em across. No problem."

"Too bad we didn't get Zeke when the Grand Master sent his trackers and those vamps. We didn't know Zeke wouldn't be at home when they came to call."

"Somebody may have. Jack Howard comes to mind."

"Now it all makes sense. Howard is in this guy's pocket. Information is passed to Howard, Howard passes it to Tanner. Tanner makes the move he plans to make anyway, going after the shifter kids and Ashe in Star Cove. Leaves only a few of his behind, just to make it look good. Man, this gets worse as it goes along," Matt said. "At least Obediah didn't see it coming."

"Obediah had his own source of information, who only failed once," Winkler stood abruptly. "The source managed to escape, too, and is probably working for somebody else right now."

"Wildrif," Matt's voice was flat. "He had the best security we could provide around him, and he still managed to get away. He's like a ghost. If you manage to catch him, you can't hold onto him."

"Trouble seems to follow him, too. Do you think that maybe—yes. That has to be it. Wildrif can't sense the kid. That's what this is. The best informant ever can't sense the kid. I'd bet money that he can sense those around the kid, though." Winkler muttered a string of expletives. "What the hell is going on here, Matt?"

❧

"Six of the Dark King's subjects were murdered by the Ir'Indicti. For no reason. How soon do you think it will be before he begins to murder yours, too?"

Wildrif's poisonous lies poured forth as Friesianna listened on her cell phone; the cell had been a gift from her Jewels. All four were now dead—at the hands of that hateful boy if her sources were correct—and she still mourned their loss. At first, she'd been unwilling to believe the boy responsible. After the events in Canada, that was no longer true.

"He is after your crown, Bright Queen, and he will stop at nothing to obtain it," Wildrif continued. "The six who died blocked his path to the Dark Crown, and paid for their protection of Baltis with their lives. If the boy is not stopped, he will achieve his objective."

"I curse the day he was born," Friesianna paced inside her tent as Parlethis and Rabis looked on. "Why is this happening to me? Why?" She flung out an arm in frustration.

"You must send your best after him. He must be stopped before he attacks. He appeared in Canada, with none the wiser. Your captains tell you this. How simple will it be for him to come for you? How easy will he find it to wrest the crown away while he grinds you into the dirt beneath his heel? My Queen, I have read the H'Morr, and I have seen much. Your Miriasu cannot see him—he depends upon the H'Morr for guidance. Yes, parts of that book are true, but it is not completely accurate and has not predicted everything. You think to stay alive if the Ir'Indicti comes after you?"

"I will gather my best. The boy will die." Friesianna jerked her head at Parlethis, who took the phone and ended the call.

"Rabis," Friesianna snarled, turning to her Miriasu. "Tell me true. Will the boy have my crown if I do not stop him?" Friesianna employed le'meruh as she commanded Rabis. Le'meruh was a gift few

Elemaiya had ever possessed. It was extreme coercion, and by nature had to be used sparingly.

While several among the race might hold the gift of compulsion, le'meruh could not be denied—even among the strongest and most talented. Friesianna had gained the Bright crown by employing her gift. Rabis, as strong as he was, was unable to deny Friesianna's order.

"If the boy survives, he will take your crown," Rabis muttered unwillingly.

CHAPTER 9

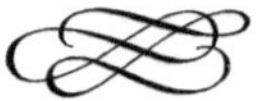

"Talked to Sal earlier." Ashe elbowed Marco as Marco took a seat at the kitchen island and snagged a large slice of pizza.

"How?" Marco blinked at Ashe for a moment. "Never mind. He's grounded, but you can get around that, can't you?" Marco bit into his pepperoni pizza with a sigh.

"Took him a couple of burgers. I heard he was starving himself," Ashe grinned. Marco almost choked as he laughed with a mouthful of pizza.

"What's that?" Winkler strode into the kitchen and opened a box containing a sausage and mushroom pizza. Pulling out a slice, he folded it in half lengthwise and took a bite.

"Sali got grounded," Marco swallowed and chuckled.

"Heard that already," Winkler grinned. "Kid, the vamps are up in England. Wlodek had money transferred into your account. You'll have an extra hundred grand to spend for helping take down Rydley. I can put half that in your savings and let you decide what to do with the other half."

"Mr. Winkler, I'd like to buy a car," Ashe said right away.

"You serious?" Marco stared.

"Yeah. And I know what I want already. Price might be right, too."

"What is it?" Winkler took another bite of pizza.

"A classic car. A red, 1959 Cadillac convertible. The fins are awesome."

"Where is this car?" Winkler asked.

"It's in Austin. Belonged to a collector there, who died recently. His heirs are selling his collection. The price they're asking is seventy-five thousand, but I might get it for less."

"All original?" Trajan walked in and grabbed a slice of pizza. He'd heard the conversation as he walked to the kitchen.

"Yep. The price is a bargain. Others are selling for more," Ashe grabbed a slice of sausage and mushroom before Winkler could get it.

"I'll let you buy the car for whatever you can get it for, and put the rest in your savings account," Winkler agreed. "You deserve it. Planning to drive much?"

"Nah. It's just to show off," Ashe grinned.

∽

"I'm not kidding, Sara. Mr. Winkler will lend us his condo in San Antonio. It won't be the beach, but I know things didn't go so well when you were here. You trusted me with something, and I feel like I let you down." Randy gripped his cell tightly as he spoke with Sara.

"Randy, stop worrying about it, all right? San Antonio sounds fine when I visit again."

"Sara, I wish we were together. Right now. I want my hands on you, baby."

"Randy, don't do that. It's hard enough as it is, being this far apart."

"I know. I never should have let Mom talk me into moving."

"Randy, she's your mother, no matter what. I'm just the girlfriend, remember?"

"Sara, don't ever say that again. You have no idea how important you are."

"I'll remind you that you said that after our first big fight," Sara teased.

"You do that. It'll still be true."

"Here's the information." Gavin set a folder in front of Ashe while Tony lifted an eyebrow in surprise. Gavin, the crusty old vampire, never allowed anyone except another vampire Assassin to see information provided by Wlodek and the Council.

"Kieran Ormonde?" Ashe blinked at Gavin as he flipped through three pages of printed information.

"May be responsible for murdering six people in the San Francisco area. Considered quite dangerous. He was last heard from when he reached Oakland, where we lost touch. You see his financial status, before and after the crisis." Gavin barely nodded.

"I see it. He has more money now than he did before the meltdown, with not much in between."

"Precisely. All the victims have made recent large transactions, transferring funds into specific investments. We believe Ormonde has placed compulsion on a human, who is in charge of these investments. Most of that money has disappeared, leaving the human in the hands of local authorities. He has been charged with fraud and running a Ponzi scheme."

"Doesn't sound good for old Kieran, does it?" Ashe shook his head.

"No, it does not."

"I'd say you're right. Except Kieran isn't the only one involved. Got any other folders containing the names Brinkley Addison and Ellis Kline?"

"Those are only suspects at this point, with recently reported locations in Ireland," Tony said. "Are they involved?"

"I'd say so. You know for sure that they haven't been to the U.S. in the past four months?" Ashe's eyes were filled with stars.

"Not completely." Gavin only blinked once at Ashe. "Private jets leave the country all the time."

"Yeah." Ashe's eyes were back to their normal blue.

"Are we traveling to two locations tonight?" Gavin asked, taking the folder from Ashe's outstretched hand.

"Yes. San Francisco and Dublin."

"I haven't been to Dublin in a while. Kid, dress warm. For both places," Tony said. "Maybe we should hit Dublin, first. It's ten p.m. here. We have less than two hours before sunrise in the U.K.," Tony consulted his watch.

"I'll go change," Ashe hunched his shoulders. He was destined to see more vampires die.

"Hi, Thomas," Wynter said brightly when Thomas Williams called her cell. "I heard you had some trouble in Amarillo. Are you okay?"

"I'm good. The vamps did most of the work. Weldon and I only got two and that's because Dalroy and Rhett were too polite to interfere," Thomas chuckled. "How about you?"

"School starts again in a week. But I'm almost done."

"Good for you. What I called about, well, I'll be looking for a ring. Is there anything special that you like?"

"I love chocolate diamonds surrounding a diamond," Wynter squeaked. Thomas was buying her a ring!

"I'll see what I can do, then."

"Did Daddy give you a hard time?"

"Not much of one. I told him I'd take good care of you. Twice. And he said you can fly out one weekend a month, as long as you're supervised by my sister."

"Daddy has to stick his nose in everything. It's not like I'm an adult or anything."

"Sweetheart, we have to get to know each other. I want you to be sure when I put that ring on your finger."

"I'll be sure."

"We know where he is, but he's guarded most of the time," Parlethis informed the four who stood before him. "By werewolves and vampires. We have devised a plan to draw him away from that place so your attack will be easier. You are the fastest we have at relocating, and you must take him by surprise. I have these." Parlethis handed capped darts to each Bright Elemaiya soldier. "These darts contain lion snake poison and will kill almost anything quickly."

"We know about lion snake poison," one of Parlethis' chosen assassins handled the dart carefully, examining the cap and how solidly it was positioned over the point.

"Good. You go in two days. Here is the map and photographs we received from one of our contacts." Parlethis handed out paper copies of what he'd been given. He'd also sent two darts to the contact in question by return mail. It was the first time he'd mailed anything, and found it quite simple to accomplish. He'd lied, too, telling the clerk the box contained photographs.

"You'll do it because I tell you to do it," Zeke snarled at Josiah's contact over the phone. "Wildrif is here, and he was happy to give me your information. You'll hit the target I told you to hit. You get two darts, in case somebody else is there."

Zeke listened for a moment while the contact argued on the other end. "Look, either you do this or my trackers come hunting you. If they don't get you, I can always send information anonymously to the Grand Master. I'd say that one of us will have you. You don't stand a chance." Zeke listened again while the contact called Wildrif many names. Most of them had profanity involved and none of them were nice.

"You gonna do this?" Zeke's mouth turned up in a smile when he received a sulky "Yes."

Kid, I don't know how you do this. I'm not arguing, though. Tony waved a hand to keep Ashe from defending himself. He, Ashe and Gavin stood across the street from a house in Dublin, a narrow, cobbled lane lying in between. Inside the house, dim lights shone from behind heavy curtains. *You're sure they're here?*

Yeah. With humans. Women, Ashe added, swallowing nervously.

"I think they're engaged in sex," Tony breathed softly to Gavin, who nodded and gripped Ashe's arm.

"Young one, stay outside unless you are needed," Gavin whispered next to Ashe's ear.

No problem, Ashe agreed mentally. Gavin nodded. Ashe watched as Gavin and Tony approached the house. Surprisingly, Tony drew a lock-picking kit from a pocket and went to work on the door. The faintest of ticks sounded and Ashe nodded respectfully when Tony had the door open in seconds. Gavin led the way inside the house, Tony close behind.

"I can meet with you tomorrow night. You can choose the place," Peyton spoke into his cell. He'd been more than surprised that William Winkler called him back. It didn't matter that he might be walking into a trap—Peyton had spent the last twenty-four hours evading Zeke Tanner's trackers. Not for the first time did he wonder why the trackers didn't go after Winkler, but shoved that thought aside. Winkler was on the phone, asking for a meeting.

"Come to the house. I'm sure you know where it is anyway," Winkler said.

"I'm being followed," Peyton admitted.

"No surprise. Know where those followers might be?"

"They're here in Corpus Christi," Peyton said. "I managed to lose them last night, but they're here. I figure they'll catch up with me soon enough."

"How about letting them follow you here?" Peyton could almost hear the grim smile in Winkler's voice. "I think we can arrange to give them a traditional, rogue welcome."

"That would be mighty fine, Mr. Winkler," Peyton released a sigh. "I'll give you every bit of information on Zeke Tanner I have. He doesn't tell me everything, but I know enough."

"Just telling me where his compound is will go a long way," Winkler muttered.

"I can do that, but if I know Zeke, he may be making a move. He does that a lot, if he thinks somebody might come to visit."

"Know anything about that nutjob, Wildrif?" Winkler asked.

"Yeah. Scary as hell," Peyton shuddered. "I think Zeke's been in contact with him all along."

"That's what I was afraid of," Winkler replied.

"I was mighty surprised when Zeke sent him to Obediah, but that was probably Wildrif's doing," Peyton said.

"Not surprised about that, either," Winkler agreed. "How long have you worked for Tanner?"

"Since I was twelve, so that makes it twenty-three years. Said he found me when I was a baby, abandoned by my parents. Now, I don't know how well you know Zeke, but I haven't believed that lie for a long time. He had some of his raise me, so most manners I know I learned from books. At least one of 'em taught me to read before Zeke took him down."

"Know anything about your parents?"

"No. I was too little to know anything, I guess."

"Where were you when that mess happened here?"

"Going after a rival dealer outside Chihuahua."

"Ever hear Zeke talk about a contact in D.C.?"

"Yeah, but I never got a name. Look, I can explain what I know when I get there, if that's okay."

"That's fine. I may have a couple of others here with me. They might have questions, too."

"Sounds good. If the Grand Master wants an execution after that, well, I'd appreciate it if he made it quick."

"I'll mention that to him."

"Thanks."

"Weldon, he's coming tomorrow night and he may have Zeke's trackers on his tail. I had Matt connected to the call—he was in Chicago, so he's flying down. Matt's ears perked right up when Peyton said he had information on that contact in D.C." Winkler toyed with a pen on his desk while he spoke with the Grand Master.

"I can be there in no time—I'm in Dallas, now, waiting on a flight."

"I'll make a call and have my pilots warm up the jet," Winkler said.

"Sounds good. I'll see about getting my bags off the plane."

"Kid, we'll place compulsion and send these to the nearest hospital. That's all we can do."

Ashe stare at the bloody cuts on two women—both huddled against a wall inside the house. Addison and Kline were dead, their ash scattered across the floor where Gavin and Tony had surprised them and taken them down.

"They meant to kill them. After." Ashe's mouth was set.

"Yeah. Don't think about it. We found them in time."

"Addison and Kline did this before. Those other women didn't live."

"Yeah. We figured that out." Tony kept the sarcasm from his words.

"Do the compulsion thing. I'll get them to the hospital," Ashe muttered, hunching his shoulders.

"Come back immediately, young one," Gavin said gently. Ashe's head jerked up as Tony knelt before the two women.

"You will not recall the events of this night. You were attacked by an animal. Say that to the hospital employees. You did not get a good look at the animal, only that it was dark and you were walking down the street. You will not recall how you arrived at the hospital either.

You will tell the hospital employees that a kind driver dropped you off."

The women nodded their compliance. Ashe skipped them to the nearest hospital, located three miles away.

❧

"The Grand Master and Matthew Michaels will come. William Winkler thinks to take our bait," Wildrif giggled.

Zeke Tanner frowned at Wildrif. Was it his imagination, or did the seer seem crazier than when he'd seen him last? It didn't matter. Zeke had fifteen trackers, all poised to follow Peyton straight to Winkler's beach house. If he were lucky, he could take out the Grand Master and Matt Michaels, too. Curtis would certainly be happy with that news—Matt Michaels was a straight shooter and often got under Curtis Roberts' skin.

"Glad you told me that Peyton was ready to run," Zeke said, causing Wildrif to stop his wild chuckling. "At least he never found out what really happened to his parents."

"It won't matter what happened to anyone. Not anymore." Wildrif's wild chuckling began again as he brushed past the stuffed white buffalo in Zeke's study. Zeke's eyebrows lifted in alarm.

❧

"I need a word with the President." Curtis settled into a comfortable, plush chair inside Congressman Arthur Vaine's office.

"Are you sure?" Arthur Vaine, Head of the Special Committee on National Security, steepled his fingers and studied Curtis Roberts. "Keeping you out of the President's line of sight has worked pretty well, so far." Arthur looked the part of senior statesman; he was tall and handsome, with carefully styled thick, dark hair sprinkled with gray at the temples.

"But I never got information like this, before." Curtis tossed a folder onto Arthur's desk. "I have it on good authority that the

President and that wanna-be Matt Michaels knew all about this, and the intel wasn't shared."

"What is this?" Arthur opened the folder. The first image was that of a boy—perhaps fifteen or sixteen, standing with Matt Michaels and two other men he didn't recognize, behind a barrier of crime scene tape. Six special agents were nearby, seemingly waiting for Matt Michaels' orders. The British Embassy was in the background—Arthur recognized that, easily enough.

"Well, Arthur, tell me why a boy needed to be at the scene—this photograph was taken with a high-power Telephoto lens from a long way off on the day the British Embassy was overtaken by terrorists. You see the time and date stamp there at the bottom?" Curtis, whose sharp blue eyes studied Arthur's reaction, smoothed back thinning brown hair as he waited for Arthur's response.

"There's no reason for a boy to be there," Arthur lifted the photograph for a better look. "The media and everybody else was held back from that location by security. How did he slip past the police?"

"What if I told you that Matt Michaels brought the boy in? That's William Winkler, of Winkler Security, there with them. You know how many government contracts we have with him. What if I told you that the boy is one of Winkler's employees? I have tax records to prove it. What if I told you that Winkler is paying the boy a hundred grand a year, for undisclosed services?"

"Undisclosed services?" Arthur lifted his gaze to stare at Curtis.

"Yeah. And what if I told you that the second photograph was taken only a couple of seconds later? Take a look and tell me what's missing."

Arthur set the first photograph down and lifted the second. Just as Curtis said, the time and date stamp indicated that only two seconds had passed. His eyes widened in surprise—the boy, the tallest man and the six agents had disappeared. Even if they'd walked away from the scene, they would still be in the photograph somewhere. That wasn't the case.

"Explain this." Arthur flipped the photograph around, then held up the first one.

"I can't. Think hard—you know what happened shortly after the time stated on that photograph—hostages were rescued from the British Embassy, just before it conveniently blew up. I don't know how that was accomplished because frankly, the times don't sync with the official report. I know somebody who might be able to explain it, though. I'd prefer to put the President on the hot seat."

"And I'd prefer to keep the President out of the loop. For obvious reasons."

"Then I'll get the information from one of my informants. He said he might be willing, for the right price."

"Who?"

"One of my informants." Curtis wasn't willing to release any names —Arthur wasn't aware of everyone on his payroll and he wanted to keep it that way.

"Some of your informants could ruin us," Arthur placed both photographs in the folder and slapped it shut. "It's damn difficult to keep attributing those expenses to other—let's say *legitimate*—sources."

"You think they'd say anything? We can ruin them, remember? I can find them, remember? These relationships are based on mutual trust."

"We're not married to them. I hope you remember that," Arthur muttered dryly.

"But we've gotten good intel from them. All of them think they're the only ones on my payroll, and when it's advantageous, they pass information on their rivals straight to me."

Arthur sighed. Curtis was becoming a liability, in his opinion. The U.S. Intelligence and Foreign Relations Division was supposed to be actively hunting and arresting criminals, not paying them and keeping them in power.

During his tenure, Curtis had managed to arrest many lower and a few midlevel criminals, but the bosses—the ones who kept the criminal activities going across the globe—were not only still in power, but growing fatter from secret payments funneled through Curtis' department.

"Nothing like job security," Arthur mumbled.

"What's that?" Curtis asked.

"Good work. Investigate this further with your source and let me know what you find." Arthur dismissed Curtis with a nod.

"Sure." Curtis took the folder and slipped it inside his briefcase. "I'll keep you posted."

~

"It's a Friday night and my target manages a restaurant," the voice complained over the phone. "That means she won't be home until after midnight at the earliest. There is another person who is with her most of the time. He may be there as well."

"Then get them both. Make it look good, like you need help or something. Those darts you have will kill quickly, according to my source. Four others will appear to kill the boy when he arrives, and he will arrive. I'll bet money on it."

"What am I supposed to do, then?" The question was almost a wail.

"Get the hell away. Turn and run. I don't give a damn what you do."

"Are we done if I do this?"

"Sure. We're done after you do this," Zeke Tanner laughed and hung up.

~

"I'll call when everything is in place," Wildrif assured Friesianna. "Once the original target has been hit by our agent, the boy will arrive. Yours can come then and take him."

"We don't intend to take him. We intend to kill him."

"I know that," Wildrif snapped.

"I remind you that you speak to royalty, Dark Seer."

"Of course, my Bright Queen." Wildrif's voice sounded contrite.

"Do not forget it."

"I will not."

~

Ashe sighed as he stared at the tall pyramid in San Francisco. He wanted to see it during the day. At least the fog was light and only obscured the city skyline a little.

"Young one, we cannot sightsee," Gavin pulled Ashe away.

"Yeah. How good are you guys with bullets?"

"Bullets?" Tony's one-word question held worry.

"He's waiting for us. Ellis Kline was supposed to check in. Kieran Ormonde knows he's dead. Thinks the Council is coming for him, now. He's right. He's also ready. Has two humans with him. Thinks machine guns will slow you down enough so he can get away."

"We need your misting ability, then. Is it possible to carry us behind the humans—we can dispatch them easily and then go after Ormonde." Gavin sounded grim.

"I can do that." Ashe nodded. "Ormonde is in the basement of an old store near the wharf. The humans with guns are positioned at the bottom of the stairs. Ormonde is waiting in the back near a high window. If he hears anything, he's gone and we'll have to chase after him. My worry is he'll head for the most crowded place he can find, and at this time of night, that's a bar."

"Not good," Tony muttered.

"We do not need that many witnesses," Gavin agreed. "Compulsion is difficult to place on so many."

"Then let's do this," Ashe said. "I drop you behind Ormonde," Ashe nodded at Gavin. "I'll take Tony to the humans and help him take them."

"In what way are you going to help me?" Tony asked.

"I'll gather them in my mist, one at a time, and then dump them in the same spot. Right now, they're at different positions at the bottom of the stairs, hiding behind brick columns. Hard for you to get both without getting shot. I can bring them together," Ashe explained.

"Yeah. That's feasible," Tony agreed. "Gavin?"

"I agree," Gavin nodded slightly.

"Ready?" Ashe asked.

"Ready," Tony said.

Dropping Gavin behind Kieran Ormonde went without a hitch.

Ashe left Gavin only a few feet behind Ormonde and then flew his mist toward the steps leading into Ormonde's basement. That might have gone without a hitch, too; Ashe gathered both gunmen inside his mist, leaving their machine guns behind. He then dumped the gunmen in a corner, where Tony removed both heads quickly.

Neither Ashe nor Tony expected a third gunman, who seemingly appeared from nothing and shot both of them from behind. Ashe cried out as he was hit and Tony, even wounded, moved like the wind to remove a third head before hauling the body and head toward the first two. Dropping both parts amid the others, he spared a pain-filled glance for Ashe.

Ashe had taken a bullet in his right arm and Tony had been hit twice in his left shoulder. Ashe and Tony pressed hands to bullet wounds and stared at the headless bodies lying on the floor.

"What are we going to do with the bodies?" Tony's breaths were short and labored.

"I'll take care of it," Ashe muttered before lifting his left hand and turning three bodies to flying sparks.

Tony, bleeding and in pain, dropped to his knees in shocked reverence as three bodies winked out of existence.

CHAPTER 10

"Hold still, I will remove the bullet." Gavin's claw was at least a foot long as he carefully inserted it in Ashe's wound. Ashe had insisted that Tony be tended first—his wounds were worse.

"Ow." The pain of the removal was nothing next to the pain Ashe was already experiencing. He watched, fascinated, as Tony snaked out a hand and neatly caught the bullet Gavin flipped out of his arm.

"Leave no evidence behind," Tony mumbled, stuffing the bullet in a pants pocket.

"Child, I hope you weren't overly fond of this shirt." Gavin ripped the sleeve and tied a strip of it above the bullet wound in Ashe's arm.

"I have others," Ashe attempted a grin. It failed—he was in too much pain.

"Can you still get us home?" Tony asked. His bullet wounds were already closing.

"Yeah. Too bad I don't heal as fast as you guys. Ready?" Ashe asked, working to keep his concentration. Gavin was now stanching blood from the wound with the rest of Ashe's torn sleeve.

"Yes," Gavin growled. Ashe skipped his passengers to Texas.

"What the hell happened?" Winkler snarled while Trajan phoned the werewolf nurse. Blood was all over Ashe and Tony's clothing. Winkler wasn't worried about Tony—he could replenish what he'd lost easily enough—Gavin and Tony's fridge in the basement was packed with bagged blood. Ashe didn't heal as swiftly as the vamps. He'd be down for a day or two at least.

"Miscalculation," Ashe grimaced as Trace moved Gavin aside, ripped the rest of Ashe's shirt in half and pulled it off as he sat on a barstool in Winkler's kitchen. "On my part," Ashe added, as Loren and Andy walked in with Marco. "Somebody showed up that I wasn't expecting and didn't see."

"Damn, Ashe, what did you do?" Marco muttered.

"Got shot with a nine millimeter. Lived over it. End of story," Ashe whispered.

"He's going down," Trace snapped.

"I've got him," Gavin moved in before Ashe could drop off the barstool.

The last thing Ashe saw before he fainted was Gavin's worried face above his.

"He's sixteen," Winkler sighed. "He's bound to miscalculate, now and then."

"I'm surprised. He's very intelligent."

Winkler nodded at Gavin's words.

"Grand Master's here," Trajan tapped on Winkler's study door.

"Send him in," Winkler sighed. It was nearly four a.m. and Weldon had gone to Star Cove to talk with Bear Wright before driving his rental to Winkler's beach house. Everybody was having a late night. Matt Michaels was spending the night in Austin before flying in the following morning.

"Grand Master," Gavin rose and shook Weldon's hand.

"Gavin, good to see you," Weldon nodded to the Assassin. "How's Anthony?"

"Anthony will recover," Gavin replied dryly. "He is sleeping and his wounds are already closed. I regret the child's wound."

"He's been stuck in the middle of a dangerous time, don't you think?" Weldon took Winkler's remaining guest chair and settled on it with a weary sigh. "Probably won't be the last time he gets hit."

"As I understand it, Ashe is the one who protects others. Who will protect him?" Gavin asked.

"I don't have an answer," Winkler responded. "Wish I did."

"How's the kid doing?" Weldon asked as Trace walked in and handed a cup of coffee to the Grand Master.

"Fine. Gavin had the bleeding almost stopped when they got here, the nurse cleaned out the wound and gave him something for pain. He's asleep."

"Good. Have you told Gavin what we've got coming our way tomorrow night?" Weldon asked.

"Waited for you to back me up," Winkler said, offering Weldon a tired grin.

"We have Zeke Tanner's rogues heading this way," Weldon began. "We might need your help."

"Winkler has some business that I need to be there for." Buck told Adele Friday morning. He'd called her as soon as he'd gotten off the phone with Trajan. Something was going down, but Trajan hadn't given Buck any details. He'd only said that Winkler needed an extra guard. Buck was the one he'd called. "I was hoping I'd see you tonight after work, but maybe we can get together tomorrow night."

"That sounds good. I can cook, or we can go out."

"Will you cook? That sounds so much better than restaurant food."

"I'll cook, then."

"Thanks, Adele."

∼

"One million dollars for additional information on that boy." Curtis made his first offer. He figured it would cost at least five times that much to get what he wanted, but it was smart to start the bidding low.

"Ten," Zeke Tanner countered.

Curtis smiled. He'd estimated five million. Zeke was putty in his hands.

∼

"Dude, I need help," Sali left the fourth message on Ashe's cell. "Man, pick up," Sali added before hanging up in frustration. Algebra II was kicking his behind. Ashe would know how to work the problems. He always did.

Tossing the cell onto his desk, Sali flopped on the bed and lifted his tablet, staring at the assignment Mr. Dawkins had given the class. "Marco," Sali muttered, grabbing the cell and calling his brother.

"Hey," Sali said when Marco answered.

∼

Don't tell him about Ashe, Trajan held up a quickly scribbled note as Marco spoke with Sali.

"Sal, Ashe had a late night and he's asleep. Cut him some slack, okay?" Marco watched Trajan, who nodded in approval. "He probably has his phone turned off." Trajan gave a bigger nod.

"Will you tell him I called?"

"I will, but you already said you left four messages. I think he'll know already," Marco laughed.

"Dude, algebra is kicking my ass," Sali whined.

"Is that what this is about? Homework?"

"Oh, like you weren't on the phone with Cori every five minutes about college algebra."

"Then call Cori. See if she'll help," Marco suggested. "Let Ashe get his sleep."

"Will you call Cori for me?"

"Sal, do you need your hand held?"

"If I call her, I'm telling her what you bought for her birthday."

"Salidar, I'll key your car. I swear I will. You can't hide it, either, Dad has the keys."

"Fine. I'll call Cori. Will she blab to Dori that I called?"

"Ah. I missed the ex-girlfriend angle in all this," Marco nodded sagely. "I don't think Cori will blab. One peep about what I got her and your car's toast."

"I won't tell. I just need help with homework."

"Good."

~

"I just want to pat his head," Matt muttered as he stared at Amos Thompson. Amos Thompson's white buffalo stood amid the dunes surrounding Winkler's beach house, guarding the property with two of Winkler's wolves.

"Amos put in twenty years with the army. I'd hold off on patting his head," Winkler chuckled.

"His wife's a good cook," Matt bit into a chocolate chip cookie and chewed happily.

"She's a swan," Winkler pointed out. "Amos loves her a lot. You should see them together on a full moon. Amos tucks her under his chin and snorts at anybody who gets close."

"That's great—I'd love to see it," Matt smiled.

"Marco told me that—he's seen it, I haven't."

"Truth really is stranger than fiction," Matt said.

~

"Mrs. Thompson," Ashe wandered into the kitchen at five, after sleeping all day.

"Young man, you need to be careful," Florence Thompson shook a flour-covered finger at Ashe. Her blonde hair was pulled back in a neat bun as she shaped rolls with her hands at the island.

"I agree," Ashe said, sliding onto a barstool.

"Want a sandwich? You haven't eaten all day."

"A sandwich would be awesome."

"How do you feel?" Trace walked in while Florence "Flossie" Thompson put a roast-beef sandwich together for Ashe.

"Kinda crappy. Like my head is full of cotton," Ashe replied. "I think your nurse friend gave me too much pain medication."

"That's possible, I guess," Trace agreed. "He may have thought he was treating a werewolf and not a shifter."

"I'm not really a shifter, either," Ashe muttered. "Thanks," he said as Flossie put the sandwich in front of him. "I'm just something different who happens to shift."

"Young man, anybody who shifts is a shifter. That's that." Flossie softened her words with a smile.

"I guess I'm a shifter," Ashe grinned and bit into his sandwich.

"Spoiling your dinner?" Winkler walked in, followed by Matt Michaels and the Grand Master.

"I guess." Ashe took another bite of his sandwich.

"He's starved. He hasn't eaten all day." Flossie was back to shaping rolls for the oven.

"Are those homemade rolls? I can't wait for that," Matt sighed.

"Don't get home cooking much, do you?" Flossie offered Matt a smile.

"Nope. Those cookies were amazing."

"There are cookies?" Ashe was interested quickly.

"For dessert. Mr. Michaels was in the kitchen when they came out of the oven, so I gave him three. He's too thin," Flossie observed. Weldon Harper threw back his head and laughed.

～

"Charles, the target has been eliminated," Aedan sounded weary to his own ears.

"Something wrong, Aedan?" Charles's voice crackled; they didn't have a good cell-phone connection.

"Nothing you can fix," Aedan replied.

"I'll send the jet tomorrow evening," Charles promised.

"Thank you." Aedan ended the call and tossed the phone onto the sofa. He'd made the call from the safe house located outside Mucklagh, in County Offaly in Ireland. Dawn was still hours away and that troubled him. This would be where his life ended; in a field near the place of his birth so many years ago. Fate had sent him to Ireland when his life had become so empty.

Rifling through his small suitcase, he found a pad of paper and a pen. This would be his last letter to his wife and son. Briefly, Aedan cursed the ones who'd brought him this unbearable pain.

"Mr. Winkler, can I talk to you for a minute?" Ashe stuffed hands in the pockets of his jeans as he offered Winkler an exasperated look before ducking his head.

"Sure, kid. What is it?" Winkler invited Ashe inside his study.

"That pain medication—what was it?"

"Not sure, why?"

"I feel like my head is stuffed with cotton. And the signals I usually get—well, they're gone. I can't feel anything."

"How long is this gonna last?" Winkler motioned for Ashe to sit. Ashe took a guest chair in front of Winkler's desk with a troubled sigh.

"I don't know. Kinda makes me feel blinded."

"Yeah, I guess it would. Maybe I'll contact the nurse and ask how long that stuff stays in your system."

"I think he gave too much. Probably unintentional, but I can't tell right now."

"And you were unconscious when he gave it," Winkler stood, a frown crossing his features. "He's one of Shirley Walker's wolves. I'll ask the Grand Master to give her a call and we'll do some quick research. We don't need traitors in our midst, just as Peyton Miller is hauling a batch of Zeke Tanner's trackers our way."

"That's not good," Ashe muttered, rubbing his forehead.

"Got a headache?" Winkler asked.

"Yeah. A bad one. I kept hoping it would go away, and I sure don't want to take anything else for pain. Not if it makes me blind and stupid."

"Understood. We didn't expect you to help tonight; Gavin and Tony will be with us. It wouldn't hurt, though, to know you're able to help if we need you."

"I'll be on standby, but I don't know how helpful I can be," Ashe said. "I haven't attempted to relocate or do anything else yet."

"Maybe a workout will help. Trajan!" Winkler called on his Second, who came running.

"Boss?" Trajan wasn't even winded when he stood in Winkler's doorway seconds later.

"Give the kid a ton of water to drink and make him run on the treadmill. We'll see if we can work some of that painkiller crap out of his system."

"Sure thing. Come on, kid. Your ass is mine for the next hour." Trajan offered Ashe a wolfish grin. Ashe slouched off the chair and followed Winkler's Second out the door.

∼

"I have my talents focused on one of the vampires, that's how I knew," Wildrif sounded gleeful.

"I'm glad we were able to do something about it," Zeke tossed a pistol on his desk after making sure it was empty of bullets. "How did you know this would work?" Zeke turned to Wildrif.

"Narcotics have that effect on the race—it dampens their abilities, sometimes for months. This particular drug is the worst—it is one of the Elemaiya's few weaknesses. Only the most foolish have ever experimented with this drug, as it leaves them helpless."

"This is gonna toss a big wrench into the works," Zeke chuckled. "That kid doesn't show up when his mother gets hit. She dies; he goes crazy and then goes after both sides. They pay us even more money to give them information so they can find him first. What more can you ask for?"

Wildrif's answering laughter sounded evil, even to Zeke's ears.

"I gave him enough," Jude Gilmore, the werewolf nurse, snarled as the gun was waved in his face. "Are you going to release my wife, now?"

"You should stick to your own kind," the tracker growled. "But thanks for giving us a weak human as a hostage. Breathe a word of this to your Packmaster and we come after your wife again."

"I'll be quiet, just stay the hell away from us," Jude replied.

"Shirley can't find Jude. Tried calling his cell three times," Weldon muttered angrily.

"So we have no idea what the kid was given," Winkler said.

"We can't take him to the hospital for tests—we don't have the time and we can't explain how he got the stuff or the healing bullet wound."

"Yeah. Should have suspected something when the kid slept so long."

"Jude's been trustworthy until now. There wasn't any reason to suspect," Weldon attempted to calm Winkler, who'd started growling in frustration. "Look, we'll have our hands full tonight. No need to add to the stress."

"I want to kill Gilmore over this. If he was pressured or blackmailed, we could have helped. Instead, we can't find him now and the kid's talents are compromised."

"Is there anyone we can contact who might have information on this—on why this is causing problems for Ashe?" Weldon leaned back in his chair. He and Winkler were in Winkler's study; Matt Michaels was on the deck with Trace and Trajan, going through the weapons cache he'd brought with him.

"I don't personally know anybody else who has Elemaiyan blood except Lissa's father. I have no idea how to contact him, and I sure as hell don't want to see him if I can help it."

"I agree. He's not an option," Weldon nodded. "We don't have time to track any of the others down again, and I really don't want to do that anyway. Not after recent events."

"Matt wants them dead or off the planet. I'd feel safer if they were gone. Who knows how many deaths they're responsible for? Those kids for sure, and nobody knows who else has gotten in their way over the years."

"Salidar said there were children at the Elemaiya camp in Canada. Only a few, but kids were there," Weldon sighed. "I asked Marcus, who gave me information after he questioned his son. I had wolves check out the site, and I'm sure Matt sent some of his, but the Elemaiya never went back once they left. I don't know where they moved, but it's a sure bet they're around somewhere."

"Mrs. Evans, we're almost out of shrimp." One of Adele's new hires blinked hopefully at Adele, as if she might conjure more shrimp from a magical location to serve her patrons.

"How much do we have left?" Adele was helping out in the kitchen —there'd been a bigger crowd than usual for a busy Friday night. Adele would be lucky to get the restaurant cleaned and everything prepped for the following day before twelve-thirty—meaning she'd get home after one in the morning.

"Maybe fifteen pounds."

"Is the crowd thinning at all?"

"Maybe a little."

"I'll come take a look. Get back to your tables, I'll check into this. If we have to pull shrimp off the menu, we'll do it. I have a truck coming tomorrow at eleven with another delivery."

Adele brushed back straying strands of honey-blonde hair and smoothed her embroidered apron as she stepped out of the kitchen, gazing toward the hostess stand near the front door. Breathing a sigh of relief, Adele turned to walk back to the kitchen. Closing was half an hour away and there weren't any customers waiting to get into the restaurant. "We'll make it," she muttered and went back to preparing clam chowder.

❧

Wlodek boarded the jet as the pilots and flight attendant bowed respectfully to the Head of the Vampire Council. This was a last-minute trip that Wlodek decided to take, and he hoped for a successful and equitable outcome.

"I have bagged blood if you'd like," the attendant allowed Wlodek to settle on his seat.

"I am comfortable," Wlodek waved the two-hundred-year-old vampire away. "I will call if I have any needs."

"Of course." The attendant bowed again and backed away. Wlodek pulled out his cell phone to make a call.

"Honored One?" Charles answered promptly.

"Inform Flavio that I am traveling."

"I will. I haven't spoken with my sire for two weeks. He will appreciate hearing from me."

"He will." Wlodek agreed and ended the call.

❧

On my way, the text read. Winkler glanced up at his waiting army and nodded. They'd gathered on his wide, back deck. Winkler had Gavin and Tony, but found himself wishing he had Nathan Anderson and Aedan Evans with him, too. It never hurt to have vamps backing you up when you didn't know how many enemies to expect.

The Grand Master stood beside Winkler, surveying their troops. Matt Michaels was dressed in body armor and had a semi-automatic rifle slung over a shoulder. Gavin and Tony stood together, both dressed comfortably in jeans and pullovers for ease of movement. Trace, Marco and Ace had turned to wolf, while Trajan was prepared to do the same. Nobody knew how many of Tanner's trackers might appear, so it was best to cover all bases. Buck, Andy and Loren stood behind Trajan, each armed with a rifle and a pistol.

"They're on their way," Winkler said softly, pocketing his cell.

"Everybody ready to go?" The Grand Master asked. Nods came from everyone.

Ten minutes. Ten minutes before daylight would arrive, bringing with it an end to his suffering. Aedan settled on a large, flat rock positioned outside the underground safe house. For centuries, the stone had guided vampires to the safe house, which offered sanctuary from the rising sun.

On this day, the stone would witness the destruction of vampire life instead of its salvation. Aedan knew the winds and coming rain would wash away his ash. A fitting end for any vampire born in the country called Ireland.

Adele always waited for her employees to get in their vehicles and drive away safely before putting her car in gear and rolling out of the parking lot. The ferry would take her to the mainland, and then a twenty-minute drive would get her to Star Cove and bed.

Weekends always meant long days and exhausting work, and she was happy that she was working a later shift on Saturday. It meant she could sleep in and still have breakfast before driving to work again.

The ferry worker guided her onto the boat with repeated hand waves, indicating that she park in the center near the front. Only three cars were aboard, and one of those belonged to a restaurant employee.

The ferry's engine rumbled as the boat moved away from the dock and glided through darkened gulf waters. Adele slipped out of her car and stood with an elbow propped over her open car door, letting the night breeze flow about her, lifting and toying with strands of her hair as she allowed the stress of the day to leach away.

How's everything in Star Cove? Ashe texted Sali. Winkler had asked him to stay inside his bedroom with the blinds shut and the curtains closed. Winkler hadn't asked him not to use his cell, and Ashe was restless. He felt that something might be wrong, but the headache persisted and he still couldn't sense anything.

Dude, it's almost one, Sali texted back.

Come on, you're probably playing video games, Ashe grumped back via text.

Hey, mind your own beeswax, Sali replied.

You were playing video games. Admit it.

Yeah. If Dad catches me, I'll probably get a life sentence of grounding.

I'll visit you in the slammer.

Gee, thanks. No offer of busting me out? Man, that's just cold.

Speaking of cold, I think I wouldn't mind some cold weather. Heat and humidity is awful here in August.

Dude, you're discussing the weather? Man, you must be bored.

Nope, just need a distraction. I'm kinda itchy right now, and I can't figure it out.

You can't figure it out? I thought you knew everything. Where were you earlier, when I needed help with Algebra? I had to call Cori and grovel.

I was asleep. Had some extracurricular activity last night. Will explain sometime.

Dude, I just heard your mom's car drive past. I think Dad's coming down the hall. Gotta go.

$\mathcal{A}$dele shut the garage door and climbed out of her car. The blue Cadillac gleamed in the dim light cast from the garage door opener overhead. Buck kept the car washed and filled up for her. He was good to her in every way, but she couldn't help but think something was missing from her life.

Oh, she'd be comfortable enough with Buck, but that wasn't the problem. She wanted something more, and there was no way to explain it or to understand what it might be.

Adele glanced at the tornado shelter cut into the garage floor and reflected briefly on its original purpose before punching in the code to deactivate the alarm. Sighing, she walked through the door into the kitchen and dropped her purse and keys on the island.

Winkler growled a curse. Tanner had sent fifteen, and more than half had come as wolves. Peyton had arrived with the fifteen on his heels. Gavin and Tony had six to deal with, while Weldon and Trajan had gone to wolf to combat the others with Trace, Marco and Ace. Buck, Andy and Loren were backing Matt, who was firing his rifle with a sharpshooter's eye. Winkler growled another curse and shucked his clothing. No way was Tanner going to take any more of his. No way.

~

The first fingers of light appeared in the east and Aedan blinked. He hadn't seen sunlight for more than eight hundred years. A curl of smoke lifted from his hand, just before the pain came. Aedan threw back his head and keened.

~

"Who could that be?" Someone rang the doorbell, catching Adele halfway up the stairs. It had to be someone from the community—the vampires wouldn't allow a stranger in past nightfall.

"I'm coming," Adele called as she turned to make her way down the steps.

~

Winkler exploded against three humans with guns; they'd appeared from nowhere to join the other fifteen, firing right into the knot surrounding Matt Michaels. Screams and shouts erupted around him —two humans were down swiftly, their throats torn open. The third thought to run. Winkler leapt after him.

~

Ashe could hear guns firing from his bedroom. He cursed and huddled away from the windows. He'd already attempted to turn to mist; he'd failed. Relocation attempts met with the same results. He doubted that he could send mindspeech, but his hearing was fine. He heard shouting, then, and knew someone had been hit. Whether friend or foe, he had no idea. Ashe hadn't felt this helpless since he was twelve and standing in Transformational Arts class, praying to turn.

$\sim$

"Oh, hi. Is something wrong?" Adele stepped aside to allow her visitor inside the house. She was stunned and then slumping to the floor as the point of a dart bit into her chest. Her heart slowed as she gazed in wounded confusion at her attacker.

"Why?" Adele whispered before her eyes lost their light. Her attacker became werewolf and ran silently through the streets of Star Cove.

$\sim$

"Where is he?" The Bright Elemaiya frowned at the dying shapeshifter, whose body lay slumped against the front door. He and three others had appeared as instructed, once the call came from Friesianna's spy.

"He's not here!" Another shouted as he raced down the stairs. He'd quickly searched the bedrooms—nobody else was in the house.

"What's happening?" A third managed to say before three vampires stormed into the house, removing heads before relocation could be achieved.

And then the light came.

$\sim$

"Child, what did you think to do? Speak quickly; it is nearly time for me to sleep." Wlodek handed a unit of blood to Aedan, who blinked in confusion at the Head of the Council.

Wlodek had arrived inexplicably, hauling Aedan out of the sun and into the safe house before he was burned beyond help. Wlodek, dressed in a suit made specifically to cover a vampire in sunlight, tore the visored hood away and removed thick, black gloves.

"I have no reason to live," Aedan whispered. He stared at his hands

—the skin had burned away, leaving raw, red flesh behind. He realized his face and other exposed skin looked the same. Why had he not thought to remove his clothing? Aedan shook his head. Would he have enough strength and courage to make a second attempt? The Honored One could not watch him every moment.

"Enough," Wlodek sighed. "Aedan, I had no intention of robbing you of your family. I have made a mistake, and it almost cost the race an honorable vampire. We have few enough of those as it is. I release you from your service until the death of your wife. Tomorrow, if you are able, you will board the jet and fly home. Make things right with your family. I will see you again in fifty years, perhaps."

"What about Casimir and the others?"

"Casimir may stay to assist you and Nathan in guarding the community. I am recalling Hector and Edmond. Your child will be approached by me or one of my agents when he is of age. If he does not choose vampirism, then perhaps he will consent to work for us."

"That is all I can ask," Aedan bowed his head. "I must sleep soon."

"I know. We will talk again when you wake."

"Why did you change your mind, Honored One?"

"Someone came to me and pointed out the error of my ways."

"What happened?" Ashe ran downstairs as Winkler and Trajan carried Buck inside the beach house. Blood dripped off Buck's fingers, causing Ashe to stop still in dread.

"He's not dead," Trace was slipping into a shirt after becoming human again. "He's in bad shape, though. Matt got wounded too, but he was wearing body armor. Has a bullet in his arm and two in a leg. He's still working to get a doctor out here for him and Buck. Vamps are putting tourniquets on while he makes calls. Andy's dead," Trace added, the words mumbled.

"Oh, no," Ashe dropped to a sitting position on the steps. And then he cursed while brushing away tears.

"Kid, he died a hero. He stood in front of Matt and took those bullets. They would have hit Matt in the head, if Andy hadn't stepped in."

~

Winkler's cell phone rang as he and Trajan laid Buck on the sofa in the media room. "Marcus?" Winkler growled low. "We're a little busy here, right now."

"Somebody needs to come. We almost had a murder here, tonight, and we have four of those Elemaiya bastards here that the vamps took down."

Winkler cursed. "Look, I have problems of my own. How the hell did they get past the Witch's boundary?"

"No idea. We have an attempted murderer to track, though."

"Who almost died?"

"Adele Evans."

~

Ashe heard. From yards away he heard Marcus' words on Winkler's cell. "Kid, somebody will drive you. Just hold on, okay?" Trace had an arm around Ashe as he rose to storm out of the house. "They said attempted murder. Your mom is alive, all right?"

"When? When can I go?" Ashe was shaking and brushing away more tears.

"Kid, we have to get help for Matt and Buck. And we have to find a temporary place for Andy and get bodies cleared away," Winkler moved Trace aside and pulled Ashe down to sit on the steps again. "Everybody's had a bad night." Winkler settled beside Ashe and raked bloodied fingers through thick, black hair.

"Andy was a good friend."

"I know. The best. Loren is standing guard over the body. I think Gavin and Tony will help get the other bodies hauled in, but I need to call Shirley to take the rogue wolves out by boat and dump 'em twenty miles out. Matt wants to ID the humans if he can. I get the idea that somebody else might be involved because Matt was their target. They didn't care about the rest of us."

"Can I talk to somebody—just to make sure Mom's okay?"

"Sure. Here, call Lavonna Anderson. I have a feeling she's there with Nathan."

"Yeah." Ashe took Winkler's offered phone and called Lavonna's cell.

"Ashe, we're not sure what happened," Lavonna sighed. At first, she couldn't imagine why William Winkler's cell number appeared on her caller ID. She'd learned quickly enough that it was Ashe calling.

"Is Mom okay?"

"She's fine, and we don't understand that. She said herself that she was dying, so something had to happen to change that. It's really confusing, and Nathan and Casimir are still asking questions."

"Trace said he'd find somebody to drive me over," Ashe mumbled.

"You have to find somebody to drive you?" Surprise coated Lavonna's words.

"It's a long story," Ashe said uncomfortably.

"Dori's here, would you like to talk with her? I need to see if your mother wants something to drink."

"Yeah."

"Ashe?" Dori's voice came through clearly.

"Dori, do you know anything?"

"No. Half the community is outside your house, though, and all of 'em are asking the same thing. All I heard was there was a bright flash of light after the vampires killed the four Elemaiya. They showed up after your mom was stabbed."

"Mom was stabbed?" Ashe's voice cracked.

"Yeah. Marcus thinks it was a poison dart. I don't know why it didn't work, and I heard somebody say that the wound was closed already."

"That doesn't seem possible," Ashe muttered.

"I don't know whether it's true or not. Your mom is alive, though, and she's answering questions for Daddy and Mr. Casimir."

"Who did it? Do you know?"

"Marcus is in there and he won't tell what your mom said."

"This is ridiculous," Ashe said, rubbing fingers against his forehead. The headache was still alive and pounding out its presence inside his skull.

"For sure. Look, do you think you might come tonight? Things are only gonna get worse, because Principal Wright is expecting shapeshifters to arrive tomorrow morning. Marcus wants to lock everything down and not let anybody in or out, so things might get a little tense."

"Sounds like it," Ashe agreed. "Andy died tonight, Dori."

"What?" Dori sounded shocked. "What happened?"

"Zeke Tanner's trackers happened. Mr. Winkler and his bunch fought back, but Andy took a bullet in the head, I think. He's gone."

"What about the trackers—are they dead?" Ashe could hear Dori's quickened breathing; the night's events were frightening her.

"As far as I know, they all died."

"That stupid jerk," Dori spat. "Doesn't Tanner know when to quit?"

"Apparently not. We lost a friend tonight, Dori. Andy was a good guy."

"I know."

"Look, I'll call if it looks like I can come tonight. I'd appreciate it if you'd let me know if you hear anything new."

"I will. Ashe, Wynn is coming. We'll call later."

"Thanks, Dori."

"I drain my crown to give them enough power to slip past the boundary, and you tell me they are dead?" Friesianna threw the cushion from her throne at Rabis. "I will be helpless for days because of this, and we have nothing to show for it?"

"My Queen, I can only report what I see. Nothing more." Rabis didn't point out that it had been Friesianna's decision to drain her crown.

"This is untenable. The boy must be destroyed. Where is Parlethis?"

"It is quite late, my Queen."

"Wake him. I need advice."

"Of course, my Queen." Rabis bowed himself out of Friesianna's tent and went in search of Parlethis.

"Jude, where the hell have you been and what the hell did you give that kid? Winkler is so pissed he's ready to rip your throat out."

Shirley Walker, six feet of pure muscle, stared Jude Gilmore down. "And then we can't find you for hours? Tell me what's going on. Make it good, because fifteen werewolves and three humans stormed Winkler's house tonight. All those rogues are dead, but Winkler lost one of his—his assistant. If I learn you had anything to do with this, your life won't be worth the price of a stick of gum."

"They took Tina hostage," Jude whined, wanting more than anything to turn and cringe at Shirley's feet. "I gave the kid a dose of diamorphine. On the street, it's called heroin. I only gave enough to knock him out for a day. He should be fine, now. He just won't pass any drug tests for a while."

"I hear he isn't fine, and you'll have to answer to the Grand Master for this."

"Kid, I know you want to go now, but she won't recognize you," Winkler said gently. "Try to get some sleep tonight and we'll go in the morning. Marcus said he'd let me know when the questioning was done."

"Fine." Ashe, his arms crossed tightly over his chest, watched from the deck as several of Shirley Walker's wolves moved the bodies of fifteen rogue werewolves into a waiting van. Only six of them were in human form.

Matt had three of his agents there, one of whom was vampire, to haul away three human bodies for identification at a lab in San Antonio. Ashe wanted to curse. With his abilities, he could have identified them easily for Mr. Michaels. As it was, he was still blind to everything, his mother had been attacked and he was helpless.

"Come on, let's go in. I still have some calls to make, Ace is standing guard over Peyton Miller, the Grand Master wants a meeting with me when Shirley Walker gets here and Trajan is growling at everybody."

"What are we gonna do without Andy?"

"I don't know, son." Winkler pulled Ashe into a hug. "We'll have to go on without him, somehow."

∾

"Thanks for coming in early. I had no idea we'd need your skills," Bear Wright shook hands with Kerry Slater, a tall, thin shapeshifter with gray eyes, brown hair and character in every line on his face.

Kerry had graduated from medical school five times in his three-hundred-year lifetime. He carried a case filled with medical supplies and had only been allowed inside the community because Bear had stared Marcus down over it.

"What seems to be the problem?" Kerry asked as Bear led him inside the Evans home.

"Adele Evans was attacked earlier by one of our local werewolves, and will likely have difficulty sleeping if we don't help," Bear replied, leading Kerry up the steps toward Adele's bedroom. Kerry ignored the blood covering the carpet on the steps as he followed Bear.

"I have something that will help," Kerry nodded, avoiding a deep stain of red on a step halfway up.

∾

"Mrs. Evans?" Bear opened the bedroom door carefully, nodding to Lavonna Anderson as he stepped inside. Lavonna held Adele's hand tightly as Adele wiped tears away.

"Mr. Wright," Adele attempted to keep a sob from rising.

"Adele, this is Kerry Slater, who has at least five medical degrees," Bear smiled gently. "I think he can help you get some sleep."

"I hope so," Adele wiped more tears away. "Mr. Wright, can you please tell me where my husband and son are?"

"I'm not sure where your husband is at the moment," Bear said, struggling to keep the surprise from his voice. "Your son is safe at Mr. Winkler's beach house."

"That's what Lavonna said," Adele nodded. "I just can't believe he's not here right now."

"You'll see him in the morning," Lavonna squeezed Adele's hand and stood up. "Let Mr. Slater help you sleep."

❧

"You saw a flash of light? That's it?" Marcus asked Nathan. He had no desire to speak with Hector or Edmond. Casimir had wisely pointed out that the community needed guarding and led them away from the DeLuca home.

"Well, perhaps not all of it, but I'll be damned if I can explain it," Nathan muttered.

"What else was there, then?"

"I swear, in the flash of light, I imagined I saw a woman. She was shining, as bright as I remember the sun shining in my youth, but that could be my imagination; my mind playing tricks," Nathan added. "Adele was dead by the time we killed the last of those intruders—I heard no heartbeat. The light came, then, and when it disappeared, Adele was alive again."

"Nathan, I hope you realize how ludicrous that sounds."

"I find it ludicrous that Dawn Smith stabbed Adele. They've always been good friends."

"I find this difficult to grasp as well. The darts are in my safe, and I hope we can get the poison analyzed. Several of my Pack are out tracking Dawn, but she must have planned this attack carefully. Her scent disappeared outside the gate."

"Has anyone informed her son?"

"I haven't called," Marcus shook his head. "Do you think she'll contact him, or go there first? Should we pay him a visit?"

"Worth a try," Nathan muttered.

"Want to come with me?" Marcus pulled keys from his pocket.

"Yes. Aedan would expect it of me."

Randy woke from a sound sleep at the pounding on his door. "All right, keep your shirt on," Randy muttered as he quickly pulled on jeans and headed for the front door. The pounding continued as he knocked a foot against the sofa leg on his way to answer the door.

"Marcus? Nathan?" Randy blinked in the brightness of the porch light as he swung his apartment door open.

"Randall, have you heard from your mother?" Nathan pushed past Randy and entered the apartment, sniffing as he went.

"Mom? No. Why?"

"Let's go inside," Marcus gestured with a hand. Randy stepped back to allow the Star Cove Packmaster in his home.

"Your phone, where is it?" Nathan asked.

"On the table. I turned it off before I went to bed," Randy replied, moving to the small kitchen and switching on the light.

Nathan turned the phone on and scrolled through messages. "Nothing," he handed the phone to Marcus, who thumbed through the messages before nodding.

"What's going on? Why are you looking for Mom? Isn't she at home?" Randy looked from Marcus to Nathan curiously.

"She stabbed Adele Evans earlier this evening, before running away as werewolf," Nathan said evenly. "If we find her, I'm afraid she will be questioned before facing werewolf justice."

"What?" Randy stared at Nathan in alarm. Werewolf justice meant one thing in a homicide or attempted homicide—death.

"You will return to Star Cove with us. If we have to place compulsion to keep you from warning your mother, we will do so. We will also place compulsion for you to reveal your mother's whereabouts, if that is known to you." Marcus' voice became a growl. Randy backed against the small island in his kitchen.

"But," he began.

"Randall, your mother attempted murder tonight, against someone we thought she cared for. We will find her and learn the truth of this. You will not interfere." Compulsion lay thick in Nathan's words.

Ashe couldn't sleep, so he pulled a book off a shelf and carried it to his bed. The *Return of the King* always made him feel better, somehow. He opened the book to a favorite chapter, and an envelope dropped out.

"What's this?" Ashe lifted the envelope with unsteady fingers. He was the only one who touched his books, and he certainly hadn't placed an envelope inside. The stationery was expensive, in a pale, cream color. Ashe lifted the flap, which wasn't sealed, and drew the single sheet of matching paper out.

You're welcome was written in lovely, handwritten script across the top.

CHAPTER 12

"*D*id you sleep at all, kid?" Trajan sat beside Ashe at breakfast the following morning. It was Saturday, and most people might be sleeping in or thinking about how to spend their weekend. Ashe only wanted to see his mother. To make sure she was all right—even if she failed to recognize him as her son.

"Not much. I read a book," Ashe replied.

"Young man, you should take better care of yourself," Flossie Thompson admonished before setting a bowl of oatmeal and a plate holding three link sausages in front of Ashe. "Want milk or juice, hon?"

"Milk," Ashe said, spooning brown sugar into his oatmeal. "Aren't you supposed to be off today, Mrs. Thompson?"

"I was, but Mr. Winkler called and asked me to do breakfast and lunch today. He explained what happened last night to Amos and me, so of course we'll help out."

"Thank you, Mrs. Thompson," Ashe nodded. "This is a better breakfast than a bowl of cold cereal."

"It is. Cold cereal is for late-night binges. Isn't it?" She smiled at Ashe.

"I always like it for that," Trajan laughed.

"Yeah." Ashe agreed. Trajan reached over and ruffled Ashe's hair.

Ashe was escorted to Star Cove by Ace, Trajan and Winkler. Winkler was in a grim mood, so Ashe didn't ask questions. He wanted to know when Andy's funeral might be. He wanted to know what was happening with Peyton Miller. Most of all, he wanted to know who'd hurt his mother and how Adele survived the ordeal. If Mr. Winkler knew anything, he wasn't sharing.

"She's sleeping." Sharon O'Neill met them at the door after Winkler parked his SUV in the Evans' driveway. Ashe stared at the dried blood on the carpet as he walked through the front door.

"That belongs to the Elemaiya," Winkler whispered. Ashe nodded and swallowed with difficulty.

"What did they do with them?" Ashe asked softly.

"Shirley's wolves picked them up, too."

Ashe didn't reply; he nodded instead. Mostly the house looked the same, except for the bloodstains on the foyer carpet and those on the stairs leading to the bedrooms. "There's a werewolf-owned carpet store in San Antonio. They're on their way," Trajan murmured next to Ashe's ear. "We'll have this out of here and new carpet laid before the day's out."

"Ashe, it's good to see you," Sharon O'Neill smiled at him. "You, too, Ace. Heard you had a bit of excitement your way last night as well."

"We did, Mrs. O'Neill," Ace nodded respectfully. "Is Wynn all right?"

"Wynnie's fine. She's probably having breakfast if you want to go visit."

"Go ahead," Winkler gave permission. Ace was through the door as fast as possible without appearing disrespectful.

Adele woke when her bedroom door creaked open. She was surprised to see Sharon O'Neill, closely followed by Winkler, Trajan and *Ashe*.

"Honey, where have you been?" Tears slipped down Adele's cheeks as she held her arms out to Ashe.

Ashe was beside her on the bed in seconds while Adele held him as tightly as she could. "Mom, what happened?" Ashe mumbled as he hugged her and wept.

"Honey," Adele let him go and leaned back to look at her son's face, "Dawn Smith showed up right after I got home from work last night. I thought she needed something. She stabbed me with something sharp and ran away. I can't explain any of this."

"Mr. Winkler," Ashe turned to Winkler and Trajan. "Dawn Smith is Zeke Tanner's informant. No, I don't have any of my stuff back yet," Ashe held up a hand. "I've known this for maybe a couple of weeks. Might have suspected before then, but suddenly it all came together. She was supposed to get caught with Josiah Dunnigan, but she punked out on him during the full moon."

"And you're telling us this now?" Winkler wanted to growl. He didn't.

"Because of Randy," Ashe hung his head. "Randy's always gotten a bad deal from the werewolf community. His dad died. I didn't want to take his mom away, too, unless she got caught in the act. I was hoping she'd finally turned things around, when she didn't participate in Dunnigan's attempt at murder. If I get my ability back, she's toast." Ashe clenched a hand in anger.

"Randy's here in the community, with a guard," Winkler sighed. "He's at his mother's house. Marcus has extra guards around the community, but Dawn probably won't be back. She'll face werewolf justice if we find her."

"Randy will lose his job," Ashe muttered, unclenching his hand.

"I'll have a state senator call the newspaper's owner. He'll still have a job when this is over. If he wants it."

"Yeah." Ashe knew Randy would likely get as far away as he could if the werewolves executed his mother.

"Mrs. Evans, Buck was wounded last night. He asked about you, first thing," Trajan said gently.

"That's awful." Adele brushed wisps of hair from her face with a sigh. "I was thinking about telling him it wasn't going to work. Ashe, do you know where your father is? I want to talk to him."

"Dad?" Ashe's voice was nearly a squeak. "Mom, I don't know where he is. He might not answer if we try to call."

"We have to try, honey." Adele brushed fingers down Ashe's cheek. "I want things the way they were, and I won't accept no as an answer from your father."

"Then we'll give it a try," Ashe nodded.

"Adele, are you hungry? It's past breakfast time already," Sharon O'Neill asked quietly.

"I have to get to work," Adele sat up.

"No, I've called the restaurant. Your assistant manager is coming in. She'll handle the restaurant this weekend, until you're well enough to go back to work." Winkler nodded to Adele. "The restaurant will be fine."

"Thank you," Adele nodded and ducked her head. "I'm still shaky, but it'll go away."

"Dr. Slater will be by later this morning," Sharon said. "I'll go downstairs and make some eggs and toast."

～

"Sal?" Ashe blinked in surprise when Sali walked into the kitchen later, followed by Jeff and Larry. "I thought you were under house arrest."

"Dad let me off for good behavior," Sali grinned. "He asked us," Sali indicated Jeff and Larry with a finger, "to help guard the community. Everybody was briefed this morning about last night. At least on what we know so far."

"I heard they're holding Randy in his mom's house," Ashe said. "Want a soda?"

"Sure." Sali, Jeff and Larry took seats at the kitchen island while Ashe went to the fridge and pulled three bottles of cola out.

"This okay?" Ashe asked as he set the bottles down on the island.

"This is good," Larry nodded.

"School just isn't the same, Ashe," Jeff said, twisting the cap off his soda and drinking.

"Yeah. Not much is, nowadays," Ashe agreed, taking his seat beside Sali.

"Where do you think Mrs. Smith might be?" Sali asked.

"No idea," Ashe mumbled.

"You don't know?" Sali stared at Ashe in disbelief.

"Long story, Sal," Ashe replied, bitterness in his voice.

"Ashe?" Wynn and Dori walked in. "How's your mom?"

"Case in point," Kerry Slater, physician and shapeshifting lion, nodded his agreement. "The werewolves will dispense justice in this case, if they can track the Smith woman down. This should be shapeshifter justice. We should have our own trackers, and a team in place to make judgments. I've watched too many shifters go down in the past three centuries. Most of them victims of vampires or werewolves. They generally took those they could easily kill, since we're so varied in our animals."

"We only have a temporary truce with both vamps and wolves," Thurmon Novak pointed out. Thurmon was a polar bear shifter, and as such had been friends with Bear Wright for a long time. "I was hoping it might become permanent when the vamps approached us about having kids with some of theirs. Turns out the vamps had their own agenda, and when things didn't turn out exactly like they hoped, they shut down the program and we're back on tenuous ground."

Midmorning sunlight made Thurmon's pale blond hair appear even lighter, and glinted off the gold watch on his wrist. Thurmon owned an alternative energy company, and made important advancements in the solar and wind energy business.

"I'm with Thurmon on this," Bear's third visitor spoke up. "The vamps always seem to have an agenda. We need our own council, our own trackers, our own justice system. Keep this in mind, though—we still need the vamps and the wolves. Sure, we have a few shifters who might take a werewolf down. Maybe. We don't have anybody who can take a vamp down, unless it's daylight and they're sleeping. The rule has always been that they deal out their own justice. What we need is a joint council or judiciary, with two or three members from each race, to make sure justice is done across the board. This will ensure a balance of power, with each race having an equal say if one race is involved in crimes against another."

Bear nodded at Opal Tadewi. Opal was the oldest among the known Old Ones, at four hundred. Born to a Native American shapeshifter mother, Opal had endured the most difficult times as a velociraptor. Not many shapeshifters survived who became an extinct animal when they turned. Opal was one of those few.

"You're right as usual, Opal," Kerry agreed. "We do need that joint justice council. I like the idea of two or three members from each race presiding in cross-species judgments."

"That's the best suggestion I've heard all morning," Bear agreed. "Anybody want more coffee or a snack?"

"Mom's asleep again. Dr. Slater came in after she ate, gave her something to make her drowsy and said it was best if she slept most of the day. He went back to Principal Wright's house after that. I figure they're working on a shifter council," Ashe said.

Dori and Wynn had stayed with Ashe while Sali, Jeff and Larry went out again to patrol the community. "I think the carpet truck is here," Wynn half-rose from her barstool to peer out the kitchen window.

"Yeah, I heard," Ashe slipped off his stool and shuffled toward the front door.

"That looks like something we need to take care of," the werewolf nodded as he examined the bloodstains covering the carpet. "Got a call from the Grand Master early this morning. I take it this isn't shifter or wolf blood?"

"Nope," Ashe shook his head.

"Great. We'll have this outta here in no time, with new carpet laid before dinner."

"That sounds great," Ashe said. "Thanks for coming on short notice."

"Oh, that's no problem. The Grand Master says jump, we jump. Doesn't hurt that Mr. Winkler is paying us double, either."

"Do you need anything from me?" Ashe asked politely. "There are sodas and bottled water in the fridge, and we can get lunch for you if you want."

"Lunch would be welcome," the carpet tech motioned for his two helpers to come inside. "Around twelve or one, maybe?"

"I can arrange that," Ashe said.

"Thanks, kid."

∽

"I'll bring lunch for them when Amos and I head that way," Flossie Thompson promised Winkler over the phone. "For three, you say?"

"Bring enough for the kid, too. Trajan and I can eat with Marcus and Denise; we're still trying to figure out Dawn's next moves."

"I can't believe she did that," Flossie muttered. "Amos almost had a fit when he found out."

"I almost had a fit when I found out," Winkler agreed. "Thanks for your help, Florence. You're making things easier for us."

"No problem, Mr. Winkler. Take care of Ashe. He's having a hard time."

"We will."

∽

"I don't know what happened," Ashe sighed. "I walked in behind Mr. Winkler and Trajan, thinking she wouldn't recognize me or would just ignore me. When she said my name, I felt dizzy. It's almost too much to understand."

"Beyond comprehension," Dori agreed with a nod. Ashe was wedged between Dori and Wynn on the back deck of his house. They'd left the carpet layers inside, ripping up bloodied carpet and padding.

Ashe propped wrists on his knees as he stared at the back fence surrounding the yard. "When Mom asked where Dad was, I knew something had happened," Ashe continued. "I just don't know what it was."

"At least your mom seems normal, now. You don't think it's because she almost died, do you? And there's still that whole thing about the light," Wynn huffed.

"Light?" Ashe jerked his head toward Wynn.

"Yeah. Ace told me. Said Nathan told Marcus, who told Mr. Winkler. Nathan said there was a bright light that came when he and the other vamps were taking out the Elemaiya who showed up. Ace says that Nathan swears he saw a shining woman."

"What?" Ashe goggled at Wynn. "That's just, that's, I don't know." Ashe tossed up a hand in exasperation. Memories flooded his mind, however. Memories of a shining woman, standing at a gate while Edward and the other half-Elemaiyan children escaped through it.

He still didn't have any idea where they'd gone, he only had Ren's assurances that they would be safe. He had the memory of a second woman, too, who'd stood on the opposite side of the gate. A beautiful woman, with black hair and piercing blue eyes. She had mindspeech. Had told Ashe she loved him. He still hadn't sorted that out. Was afraid to, if he were honest with himself. Her image infiltrated his dreams at times, when he imagined himself older than he was.

"I need to run home; I only told Mom I'd be gone an hour," Dori rose and dusted off her shorts.

"I'll go, too. Ace had to go to Marcus' with Mr. Winkler, but they may be done, now."

"Ace is a good guy," Ashe rose and helped Wynn stand.

"Yeah. I know," Wynn nodded shyly. "Call us if you need anything."

"I will." Ashe walked them down the deck's steps and saw them through the side gate in the fence before climbing onto the deck again.

"I suppose you'd like to know what happened last night." Griffin settled onto a chair and blinked at Ashe.

"Yeah. I do want to know what happened last night," Ashe sat on a deck chair opposite Griffin's.

"It's called *Changing What Was*," Griffin sighed. "Six Larentii can do it, but only on a small scale. As in individual cases. There's only one who can *Change What Was* on a larger scale. The fact that this is what happened worries me."

"Why? And you know about the Larentii?" Ashe didn't mean to sound as incredulous as he did, but he couldn't hold it back.

"I'm surprised *you* know about the Larentii," Griffin half-smiled. "Perhaps I shouldn't be so surprised. If I didn't have us so tightly shielded at the moment, we could expect a visit the moment I say Pheligar's name."

"Pheligar?" Ashe asked.

"Pheligar is the Larentii Liaison for my race. He acts as a go-between for us and those who created us. He can be quite irascible at times. If he were here, I imagine he would remain standing so as to intimidate us with his eight-and-a-half feet of blue-skinned grumpiness, and ask me what I might think to accomplish by being here."

"Do all their names end in gar?" Ashe didn't want to bring up his friendship with Ren, who'd been decidedly *ungrumpy*.

"The male's names. The female Larentii names ended in lar. Too bad there aren't any female Larentii at the moment. Don't ask," Griffin held up a hand to keep Ashe's curiosity from erupting. "It's too long a tale. Perhaps someday, you'll know it."

"Back to *Changing What Was*," Ashe said, frowning at Griffin.

"Yes. Well, do you know the Legend of the Three?" Griffin asked.

"No."

"It goes like this—in the beginning, the One created the Three. Only the One was more powerful than the Three. They were named Wisdom, Strength and Love. Those Three are more commonly known as the Mighty Mind, the Mighty Hand and the Mighty Heart." Griffin's eyes became unfocused as he gazed into the distance. Ashe watched him carefully—he imagined he might hear something few had ever heard before.

"Eventually," Griffin continued, "others were made, with varying degrees of power, who served under the One and the Three. The worlds were made, both Light and Dark, and those worlds were populated with all manner of races and creatures." Griffin's fingers tapped his knees unconsciously as Ashe watched.

"What happened?" Ashe prompted Griffin, who'd fallen silent again.

"One day, the One and the Three discovered that a blight had infected their ranks," Griffin blew out a breath. "Some at many levels of power had banded together and turned against them, seeking to destroy what had been created. The Three were given the task of pursuing the rogues—those Destroyers—and finding a way to turn them back to the Light or devising a way to eliminate them. Not an easy thing to do, since the ones they hunted were not only immortal and powerful, but were recruiting allies among the created races. The Three began to choose their armies carefully—part of their duty is to seek out and right many wrongs in their pursuit of the invasive evil."

"Is that true?" Ashe blinked at Griffin.

"Yes. There is another tale associated with that one, but it is something I feel you must discover for yourself."

"What has all that to do with *Changing What Was?*"

"Only one of the Three will be gifted with *Changing What Was*. It is something the One allows sparingly, as it is quite rare. None know which of the Three will have it, when they appear."

"You make it sound as if they don't exist, yet, when you already said they do." Ashe followed the logic.

"Caught that, did you?" Griffin chuckled. "Good job. Should have known the Ir'Indicti would figure that out. As gods, the Three can't interfere. But there's a way around that rule. If they're reborn into a created race—as one of them, they can interfere all they want. There are ways of becoming immortal if they're born mortal, as you well know. The problem with all that is, they may be vulnerable. Their enemies may be looking for them, to destroy them in their new forms and keep them from their duty. When all Three come together in their new existence, it means the god wars are imminent. That's not a good thing, young one. Is there anything else I can tell you before I leave?" Griffin asked.

"I wish you'd tell me how to get rid of this drug in my system. It's making me stupid." Ashe tapped his forehead.

"You were given an opioid?"

"I don't know what it was. I was unconscious, and now I can barely think."

"You were given an opioid," Griffin confirmed. "It is the bane of any Elemaiya, and dampens their talents, leaving them virtually powerless if enough is injected."

"I got pain medicine when I was twelve. Was that the same thing? I could still do stuff after that," Ashe said

"You were likely given either a non-opioid or a compound, and it wasn't enough to impair you. This—whoever gave this to you had a particular goal in mind, and injected a sufficient quantity to impair your system. I can't interfere directly in this. I can tell you that the answer to your question circles your arm. Those who currently call themselves King and Queen of the Elemaiya can't read those medallions and never knew how to use them properly. I should go." Griffin unfolded his tall frame from the deck chair and stretched. "Be careful." Griffin disappeared.

"Yeah. Sure. Easy for you to say." Ashe lifted the sleeve covering his left arm and gingerly touched the eight gold medallions circling his biceps. At least they weren't as tender against his skin as they'd first been. When they'd first appeared, he could barely stand to touch them, and it was worse if someone else tried.

"How am I supposed to read these things now, to get back what I lost?" Ashe shook his head in bewilderment. "This just gets worse as it goes along."

~

"Any improvement?" Trajan asked as he settled at the Evans' kitchen island. "Mrs. Thompson is bringing dinner for you and your mom."

"No improvement. Not since five minutes ago, anyway, when I last attempted to mist," Ashe grumbled dejectedly. "Want coffee? Mom asked for some a few minutes ago. She got up and took a shower. Said she'd be down in a few minutes."

"I'd take coffee." Trajan nodded. "Shirley says we can have a service for Andy tomorrow afternoon at the usual spot."

"He shouldn't be dead." Ashe poured water into the coffeemaker and turned on the brewer.

"True. Winkler and the Grand Master want to hunt Zeke again, but Peyton says Zeke is probably moving his compound, if he hasn't done it already."

"What's happening with Peyton? They're not thinking of killing him, are they?" Ashe turned worried blue eyes on Trajan.

"Not at the moment. He's telling everything he knows to the Grand Master, and a lot of it confirms what Weldon already suspected," Trajan sighed. "Winkler's sending Peyton to Dallas afterward, to train with some of his other wolves. Most of the education Peyton has is self-taught, so he may be enrolling in night classes, too. Loren is filling in for Andy. Winkler may make it permanent. Loren catches on pretty quick."

"Wish I could help," Ashe said. "Can't right now."

"Understood."

"Here." Ashe poured a fresh cup of coffee for Winkler's Second. "Any news on Dawn Smith? Is anybody making sure Randy has something to eat?"

"No news, and yes, Randy is being fed. He's in good shape, other than worrying about his mother and his job. Winkler let him call Sara once, but that's the only call he was allowed to make. He didn't tell her about his mother."

"What did Sara say? She's a bunny shapeshifter, you know."

"Didn't know that," Trajan shook his head. "Winkler said she couldn't come down to see Randy until things were more settled."

"Wish I could see the implications of all that," Ashe remarked.

"Is the coffee ready? It smells good," Adele walked in, dressed in jeans and a comfortable top. Her feet were bare and her hair pulled back in a single braid.

"Sit down, Mom. I'll get it for you." Ashe went to the cabinet to get another cup.

"Ashe, why are my recent memories of you so hazy?" Adele asked. "Do you think it's a side effect of what happened last night?"

"I don't know," Ashe lied, setting a cup of black coffee in front of his mother. "Mrs. Thompson is bringing dinner for us later."

"That's so nice," Adele lifted the cup to her lips.

"That's my phone," Ashe pulled the cell from his pocket and checked the text he'd received. "It's from Dad," he whispered, opening the message.

Coming home. Will arrive in New York to spend day. Be in Corpus Christi Sunday night, late. Have informed Nathan. He will pick me up. Will explain when I arrive.

Ashe read the message twice before handing the phone to Trajan. "Holy shit," Trajan swore.

CHAPTER 13

"Fifteen trackers are dead and Wildrif has disappeared," Zeke snapped. Hutch stared at the floor surrounding Zeke's desk—Ezekiel Tanner had nearly destroyed the desk inside his new study in anger, sending a laptop, files and everything else flying when he learned of Wildrif's perfidy. "Have you sent anybody out to track him?" Zeke barely kept the snarl from his voice.

"I've got three out, but they lost the scent just before he reached the river. Probably had somebody pick him up," Hutch growled low. "If it was somebody from the other side, he's long gone by now."

"I shouldn't have given him a new cell phone. He dumped the other one in the desert when we went to get him," Zeke huffed. "Who knows if he intends to sell us out, now? How's the move going?"

"Well enough. Two more loads and we're done."

"Get it done quick. It may not be enough, but at least Peyton won't be able to send the Grand Master against us."

"We don't know that Peyton is still alive."

"Thanks to Wildrif high-tailin' it out of here. If I ever catch him," Zeke's hands clenched in fury.

"Buck, I'm sorry. I just feel that something's missing," Adele sounded tired over the phone. He'd called and she'd thought to allow the call to go to voicemail. Instead, she'd answered, determined to end her relationship with the werewolf as gently as possible.

"Adele, I wish you'd think about this before dumping me." Buck didn't sound happy.

"I promise to think about it—I just can't promise that I'll come to any other conclusion," Adele brushed tears away. "You were good to me, and I appreciate that. More than I can say. It's just—not right. Not what I want. I'm sorry."

"Look, both of us got hit last night. I'll call you back in a couple of days and we'll talk again." Buck ended the call.

"That went well," Denise DeLuca sat next to Adele at the kitchen island.

"I'm sorry you had to hear it. Did Ashe let you in?"

"Yes. He went out to talk to Sali. How are you feeling?"

"Not so good, after that." Adele tapped her phone. "The good news, I guess, is that Aedan is coming home. He texted Ashe. Maybe he was afraid to talk to me."

"Things haven't gone so well, lately," Denise agreed softly.

"Anything new?" Ashe asked as he and Sali walked through the Star Cove community.

"Nope. Marco is at the beach house with Loren, and he says things are really quiet over there. Says he's talked to Cori three times today. She almost freaked when he told her about last night."

"Not many people knew what was happening," Ashe said.

"Ashe, what's wrong?" Sali stopped on his trek around the community and stared at Ashe.

"I'm blind as a bat, no pun intended," Ash muttered. "Dang. I don't know if I can even change to the bat," he added. "Sal, will you pick up my clothes if I turn?"

"I guess, but dude, it's still daylight."

"Doesn't matter. If I can't do this, I really am screwed." Ashe concentrated on turning to the bat.

"Looks like a bat to me," Sali muttered dryly as Ashe flapped in front of his face.

Yippee! Ashe sent.

"Dude, turning to an itty bitty bat is no cause for celebration," Sali pointed out.

You can hear my mindspeech? Answer if you can.

"I hear you. Won't you fry those tiny wings if you fly around too much in this heat?"

It's either that or run naked through the street to get back home, Ashe pointed out.

"Young one, perhaps you'd like a ride?" Ashe flapped around to see who'd spoken. She was ancient and lovely, with blue-black hair captured in a braid down her back and dark eyes that held wisdom and pain in their depths.

I'd accept a ride, Ashe agreed.

"He speaks with his mind? That's wonderful," she stated. "I am Opal Tadewi, one of Alvin's friends."

"Alvin?" Sali blinked.

Principal Wright, Ashe supplied.

"Oh. Man, I didn't know he had another name besides Bear."

"He does," Opal smiled. "Young one, you may sit on my shoulder," she tapped her right shoulder with a finger. "Perhaps you will tell me which house is yours?"

Sali gathered Ashe's clothing and followed Opal and Ashe down the street.

～

"Hey, Mrs. Evans. Ashe turned." Sali lifted Ashe's jeans and sneakers.

"Who is this?" Adele saw Opal as she walked around Sali.

"I am Ashe's ride for the present," Opal smiled. "I hear you had a traumatic experience last night. Is there anything I can do?"

"I'm all right, I just feel a little confused," Adele smiled. "I have coffee. Would you like some?"

"I'd appreciate a cup. Young one, perhaps you'd like to get dressed?" She addressed Ashe, who still perched on her shoulder. Ashe flapped away, following Sali up the stairs.

~

"Man, Mom will blow a gasket when she figures out I don't have any clothes here. They're all at Mr. Winkler's." Ashe came out of the bathroom, fully dressed again, his hair ruffled from pulling the T-shirt over his head.

"Marco said Cori was coming home for dinner with her mom and Dori," Sali said. "Maybe she can go by Winkler's place and pick up stuff for you."

"That's fine, but what then? Mom signed a paper, making Mr. Winkler my guardian. Does she remember that at all, or are her brains completely scrambled?" Ashe turned a worried glance on Sali.

"No idea, man. Maybe you should talk to Mr. Winkler first. Or the Grand Master."

"They've got their hands full, don't you think? Zeke Tanner is still causing trouble, Dawn Smith is trying to kill my mom, Randy's under house arrest when he didn't do anything, and the Elemaiya are showing up for who knows—uh-oh." Ashe's eyes widened in alarm.

"What? That uh-oh didn't sound good, dude."

"Sal, they were trying to get me, last night. Why didn't I see this before? Oh, man, this is a hundred times worse."

"See what?" Sali asked.

Ashe almost ran through his bedroom door, heading for the stairs. Sali trotted behind, still asking questions. "Where's Mr. Winkler?" Ashe's sneakers squeaked on the tiled kitchen floor as he sailed into the kitchen.

"He's still with Marcus and the Grand Master at our house," Denise DeLuca answered.

"I need to talk to him," Ashe breathed. Sali caught up and bumped into Ashe, nearly knocking him over as Ashe stopped still to call Winkler on his cell.

"Is he always this abrupt?" Opal smiled at Adele. Sali righted himself before pulling Ashe back from a near fall.

"Not always, unless there's something important going on," Adele replied. "Honey, what's going on?"

"I sort of know more than I did," Ashe said. "Mr. Winkler, can I see you for a minute?" Ashe asked when Winkler answered the call.

"Thanks," Ashe hung up. "Mom, I need to go to Sali's house. I'll be back." Ashe raced out the door, Sali close behind.

~

"You're sure about this?" Winkler knelt beside the chair Ashe had chosen in Marcus' den. Marcus, Sali, Trajan and the Grand Master were waiting for Ashe to explain why he thought the Elemaiya had been waiting for him to appear to save his mother the night before.

"Well, they were waiting for me in England, when they tried to take Dad," Ashe pointed out.

"So, Dawn Smith is not only involved as Tanner's informant, she may be dealing with the Elemaiya, too?" The Grand Master attempted to puzzle things out.

"I think Wildrif is pulling strings in all this," Ashe muttered bitterly. "You think he's taking money from all sides?"

"Could be," Winkler's forehead wrinkled as he considered the idea. "Kid, I never thought I'd miss that crazy talent you have, but I do now."

"We'll just have to figure this out the old-fashioned way, until the crazy talent comes back," Ashe said. "I have a headache, again. Sal, got any aspirin?"

~

"Do you have a last name?" Curtis Roberts asked.

"None that matters," Wildrif shrugged.

"You say you're the one providing all the intel? Through Tanner?"

"Yes. He has failed to pay for my services or provide proper compensation of any kind. Therefore, I offer my services directly to you."

"What can you give me on that kid? The one in those photos?" Curtis asked. He studied Wildrif as his new informant considered the request. Curtis thought Wildrif looked much like the homeless people he sometimes passed on the street. Dressed poorly in ill-fitting clothing, Wildrif wore shoes too large for his feet, his mismatched eyes made everyone around him uncomfortable and he needed a bath and a haircut.

"The child is dangerous most of the time, but I have recently learned that his power is diminished. If you can arrange to take him before his power returns, you might command it instead of the pretender, Matt Michaels."

"Where did these photographs come from?" Curtis held up the two photographs he'd discussed with Arthur Vaine.

"An acquaintance, who owed me a favor," Wildrif dismissed the photographs with a wave. "He is no longer alive—William Winkler and the boy saw to that."

"That's too bad," Curtis muttered. "Look, how about I set up an account for you and deposit what Tanner was scheduled to get, then hand you some cash and find a place for you to stay? You can clean up there and I'll have my associate, Mr. Calhoun, get shoes and clothes. Just give him your sizes and he'll take care of it."

"I'd appreciate that," Wildrif nodded, his colorless hair floating about his head.

"Calhoun, make sure he has a new cell phone, too," Curtis waved his assistant away.

⌒

"How long? Your best guess, Rabis?"

"I see your power returning in two days, my Queen." Rabis bowed to Friesianna so she wouldn't see his eyes. He was giving her truth, he merely refused to let her see what else he knew—that she would contact Baltis the moment she held enough power to do so. After that, who knew what might come? Everything was becoming unsettled with those surrounding the boy, too, and Rabis was more worried than ever.

"Where is Parlethis? I wish for him to attend me," Friesianna snapped as Rabis straightened.

"I will find him for you immediately." Rabis bowed again and left Friesianna in her tent.

"Climb up the conventional way?" Winkler settled beside Ashe on the roof of the Evans home.

"Ladder," Ashe nodded.

"Heard your dad is on his way home. Know anything more about that?"

"No. I was hoping Nathan would have more when he was up and around, but he didn't stop at the house."

"You think your dad knows about your mother's near miss and sudden memory restoration?"

"No idea. I can't really explain the memories returning, either. One minute she doesn't recognize me, the next, everything's like it was." Ashe considered telling Winkler about the visit from Griffin and the note he'd found in a book, but held off. There was enough trouble, without letting Winkler know about impending god wars. Absently, Ashe rubbed the medallions around his arm. How could he unlock their secret, when he'd lost that ability?

"Did you catch up with Shirley Walker's werewolf nurse?" Ashe asked instead.

"Yeah. He's in a lot of trouble. Said Zeke's wolves were holding his wife hostage and said they'd kill her if he didn't do what they asked, which was to give you a big dose of an opiate painkiller."

"What will happen to him?"

"The Grand Master left that with Shirley, so I don't have an answer."

"He should have told you and the Grand Master. Before he gave me that crap, I could have done something about his wife."

"After you woke up."

"I would have."

"Yeah. Water under the bridge, kid. Water under the bridge. How's the gunshot wound?"

"Not bad." Ashe pulled back his right sleeve to let Winkler see for himself. "Almost closed."

"Impressive. Have you healed that fast, before?"

"Don't think so. Last time I was shot, it took a lot longer."

"At least something's going right."

"I guess. And Dad's coming home. I don't know what's gonna happen with all the extra vampires."

"Hector and Edmond have been recalled by the Council." Nathan lifted himself onto the roof and came to sit next to Ashe. "I have heard from Aedan. I did not inform him that Adele seems to have lost whatever it was that separated her from him. Perhaps it will surprise them both."

"I hope it's a good surprise," Ashe muttered.

"Ashe, Aedan did not mean to treat you so harshly. I believe he thought to protect you. I don't have a reason for the Honored One's reversal in this, but I am inclined not to inquire. I do know that Wlodek always keeps his word, and Aedan says he has been released from his service to the Council for at least fifty more years."

"Good," Ashe bumped his forehead against his knees.

"Casimir is staying in Star Cove?" Winkler asked Nathan.

"Yes. He will help us guard the community."

"Good. I'll feel better, knowing there are three of you. I don't know about anybody else, but this thing with Dawn Smith and Wildrif has me worried."

"Yeah. It's not a good thing, either," Ashe mumbled against his knees.

～

Dawn fought off the urge to call Randy. She hadn't left a note, either. Perhaps it would keep him out of trouble with Marcus and the Grand Master. She'd dumped her cell and bought a temporary replacement so she couldn't be traced. Cursing Zeke Tanner for perhaps the hundredth time, she drove toward St. Louis, on her way to Chicago. If she were to be executed for murder, she'd like for one of the murders to be profitable to her. To Randy, too, if he'd only see the sense in it, someday.

"All three have criminal records," Matt informed Winkler over the phone. "We ran fingerprints through the database, and got positive IDs on all of them. I'd bet money they didn't have ties to Tanner, though. Their crimes were committed back east, mostly in New York and New Jersey."

"You were their target, that's easy enough to see," Winkler said. "They intended to take you down. They got Andy, instead."

"There's no reason for me to be on their radar—unless somebody sent them in my direction," Matt observed.

"I think that's exactly what happened."

"I'm beginning to agree with you. How's the kid?"

"Still impaired."

"Not good. Tanner somehow knew exactly what to do to take him out of the game."

"Wildrif knew. I'd bet a lot on it."

"You're right. You think he's playing all the pieces against each other?"

"I do."

"How much are they paying him?"

"No idea. Bear in mind, though, that he didn't look wealthy to me when we picked him up with Obediah's bunch."

"True. Is he not spending the money, or is he being compensated in another way?" Matt asked.

"Something to think about," Winkler muttered. "I've got mine working on the Smith woman, hoping we'll get a hit on her credit cards."

"I've got her tag number and vehicle description distributed, but it varies, state-to-state, how actively they search for that," Matt said. "It's probably safe to say she's left the state of Texas."

"Long gone," Winkler agreed. "Her son says he has no idea where she might go, and New Mexico would be the first logical choice, so I'd bet she didn't go in that direction."

"Will Tanner send more after you?"

"No idea. If that were me and I'd just lost fifteen of my best wolves, I'd take time to regroup and form a better plan before making another attempt."

"Something must have made him think he'd be successful in this attempt," Matt said.

"Wildrif," Winkler growled.

"You have to ask yourself what Tanner actually accomplished in that raid, since I'm pretty sure the humans weren't on his payroll."

"All Tanner accomplished was taking the kid out of the game." Winkler held the phone away from his ear and cursed. Matt heard it anyway. "You think that was Wildrif's goal? What about the hit on Adele, when those Elemaiya showed up to take Ashe? Something doesn't add up, here."

"I agree."

Aedan sighed as he walked down the steps to the safe house. How would Adele react to his appearance? Would she take him back after he removed the compulsion? Would she forgive him for placing it? He didn't have many answers; all he knew was that he had amends to make—with his wife and his boy. Somehow, he'd been given another chance and he was determined to make it work.

Ashe was surprised when Trace spoke at Andy's funeral. Six werewolves, per tradition, had guarded the carved wood box holding the body since the evening before.

"I have hope," Trace said, "that this is not the end. That something else waits for us. A better time. A better life. Perhaps a better world. Andy certainly deserves all those things. What more can we ask of anyone, than that they give their life to save another? What greater gift is there?"

Ashe turned to watch Winkler as Trace delivered Andy's eulogy. Winkler's head was bowed, leaving his face in shadow. Ashe turned away, giving the tall werewolf privacy in his grief.

"Honored One, William Winkler has offered the use of his jet and a safe place to sleep while we work in the states." Tony had offered to make the call and Gavin allowed it, shortly after nightfall. "It appears Ashe's talents have been disabled through treachery—he was wounded during our last assignment, and the werewolf nurse was compromised. The boy was given a large dose of opiate and, as Winkler puts it, can't touch his talents because of it. We have no idea how long the effects might last."

"This is evil news," Wlodek said.

Gavin, who stood nearby as Tony placed the call, nodded his agreement. "Honored One," Gavin began, knowing Wlodek would hear his voice clearly; "it is evil news. The boy was more than cooperative, and surprised both of us with his willingness to help. The talents he possesses are, if anything, even more astounding than originally reported. It is my suggestion that we court him for future work. His ability to move about in the day will be a decided asset. I see no need for vampirism in this case. The Council can pay him fairly and the boy is not greedy, if my sources are correct."

"Yes, I have had information on that as well." Wlodek didn't elaborate and Gavin didn't press the matter. "I will agree to leave you where you are; I merely expect you to keep me apprised if your situation changes."

"Of course, Honored One," Gavin replied. He nodded at Tony, who ended the call on his cell.

"I feel better now," Tony breathed a sigh. "I hope the kid can get that crap out of his system soon. We could use his help."

"I know. Our next objective is Hughes Humphrey, and he is younger and less intelligent than our previous targets. We can pursue him easily enough without assistance from Ashe."

"Where is he?" Tony sorted through folders in Gavin's briefcase, searching for the proper one.

"New York, according to his file. And then we must find Alan Everett," Gavin added.

"Where is Alan? Best guess?" Tony lifted an eyebrow in curiosity.

"Likely in New Orleans," Gavin replied.

"No. A vampire in New Orleans? That's rich."

"Anthony, this is no time for levity," Gavin offered Tony a severe frown. Tony burst out laughing.

"Marco gathered clothes and sent this," Cori handed Ashe a duffle filled with Ashe's clothes, plus a bag from a popular electronics store.

"What is this?" Ashe dug in the bag, first.

"Something Gavin asked him to give you," Cori grinned. "I already peeked. You'll like it."

"Holy cow. It's the new tablet," Ashe was tearing into the shrinkwrap-covered box quickly. "Gavin bought this for me?" Ashe stared at the tablet as he considered the possibilities.

"Look, it's one of those with an Internet connection anywhere, and the contract has been paid for a year," Cori waved the receipt in front of Ashe.

"He paid for that? Dang, that was nice," Ashe breathed, checking the tablet to see if the battery was charged. "I can use this to place calls and do face time," Ashe powered it up, finding it had a partial charge. "I'll plug this in and start getting apps loaded."

"Marco wants one," Cori grinned. "I'm saving money to get him one for Christmas."

"Cori, I'll lend you the money and you can pay me back," Ashe offered.

"Really? That would be awesome," Cori laughed.

"Here, let's order it online, and send it to your home address," Ashe began tapping on his new tablet.

"Ashe, we really miss you around here. I know you work for Mr. Winkler, but it's just not the same. And after Hayes and all that," Cori said.

"Yeah. Jimmy, too. And Andy."

"Marco says Winkler misses Andy. More than he's letting on. I know werewolves see friends and Packmates fall, but we've had more than our share."

"Yeah. I hope we don't see any more of it. If I get my stuff back, I'm going hunting." Ashe chewed his lip in determination as he ordered a tablet and entered Cori's address through an online website.

"What will you hunt?" Cori whispered, blinking at Ashe in concern.

"That's who, Cori. And there might be several on that list."

CHAPTER 14

"I just don't know how to act," Adele smoothed her dress nervously. "I feel as if I haven't seen Aedan in months." Adele had taken extra care with her clothes and hair while waiting for Aedan to arrive.

"It hasn't been that long, Mom," Ashe said. It was late—past midnight—and Nathan had left Star Cove an hour earlier to collect Aedan at the airport. He'd taken Hector and Edmond with him; they'd be boarding the Council's jet for a return flight to New York and would fly from there to the U.K. the following evening.

"I know, I just miss him," Adele breathed.

"Maybe I should go to Sali's, or go back to Mr. Winkler's place tonight."

"No, hon. You stay here. You haven't seen him, either." Ashe didn't point out that he had seen Aedan, and Aedan had sent him home. It wasn't a good memory.

"Is that a car in the drive?" Adele ran to a window near the door to peek. "It's them. Honey, do I look all right?" She turned to Ashe, a mixture of hope and terror on her face. "Will he be happy to see us?"

"I sure hope so," Ashe mumbled.

"Ready, Father?" Nathan asked as he and Aedan climbed out of Nathan's car.

"Yes." Aedan had dressed carefully in a suit and tie, and adjusted his cuffs and the tie's knot before nodding to Nathan.

Steeling himself, Aedan strode purposely toward the front porch and climbed the steps. Before he could reach out to ring the doorbell, the front door opened and Adele threw herself at him, holding on tightly and weeping as she repeated his name, over and over.

Dad's home. Mom's happy. He's in shock, Ashe texted in response to Sali's question.

Great. At least I'm out of house arrest, so we can hang tomorrow after school if you want.

Maybe. I have to go online and check my assignments. No idea what that's gonna be, Ashe responded. *Need to get with Mr. Winkler, too, and see what he wants.*

You coming back to Star Cove, since your dad's home?

No idea. I didn't say much to Dad. He took Mom to the back deck for a talk, so I went to my bedroom.

Things are kinda messed up.

Some things are worse, some things are better, Ashe responded philosophically.

I need to get in bed, it's nearly two, Sali pointed out.

Yeah. Goodnight.

Ashe tossed his cell onto his old dresser before smothering a yawn. Part of him wanted to sleep, another part wanted to ponder his current problem. He couldn't avoid the worries that plagued him, wondering if anyone might be in danger while he was so helpless.

"I got your message." Hughes Humphrey stared at the one before him. He still hadn't figured out how a stranger might get not only his cell-phone number, but have information that might save his life.

"My name is Wildrif, and I'm something of a clairvoyant." Wildrif looked better than he had in a very long while. New clothes, shoes and a haircut had done wonders for the Dark Seer.

"Your eyes are different colors," Hughes pointed out the obvious. Wildrif held his sarcasm back.

"I have a business proposition for you," Wildrif said, ignoring Hughes' witlessness. "And money to get you to the country of your choice, should you decide to help me."

"It depends on how much money and what you want. I don't mind killing, but it has to be somebody who won't be missed too much. I'm in enough trouble as it is."

"That isn't what I want," Wildrif smiled.

"What do you want?" Hughes' curiosity was piqued.

"I want to be a vampire. Just make the turn and leave me in a safe place. When I wake up, I'll give you the number to a private account holding three million dollars."

"I don't have to stay and take care of you?"

"Certainly not." Wildrif sounded offended.

"Sounds good," Hughes shrugged. "Maybe if you cause enough trouble as a vampire, it'll take some of the heat off me."

"Precisely what I was thinking," Wildrif agreed. "How long do you think it might take?"

"Oh, you seem in pretty good shape. Maybe five or six days."

"Good enough. Is there somewhere nearby where we might do this quickly? I'll make sure you're safe enough from the ones who hunt you."

"Gavin Montegue never misses," Hughes agreed. "I need as much help as I can get to stay out of his way."

"Do what I say and your safety will be assured," Wildrif lied smoothly. "Shall we go? I've written out precise instructions for making a vampire. Be sure to follow them exactly."

"Okay."

~

"We have a message from the Bright camp." Raze fingered the envelope in his hand.

"They know where we are?" Baltis rose from his throne in alarm.

"Not at all. This was handed to one of ours outside the gate in Kansas City. I doubt there's reason to worry; from what I heard from the messenger, there may be good news inside this." Raze offered the envelope to Baltis. "I hear they have someone waiting for a reply from you, should you choose to respond, at the same location."

"This is rather unusual; I can't recall getting a message such as this before." Baltis warily accepted the envelope—it was addressed to him in the Elemaiyan language. Cautiously he lifted the flap and withdrew the paper.

Greetings, Exalted Baltis, the message began.

~

Ashe slumped at the island in Winkler's kitchen. His parents had spent the night together, and Aedan was now in his bunker while Adele slept late. Marco had gone to Star Cove to pick him up early; Ashe had left a note for his mother and quietly closed the front door behind him so he wouldn't wake her.

He was now going through assignments for his college courses; he had English Comp I, College Algebra and History, 1865 to the Present, to deal with. He envied Sali and his high school curriculum after reading the online syllabi for his classes.

"Read the syllabus?" Winkler asked, sipping a cup of coffee at the kitchen island while Ashe made notes for his first assignments on the new tablet. Flossie Thompson had set a plate of food in front of Ashe, and he was absently eating bacon and eggs while he scrolled through information.

"Syllabi, and yes, I have," Ashe mumbled, biting into a strip of bacon.

"Did you get to talk much with your dad?"

"No. Mom jumped in his arms and started crying, so I sort of kept out of their way," Ashe shrugged.

"Wise," Winkler agreed. "Kid, your dad will probably talk to you tonight, and I need to see him, too. We'll get this mess straightened out. I won't revoke the guardianship until I'm sure he won't leave again."

"I don't think Mom remembers that she even signed those papers," Ashe set the tablet down on the island and turned to Winkler. "Stuff happened and I still can't explain it."

"No improvement on the ability front?"

"Not as of this morning. I'd have come without bothering Marco for a ride."

"Understood."

"Mr. Winkler, you're not obligated to keep me on the payroll. Without my talent, I'm a glorified file clerk."

"I doubt you'll ever be that," Winkler patted Ashe's shoulder. "It'll come back. How long to finish your first assignments? Loren could use some help with Andy's computer."

"Yeah." Ashe's shoulders slumped at the mention of Andy's name. "I figure I can finish this stuff in four hours or so."

"So, maybe after lunch, then?"

"Sure. Tell Loren to hang in there until then. At least they couldn't take some things away."

"Kid, you healed up quick from that bullet wound. Maybe this will go away faster than normal, too." Winkler's dark eyes stared at the cabinets lining the walls as Flossie bustled through, preparing spaghetti sauce for lunch.

"I sure hope so, but I don't know what the normal healing time for this is. Mr. Winkler, I had another visit from Griffin."

Winkler's head swiveled toward Ashe. "What the hell did he say or do this time?"

"He says that opiates are the bane of the Elemaiya. That it dampens their talents, leaving them virtually powerless if enough is injected. I didn't think to ask how long those effects last."

"We've pretty much figured those things out for ourselves," Winkler muttered dryly and took another sip of coffee.

"He said something else, but didn't bother to explain it, so it didn't help at all," Ashe added.

"What was that?"

"He said the answer to my problem is around my arm." Ashe pulled back the left sleeve of his T-shirt, revealing the eight gold medallions. "Griffin said that the Elemaiya can't read them now and don't know how to use them properly."

"Maybe you should focus on those tonight, then. After you get your work done."

"It may not do any good," Ashe sighed. "I can't read them, either. Never really tried. I thought the symbols were decorations and didn't mean anything."

"They don't look like letters, but what do I know?" Winkler shook his head. "I flunked Alien Studies in college."

"That's so funny," Ashe grinned. "You never flunked anything."

"My dad would have killed me." Winkler gave Ashe a quick hug. "Come on, finish your food and get to work. I have a meeting with the Grand Master and Matt before they leave for the airport."

"Have fun storming the meeting," Ashe quipped, going back to his food.

~

"I can't say it for sure," Matt said. "I wish the kid was okay—he could help with this."

"What can you do if you think he's tailing you?" Winkler asked.

"Curtis isn't known for being ethical about anything he does," Matt replied. "The President isn't really aware of the scope of his program, either. It sounds innocuous to anyone who isn't familiar with Curtis and his methods."

"U.S. Intelligence and Foreign Communications Division sounds innocent enough," Weldon agreed. "Sounds as if they monitor phone calls and email messages."

"They do that, too, even though other agencies are doing it. Supposed to be watching the watchdogs, if you can believe Curtis. I think it's just his way of collecting dirt on everybody, including highly-placed government officials."

"Including you?"

"Including me, I believe." Matt didn't sound pleased. "It would be easy enough to send those three criminals after me, when he had intel from Zeke, who likely informed him that he was about to take Winkler down."

"Killing two or three birds with a single blow?" Weldon growled softly.

"That's what I think. Curtis has a lot of influence, so it wouldn't be hard for him to set up one of his puppets in my place if he can eliminate me. That will give him even more power. I have better, more reliable agents, and we can move faster. At least he doesn't know about the vamps and wolves."

"He doesn't need to know about us," Weldon snapped. "He certainly isn't trustworthy. Is there anything we can do about this? If he's trying to take you down, he knows you're associated with Winkler. It's only a matter of time before he gets something on me or somebody else just as important. It's a sure bet that Wlodek would be interested if this guy learned about the vamps."

"Maybe you should contact him, then," Matt said quietly. "If we can all arrange to have him watched," Matt didn't finish.

"Agreed. I'll give him a call," Weldon nodded. "At nightfall in the U.K."

"Gavin said he and Tony are going to New York to track a rogue in the area tonight," Winkler offered. "Maybe Tony can give us a hand with this."

"Even better," Weldon said. "Perhaps Wlodek will allow him and Gavin to keep an eye on Curtis Roberts after they eliminate the rogue."

"That would be the best option," Matt agreed.

~

"Hey, Mr. Thompson," Ashe nodded to Amos Thompson, who walked across the deck to go inside for a break.

"Ashe, how are you, young man?" Amos offered Ashe a smile as he reached for the door handle.

Ashe had settled on the back deck with his new tablet, working on a reading assignment for the History course. Amos Thompson, more than six feet of tightly muscled shapeshifter, looked a bit ruffled after spending most of the morning guarding the property behind Winkler's beach house.

"I'm okay. Still not back to normal, though," Ashe replied, blinking up at the buffalo shapeshifter. Ashe knew Amos kept his clothing behind a dune on Winkler's property, so he could shift when necessary.

"Just give it time," Amos nodded and walked inside the beach house, closing the door softly behind him.

~

"What is your opinion?" Baltis handed the message to Laridael. "The Bright Queen has lost four of her trusted captains. We have lost six. Her Miriasu has said the boy intends to take our crowns. Shall we form a temporary alliance with the Bright race in order to eliminate this threat?"

"Do you believe she can be trusted, my King?" Laridael said, handing the letter back to Baltis. "Wildrif is dead—perhaps his death can be attributed to the boy as well, since his death coincided with that of our six. We found his mangled body in the desert."

"He had difficulty seeing the boy, that much is certain," Baltis agreed. "Shall we draft a response to this message, then? She designates a time and place to deliver a reply."

"If this is treachery, we will only lose one," Laridael observed. "If she is truthful in her desire, then I say yes. Let us ally and take down this threat. Then we can decide how to resume our long war, if that is your desire." Laridael bowed to Baltis.

"Exactly my thoughts," Baltis nodded regally. "Bring paper. We will reply."

~

"Everything is backed up here, so don't worry that you'll delete it forever," Ashe said. "See, here's the file." He clicked an icon on Andy's computer. "It's in the cloud."

"This is easier than I thought," Loren said. "Thanks."

"No problem." Ashe's cell rang as he slid off the office chair and let Loren take over.

"Mom?" Ashe answered the call.

"Hi, honey. I was wondering if you were planning to come home for dinner."

"Uh, I don't know. I have to ask Mr. Winkler," Ashe hedged.

"Marco can drive you home, if that's how he wants you to get here."

"Okay," Ashe said, suddenly uncomfortable. It was almost like speaking with a stranger, and his mother was completely out of touch. "I'll go ask," he added.

"Talk to you soon," Adele said and hung up.

"This is so weird," Ashe muttered and left the office behind, searching for Winkler.

~

"Mr. Winkler, I don't know what's happening, and I'm almost afraid to tell her what's really going on," Ashe said, settling on Winkler's guest chair.

"You can go home with Amos and Flossie, if that's all right. If you don't want to spend the night in Star Cove, call Marco, he'll pick you up. If you spend the night, come in tomorrow morning with the Thompsons."

"Thanks Mr. Winkler. This is so confusing for me, and I still haven't talked to Dad."

"This hasn't been easy on you, son. If things are uncomfortable in Star Cove, I'm just a call away." Winkler turned dark eyes on Ashe before nodding.

"Yeah. I'll let you know."

~

Dude, are you coming home, tonight? Sali's text caused Ashe's cell to beep as he rode in the back of the Thompson's car.

Coming now. Got a ride with the Thompsons, Ashe replied, his thumbs clicking swiftly on his cell.

Sucks, not being able to travel in your usual way, huh?

Sucks rocks, Ashe replied. *Mom called and asked if I was coming home for dinner, like nothing happened.*

Seriously messed up, Sali responded.

Seriously to the eleventh power, Ashe agreed.

What about your dad?

Haven't talked to him, yet.

Worse.

Yeah.

What do you think he'll say?

No idea. I don't feel comfortable about it, considering how things went when I saw him last.

That's what Marco said.

He was there, so he'd know. Cori, too. Took a lot of guts for them to stand against a bunch of asshole Elemaiya.

You should have taken me, Ashe. I would have helped.

Sal, don't go there. We have a truce going, remember?

Yeah. Sorry, dude.

~

"The money was moved and now he's disappeared," Calhoun dropped a folder on Curtis Roberts' desk. "He sent this, though. Gives two possible locations for the boy on the Texas Gulf Coast.

One of the locations is William Winkler's vacation home in Port Aransas."

"Where the three I sent disappeared," Curtis grumbled.

"No word on bodies, and no answer on any cell phones," Calhoun said.

"Michaels is still around, so that means they either chickened out or they're dead."

"My vote is on the latter option," Calhoun nodded. "You've paid those three too well in the past and it should have been an easy hit."

"It was the ideal opportunity, to hit him while Tanner's thugs went after Winkler."

"I hear Winkler survived as well."

"Too bad. I could have offered those government contracts to someone else, in exchange for a few favors."

"Winkler's security software is still the best available."

"You think I can't get somebody to crack that code and duplicate it?" Curtis huffed at the thought.

"I figure you can," Calhoun chuckled.

"Sunset in an hour," Adele said the moment Ashe walked into the kitchen. Ashe felt as if he were twelve again, as his mother counted the minutes until his father would wake while she cooked dinner.

"Yeah," Ashe sighed. "Need any help?"

"You can put the salad together," his mother pointed to the fridge.

"All right." Ashe pulled romaine lettuce from the crisper and washed it before tearing it into bite-size pieces and dumping it in a bowl. Tomatoes and sliced red onion went in next.

"The salad dressing mix is in the pantry," Adele said, pulling freshly baked lasagna from the oven. "There's shredded parmesan in the fridge, too."

"Okay. When do you have to go back to work?"

"Tomorrow, at three. I'll be doing the late shift, but that works out pretty well, since your father will be wide awake when I get home."

"Yeah."

"Is something wrong, honey?" Adele glanced at Ashe, a look of concern crossing her features.

"Nothing more than usual," Ashe shrugged, dumping salad dressing mix in the prescribed amount of oil, capping the container and shaking it.

"Talk with your father, then. He'll sort it out."

"Yeah."

~

"We have a message from King Baltis," Parlethis handed the envelope to Friesianna with a flourish. "I hope it contains encouraging news."

"Let me see," Friesianna accepted the envelope and lifted the flap.

~

"Adele." Aedan went to her the moment he entered the kitchen and gave her a kiss.

Ashe placed the lasagna pan in the dishwasher and shut the door, switching on the machine. He wiped crumbs off the counter with a cloth and dumped them in the trash.

"Ashe?" Aedan's voice caused Ashe to freeze.

"What do you want?" Ashe's voice was flat.

"Son, come to the deck with me."

Ashe silently followed his father through the house. Aedan opened the door leading to the deck and allowed Ashe to go through first before closing the door behind him. "Sit down, son. We have to talk." Aedan's gray eyes seemed troubled as they briefly raked Ashe's face.

"You didn't want to talk the last time I saw you." Ashe knew his voice sounded sullen. He couldn't help it.

"I know." Aedan settled on the same chair Griffin had occupied a day earlier. Ashe felt as if a century had passed since then. "Sit down. I want to explain."

Ashe took the same chair he'd taken when he'd spoken with

Griffin. Briefly, he wondered where Griffin was and whether he had a permanent residence or if he spent his time going from place to place, never staying long in any of them.

"Son," Aedan lowered his head and stared at his hands, "Nathan tells me there's something wrong. Not just between the two of us, but wrong with you—because you were given too much of a drug and it has impaired you."

"Yeah. On both counts."

"Ashe, I know you feel abandoned, and I don't know how to make that right."

"I don't know, either. I don't think things will ever be the same, since I'm not your son anymore."

"Ashe, people don't turn love on and off, like a faucet. I did what I thought I had to do, to protect you."

"I wish you'd let me in on it, then. You weren't here, Dad. You didn't hear Mom calling me *that boy*, like she'd never seen me before in her life."

"I know. She doesn't remember that. A part of me is glad, because it made things easier for me last night. I don't know if the near-death is responsible for that, or if it's something else. Somehow, I wish it had been the same with you, but I knew it wouldn't be. I knew the moment you walked out of the house, last night."

"At least she broke up with Buck."

"She told me. As if that has disconnected with her reality in some way."

"I don't get that, Dad. I heard he proposed."

"I heard that, too. From Nathan."

"Figures."

"He's my first—and only—vampire child. You're my son, Ashe. In my heart, you will always be my son, even when I refuse you so Wlodek won't find you so easy to take. He's agreed to approach you honestly in the future, with his offers. Reject vampirism, son. You have no need for it."

"Don't you think I can figure that out on my own?"

"I know you can. We don't give you enough credit for knowing these things. Many of us wouldn't be alive if it weren't for you. I'm concerned—really concerned—about what that drug has done to you, and can only imagine why it was given."

"They mean to have me or kill me, Dad. One way or another. It may be in your best interest to leave me with Mr. Winkler. That'll leave Star Cove out of this mess."

"I don't know what to do, son. You can't trust me, now, but I hope that changes. I'd like to see things the way they were, when you were younger and our lives weren't so complicated."

"They are complicated, and it looks like it may get worse. Cut your losses, Dad. Tell Mom to do the same. I can get Marco to take me back to Winkler's house tonight."

"You moved all your things away. I checked last night."

"There wasn't anything left for me here."

"I'm sorry, son. More sorry than I can say that we've hurt you."

"You can't be near as sorry as I am."

CHAPTER 15

"I'm afraid to ask. Marco says the kid didn't say a word on the drive between Star Cove and here last night."

"Have you heard anything from Aedan or Adele?" Trajan shook his head at Winkler's comment before asking the question that concerned him most.

"Nothing yet. As of now, I'm still the boy's legal guardian and his sole means of support."

"This has to be hard on him, Winkler."

"I know. I don't know what to do about it, either."

"I have a suggestion." Winkler lifted an eyebrow at Trajan's words.

"What's that?"

"I know kids in the past have sued for emancipation from their parents."

"Trajan, I'm not sure how to react to that," Winkler said. "If one of my kids suggested that," Winkler shook his head.

"But you didn't walk away from your kids. Sure, Aedan and Adele want him now, but that's confusing the kid. If he declares himself emancipated, then he can stay or go, his choice."

"I don't think this is a good idea," Winkler rubbed his forehead.

"Because everybody wants a piece of him. Walk in there now, and tell him he can make his own decisions from now on. Go on." Trajan gestured with his hands.

"Damn, Traje," Winkler blinked at his Second. "Look, maybe we can compromise. Meet with Aedan and Adele. Say we're all going to lose him eventually if we don't let him have some control over his life."

"That's the best thing I've heard today," Trajan nodded. "Let's go for that and see if it flies."

"I'll send a message to Aedan's cell and see if he replies. I'm worried that Adele won't understand if we present it to her, first. For her, it's like it never happened."

"Yeah. This is a nightmare for the kid."

❧

"It doesn't matter if you want to pay cash for a room. I still need ID and a credit card for incidentals." The hotel desk clerk wasn't budging on the rules. Dawn wanted to turn and rip his throat out. If she were to accomplish her goal in Chicago, she needed to be as discreet as possible.

"I'll find another hotel." Dawn snatched the money she'd laid on the desk and stalked out of the hotel lobby, leaving a worried desk clerk behind.

❧

"I was scared. She said she didn't have ID or a credit card. I swear she growled at me, though I know that's not possible." The manager at the third hotel where Dawn attempted to pay cash for a room called the police as soon as Dawn left. "I got a partial number from her license plate. It was a Texas tag and the last three numbers are four-three-six."

"We'll check it out," the officer's voice sounded bored.

❧

Ashe leaned back against his headboard to read another chapter of

The Return of the King, dropping the mysterious envelope on the bed as he did so.

"Wait," Ashe lifted the envelope again—had he imagined that his fingers tingled as he'd touched it? Cautiously he pulled the note from the envelope and unfolded it.

"Huh?" It no longer said *you're welcome*. Now it said *ask*.

"Ask what?" Ashe flipped the note around. Nothing was written on it except the word *ask*. "Okay, first you say you're welcome. For what? Now you're saying ask? This is ridiculous. Griffin says the answer to my problem is around my arm. You say ask. What the hell does that— wait." Ashe pulled the sleeve of his T-shirt up and stared at the medallions circling his left arm.

"This is so dumb," Ashe muttered, fingering one of the medallions. "Okay, tell me, what is it I'm supposed to ask?" His head swam with visions.

"When did Tony and Gavin leave? Is there a way to get in touch with them?" Ashe skidded into the media room where Winkler, Trajan and Ace were watching a baseball game on the large screen television mounted on the wall.

"Left last night," Winkler said, tapping the remote to mute the sound. "What's the matter?"

"If they catch the vampire they're after, they need to ask a specific question," Ashe sounded breathless.

"What question is that?" Winkler asked, hauling out his cell and selecting a number in his contacts list.

"Gavin needs to ask if their quarry has made anybody vampire lately."

"What?" Winkler exploded, just as Gavin answered the call.

"Gavin, have you captured your quarry?" Winkler asked.

"Yes. He has already been dispatched. Why do you ask?"

"Crap," Ashe dropped to his knees and covered his face with both hands.

"The kid wanted you to ask if your target had turned anybody."

"Too late," Tony's voice could be heard in the background. "Is that a possibility?"

"Yeah," Ashe mumbled. "A terrible possibility."

~

"What happened? Did you get your ability back?" Winkler pulled Ashe into the kitchen and offered him a soda while he asked questions.

"Not yet, no," Ashe said. "But I have these." He pulled back his sleeve. "Apparently, if I ask the right questions, I can get answers in the form of images." He tapped one of the medallions.

"What did you see?" Winkler asked.

"A lot of it was a blur, but what I did see was a vampire, and well, it looked like he was," Ashe slumped. It wasn't pretty, what he'd seen.

"Making a turn? Who, kid?"

"Wildrif," Ashe muttered. "Mr. Winkler, he's a seer. He knows stuff. How bad do you think that might be if he becomes vampire?"

"This isn't good," Winkler raked fingers through his hair.

"Do we need to call Gavin back?" Trajan pulled a soda from the fridge and settled on a barstool next to Ashe.

"Yeah. I guess we do." Winkler pulled out his cell again.

"Montegue here," Gavin answered promptly.

"Gavin, do you have information on that prisoner who got away from the maximum security facility in Colorado?" Winkler asked.

"Yes." Gavin only hesitated for a moment.

"The kid seems to think Wildrif may be on his way to becoming vampire."

"This is terrible news. If you are correct, I must contact the Honored One quickly. That one is Dark Elemaiya, and you know what trouble that might be, especially with the talents that one supposedly has."

"Yes, I remember clearly what kind of trouble that might be," Winkler's voice was grim. "I recall the misting, the mindspeech, the shapeshifting, the murderous tendencies—all of it. And as this one has foresight, he could be the worst of all."

"Decidedly."

"What can we do? Weldon can lend some wolves to the cause, if you need to go hunting."

"I will let you know." Gavin abruptly hung up.

"He didn't like that information," Winkler shoved his cell in a pocket.

~

"I'll agree to leave things as they are for now, but that's still my son," Aedan said. "I feel I have much to atone for, where Ashe is concerned."

"He did mention getting a car, but I've already made arrangements to get it for him. The Council paid for his services before he was given the drug."

"What car?" Aedan's interest was immediate.

"A classic car, actually," Winkler admitted. "Said he wanted it mostly for show. I had Loren make the purchase this morning while Ashe was studying. It'll be delivered this weekend."

"I will reimburse you."

"Aedan, I paid seventy thousand for it."

"I don't care. I should have bought one for his birthday. I know how disappointed he was over that."

"We can split it."

"I will pay."

"All right. I'll forward a copy of the invoice."

"Thank you."

~

"Do you think he's trying to buy his son's affection back?" Trajan asked after Winkler ended the call.

"Maybe. I'm not sure how Ashe will react."

"The kid needed his parents, and they weren't there for him. All Aedan's fault, seems to me."

"Yeah. Look, what are we going to do if the kid is right about Wildrif?"

"That sounds plain scary, boss."

"I thought Wildrif was crazy as hell before. What do you think he might do as a vampire?"

"I don't want to think about it. If he's making the turn, what's he gonna do if he wakes up hungry and there's no sire to feed him?"

"People will probably die."

"Yeah."

It had taken a bribe, but Dawn finally managed to get a room at a motel. The walls were cracking, the bed sagged in the middle and the hot water was barely warm. The desk clerk had accepted a one-hundred-dollar bribe in addition to the cost of the room, but it was a room in the barest sense of the word.

"At least there aren't any bugs," Dawn growled as she hefted her bag onto the creaking bed. Her phone needed charging, but as soon as that was accomplished, Dawn intended to find Sara's address. In a day or so, the timid shapeshifter would be dead and Dawn would be on her way to Canada in wolf form.

"How are the classes?" Trace sat beside Ashe the following morning as Ashe read his English Comp assignment at breakfast. "You get to lift weights this morning, since the bullet wound looks like it's healed." Trace grinned as Flossie put a plate of food in front of him.

"Some of it's boring. Stuff I've already read or researched for papers," Ashe said. "History, especially."

"Then passing tests will be a piece of cake."

"Got two tests on Friday. I have until Monday to turn everything in for the week."

"Too bad they didn't have an online option when I was in school," Trace said.

"You being such an old man and all," Ashe teased.

"That just earned you extra time on the weight bench," Trace's grin widened.

"Bring it on, dude."

~

"Dr. Dillon will be here until six, if you want to bring your cat in," the receptionist replied to Dawn's question. "It would be better if you can get here earlier, though, so you both won't be here so late."

"Will she be there alone if I don't get there before six?"

"No, her assistant will be here, too."

"Thanks. I'll try to come early, then." Dawn hung up and cursed Sara's assistant, who seemed to be just as conscientious as Sara Dillon, DVM. Dawn would have to wait for Sara to leave work and follow her home.

~

"How did you know about Wildrif, if you don't have your mojo back?" Trace asked as Ashe lifted weights.

"Had a visit from Griffin the other day," Ashe grunted as he bench-pressed two hundred pounds. "Told me he couldn't interfere with the drug in my system, but that the answer to my problem was around my arm. Winkler didn't tell you?"

"He didn't say much. Are you talking about those medallions?"

"Yeah. Accidentally asked one of them a question, but it gave me an answer."

"Kid, while I normally think you're scary, that's even scarier. Does it bother you that those things seem to have a mind of their own?"

"No. It's what they were made for." Ashe huffed a breath before lifting the weights again.

"There's barely a mark where the bullet hit you," Trace examined Ashe's right arm as it was extended.

"I think two of these medallions are for healing," Ashe lowered the weights. "Might explain the quick recovery."

"Two?"

"There are two of each. Two for knowledge, two for healing, two for strength and two for foresight. I got lucky and asked one of the knowledge medallions what I needed to know."

"It told you?" Trace shook his head in wonder.

"Not with words. With images. It's easier that way, to get around language barriers."

"Will they answer anybody?"

"No. Just the person they've chosen, or the person chosen by those who hold the crowns."

"The Bright Queen and the Dark King could say where these went?"

"Yeah. Until I came along. They chose me and cut out the middle Elemaiya."

"Can you choose to give them away?"

"If I want. Right now, I need them."

"I hear that. Do you know how long you'll be down because of that drug?"

"Yeah."

"How long?"

"What time is it now?"

"Ten-thirty-three."

"Then it'll be six days, seven hours and twenty-seven minutes."

"Good with math, huh?"

"I guess. Trace?"

"What?"

"Don't tell anybody except Trajan and Mr. Winkler about the time thing."

"Okay. Wasn't planning to tell anybody else, but I won't for sure, now."

"Thanks."

~

"Ashe, your father and I had a talk last night, and he says you're upset. We also talked about Mr. Winkler being your guardian."

Adele had called while Ashe was running on the beach. Trace and Ashe had slowed to a walk so Ashe could answer his mother's call.

"Mom, I don't want to do anything about that right now," Ashe said, stopping in mid-step and turning his eyes toward the east to watch the waves washing ashore. Trace stopped as well and stood a discreet distance away.

"Honey, your father said he made a mistake and made you think we'd abandoned you. I realize something happened or I would never have dated Buck while your father was gone. We're together again, and that's how it's going to stay."

"Look, this is, well, it's painful," Ashe shaded his eyes as the sun broke through low clouds hanging overhead.

"But we still love you, honey."

"I know. I'm just trying to get past recent events."

"Aedan said to let you make up your own mind on this, but I really wish you'd come home more often. You only have a few clothes left here at the house. Everything else is gone."

"I know. I think I want to leave things as they are for now. Maybe I can tell you what I want in a few days."

"All right, but I'll ask you again in a week if you haven't made a decision."

"That's fine."

"I'll fix meatloaf if you'll come home Thursday night. I have that evening off."

"I'll try to be there."

"I love you, hon."

"Yeah." Ashe ended the call and wiped wetness off his cheeks. Trace started running down the beach. Ashe caught up with him. Eventually.

∽

"She will meet with you. In four days, my King." Laridael handed the message to Baltis, confirming his words.

"Good." Baltis couldn't help but release a sigh. "Laridael?"

"What, my King?"

"What has brought us to this?"

"May I speak my mind, my King?"

"Of course."

"Since I was a child, all I have seen between the races is bad blood, hatred and death. What has brought us to this, my King? How did this start?"

"I am the eighth King, in a long line of Kings. Old tales said it had something to do with the first King, but I have no knowledge of it. It was not given to me when I destroyed my predecessor and took the throne. I imagine that Friesianna is the same, although she is only the fourth to hold the Bright throne."

"I was born shortly after she came to the throne, and have no knowledge of what came before that."

"I am twice her age, and in my lifetime, things have gotten worse as time passed."

"Do you think any of it might come to an end?"

"Do you know the Legend of the Ir'Indicti, as it is written in the H'Morr?" Baltis asked. "Yes, I have read that cursed book," he added at Laridael's shocked expression.

"No, my King. I have never heard it. I have only heard rumors."

"Ir'Indicti is an ancient word in our language," Baltis said, settling on his throne and flipping back the red robes he wore. "It means Rebuilder, as well as I can determine. You have to understand the ancient language, however, to realize that this Rebuilder will rebuild from the ashes of our races. That our people will die, first, before they can be raised up again. The H'Morr says the Ir'Indicti will attempt to take both crowns. Should he do so, it will leave the races defenseless."

"If he is successful, will he kill us, then?"

"The H'Morr is quite vague in that area, so I cannot say for sure. It does say that after the crowns are taken, if we ally with an ancient and deadly enemy, justice will come."

"What kind of justice?"

"I do not know and the H'Morr does not explain it."

"This is quite frightening, my King."

"It is. That is why the boy must die—I will not give up my crown. The Dark race will survive." Baltis clenched his fists in determination. Laridael nodded respectfully at his monarch's resolve.

"We have much to do to prepare for the meeting. I do not have time to listen to your bluster about that blasted book!" Friesianna swished her skirts and turned away from Rabis, dismissing him from her presence.

"My Queen, calm yourself. We will have the advantage in this," Parlethis smoothly interjected as Rabis left Friesianna's tent. "That book is a worthless piece of parchment and a waste of the writer's time. It contains nothing but lies and tales to frighten children."

"You are correct," Friesianna snapped. "Where is my tea? Why have they not brought it?"

"It is coming, my Queen," Parlethis soothed.

"What's wrong?" Loren saw Ashe rubbing his forehead.

"Something, I just can't put my finger on it," Ashe mumbled. Ashe had come to Andy's old office to help Loren with another computer problem. Halfway through, Ashe began to fidget and then rub his forehead. "Can we finish this later? I think I need to go to my room for a little while."

"Sure. Whenever you're ready. I have other stuff I can do."

"Thanks, Loren." Ashe almost ran from the office, heading for the stairs and his room on the third floor.

~

"Show me what I need to know," Ashe hissed, frightened beyond comprehension. Something was happening, he just couldn't determine what it was.

~

"Trajan, will you get a company credit card for Flossie, so she can buy groceries without dipping into petty cash?" Winkler asked his Second.

"Sure, boss," Trajan nodded.

Neither he nor Winkler missed the shouted, "No!" coming from Ashe's bedroom. Both were out the door and running toward Ashe's suite in a blink.

~

I need help! Ashe wailed in mindspeech. Would anyone hear him? Could anyone respond to his desperate cry for help? He was terrified and helpless to provide assistance where it was most needed.

~

"You think you'll live to marry my son, you sorry excuse for a shifter?"

Sara stared in terror at the gun in Dawn Smith's hand. Her death was coming swiftly. She knew it. Dawn was crazed and angry, her eyes going feral. If the bullet didn't take her down, Sara knew Dawn's werewolf would.

"Randall hasn't asked me. Why do you think he would?" Sara quavered, attempting to delay the inevitable. Her cell was in her purse, but there was no way to call 911; Dawn had taken the purse away the moment she'd appeared behind Sara, who'd been innocently unlocking her front door after driving home.

"Oh, he has it bad for you. I know the signs. I'm here to remove that temptation. He'll have to find someone else when you're dead. Somebody more suitable for the son of a werewolf."

"But what if I have no intention of marrying him?"

"You do. I saw it in your eyes whenever you looked at him. That would be a mistake, and one I'm here to prevent. Back up against that wall, over there. I want as much blood spatter as I can get from your worthless body."

Dawn waved the gun at Sara, indicating the wall separating Sara's living area from the kitchen. The wall's surface was painted white, and the red of Sara's blood would make a definite contrast against it.

~

"What's wrong, kid?" Trajan had outpaced Winkler and burst into Ashe's bedroom first. Winkler skidded in behind Trajan.

Ashe blinked at both werewolves in terror as a voice—a male voice —filtered into his mind.

You ask, Mighty One. I answer.

~

"Maybe I'll kill you as wolf. No bullets left behind," Dawn snarled as Sara cringed. "Turn. Turn to that helpless little bunny. I feel hungry." Dawn's teeth were bared as she made the demand.

"You will not."

Dawn stared in shock at the man who'd appeared. Sara turned her eyes to the one who'd appeared beside her before sliding down the wall in a faint.

"I'll kill you for interfering." Dawn aimed her pistol at the newcomer and fired.

CHAPTER 16

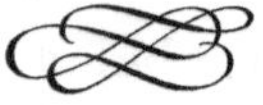

The bullet never reached its target, leaving Dawn blinking in surprise. Aiming the gun, she attempted to fire again.

"Clumsy weapons, these," the pistol disappeared from her hand and reappeared in the newcomer's grip. "It is useless against me." The gun turned to dust and became sparks that dripped from his hand. Dawn blinked in horror before attempting to turn and run.

"No, you will not leave," the man smiled grimly. At any other time, Dawn might have stared at him for another reason—he had the face of an angel.

"Who are you?" Dawn almost stuttered her question.

"I call myself Li'Neruh Rath. In an ancient language, it means Darkest Star. The one who serves the Dark Realm beneath me made a mistake long ago. He promised not to interfere with the Dark races. I made no such promise, and I will rectify part of that mistake now, at the request of one above me. Tell me, do you wish to die at my hand, here, or do you prefer to submit to the justice of your own race? It matters not to me what you choose."

Dawn trembled as the man lifted a hand, as if examining his fingernails. Only the nails lengthened until they were black claws, and his body changed. Grew. At least seven feet tall, he became a creature of nightmares, his body turning to black scales. Horns extended from his forehead and curved around pointed ears, much like a ram's might. Eyes widened and became a deep red, while flames licked their depths. Smoke curled from wide, flattened nostrils as he breathed.

"I—I'll, I choose my race's justice," Dawn whimpered. Something held her up—some sort of power, otherwise she would have dropped to the floor in fear.

"Very well," the voice had become rough and guttural, as if he weren't used to speaking in the form he'd taken. "Go." He waved a hand and Dawn shrieked as she was jerked away from Sara's home in a Chicago suburb and dumped in front of Marcus DeLuca, as he was finishing dinner with his family.

"We have her restrained, but she's crazy," Marcus reported to Winkler and the Grand Master on a conference call. "I wouldn't have believed half the crap she's saying, except she was dumped on my kitchen floor from thin air."

"Any chance she might escape?" The Grand Master asked. "I'd like to be in on the questioning."

"I'll make sure she's guarded at all times," Marcus replied. "How quickly can you be here?"

"By tomorrow evening, at the latest," Weldon said. "Hold her until then."

"I'll make sure she's guarded well. Not sure she'd go anywhere, anyway. She just keeps babbling about the devil who kept her from killing Randy's girlfriend."

"She was in Chicago?"

"About to shoot Sara Dillon, Randy's shapeshifting girlfriend, yes," Marcus confirmed.

"Does Randy know about this?"

"I think I'll have Nathan tell him, as soon as the vamps are up. Ask him to place compulsion, too, not to interfere with his mother's judgment."

"Probably a good idea. This isn't going to go well, any way you look at it."

"Yeah."

~

Ashe fingered the medallions circling his arm gently, as if they were tender to the touch. Winkler found him like that, sitting cross-legged on the floor beside his bed.

"Ashe?" Winkler's voice was soft.

"She got James Johnson killed," Ashe said.

"Dawn?"

"Yeah. Made up some story that she wanted to see him about Randy. She knew Randy kept in touch with James. They were best friends." Ashe stopped stroking the medallions and dropped his hand.

"She got past the barrier?"

"After she lied to James. Paul Harris wasn't the only one involved with the Elemaiya. He was only involved with the Dark side. Dawn was feeding information to both sides, through Josiah Dunnigan at the time."

"Not good. Why did she want James dead?"

"She wanted information from him. He refused. She called the Elemaiya, who'd followed her inside the barrier. James knew they were trouble and tried to run to Marcus, to let him know we were under attack. Instead of challenging him herself, Dawn Smith sent those two Dark Elemaiya after him. Watched while they killed him, too. The Elemaiya went to Mr. Harris afterward and told him that James had seen them accidentally and was running to tell Marcus, so they had to kill him. Mr. Harris told them to dump the body behind our house, to make it look like Dad or one of the vampires was involved. When Mr. Harris got caught, he gave us what he thought was the truth. He never knew Dawn was in it, more than he was."

"But you were supporting Randy's cause through all this."

"Because Randy didn't know about his mother. I didn't know about his mother, either, until just before we got Josiah. Things started coming to me, then. I was hoping, when she didn't participate in Josiah's attempted takedown, that she'd had a change of heart. That obviously wasn't the case."

"The Grand Master is coming tomorrow, to sit in while she's questioned. I'll pass this information to him, so he can ask about it, too."

"James' dad may want the execution."

"Will it be all right if he takes it?"

"Yeah."

"She keeps talking about a devil who showed up in Chicago to keep her from shooting Sara."

"I don't know much about that. Couldn't see it with these," Ashe brushed fingers across the medallions again. "Must have been too powerful for them to get the images."

"My question is this—how and why did he show up?"

"Mr. Winkler, I can't really explain that right now."

~

"Your mother has been captured. You will not interfere," Nathan placed compulsion. "You will also refrain from discussing this with anyone except those from the community."

"May I see her?" Randy's voice trembled.

"Ask Marcus."

"You may visit her once," Marcus agreed. He'd stood behind Nathan while compulsion was placed. "Tomorrow morning. Come at ten."

"Thank you." Randy sounded defeated. "I'll stay here tonight, if that's all right."

"Stay as long as you want," Nathan said before Marcus could interfere or say otherwise.

~

"I'm looking for Zeke Tanner," Craig Keller, former cook for William

Winkler, had a gun pressed to his neck as he stood uncomfortably next to Hutch.

"Why you want to see him?" Hutch growled next to Craig's ear.

"Got tired of running after Winkler and the Grand Master, if you want the truth. Those two go around, sniffing shifter butt all the time."

"That's exactly how I feel." Zeke Tanner walked into his study, skirting the white buffalo taking up the majority of space beside his desk. He sat down before carefully studying the werewolf Hutch had brought to him. "Why do you want to see me?" he asked.

"Want to go to work for a real werewolf," Craig muttered.

"You think I'm a real werewolf?"

"Yeah."

"What are you willing to do for me?"

"Anything."

"Willing to kill William Winkler for me?"

"Oh, yeah."

"Bear, I've made as many contacts as I can. Important shifters from all over the country." Opal informed Bear by cell phone. "We can be there next weekend. They're all interested."

"How many?" Bear sat at his desk at Star Cove combined, thumbing through invoices while he spoke with Opal.

"More than a hundred. Have you heard from Kerry and Thurmon?"

"Yeah. They have around fifty, each. With my choices and the shifters from Star Cove, we'll have more than three hundred. I contacted shifters from the other communities like this one, and they want in."

"Is that enough?" Opal asked.

"I think so. We've never had that many together at once. The school auditorium is big enough, barely, to hold all of us."

"Have you cleared it through Marcus DeLuca?"

"I went over his head and cleared it with the Grand Master. Marcus doesn't like it, but he'll have to deal. If we're lucky, we might have the basics hammered out in three or four days."

"I hope that happens. Will we make South Texas our base of operations?" Opal asked.

"I would prefer it, since this is where I work, but I'm willing to consider options."

~

"Matt, do you have anything?"

"I was contacted by Rockland, formerly Hancock, who explained the problem. We can't backtrack on that dead vampire's trail—it's cold. If Wildrif is making the turn to vampire somewhere, there's little chance of us finding him. New York is a really big place to search."

"This is crazy," Winkler muttered. "We don't need Wildrif as a vampire. We couldn't control Wildrif as three-quarters human."

"All I can say is if he makes the turn and shows up on the radar, we have to kill on sight. No waiting to question, we need him dead."

"Agreed."

~

Wlodek, Head of the Vampire Council, dismissed Charles from his study with a nod. He'd given Charles plenty of assignments to keep him busy. Waiting for Charles's footsteps to recede, Wlodek pulled a key from his pocket and opened a locked desk drawer. Pulling out a framed photograph, he stared at the images.

The woman who'd appeared in his office had been quite brusque and businesslike as she'd lambasted him for his unfeeling treatment of Aedan Evans and his family. Wlodek thought to defend himself. Found he couldn't move from his chair. And then the woman presented him with the photograph. Wlodek had blinked at it in astonishment.

The woman in the photograph was beautiful in a youthful, perky kind of way, with short, curly black hair and a lovely smile. She stood in sunlight on the wharf in San Francisco, where little had changed through the years.

What shocked Wlodek to his core, however, was the image of the one standing beside her. It was a photograph of him. Wlodek never allowed himself to be photographed. He knew this could not be. Yet it was. In the photograph, an almost-smile played about his lips as he held the brunette close to his side.

Wlodek felt as if he'd been punched in the gut as he gazed at the brunette's face. He wanted her, and he hadn't wanted anyone since Sarita's death.

"Is this a trick?" Wlodek's breath was short as he'd questioned the woman sitting before his desk. Her face had shone, making it impossible for Wlodek to see her features and hair color. He still found it unsettling.

"Not a trick," she'd replied. "Aedan is preparing to walk into the sun, because of your idiotic actions. There's still time to save him if you leave soon. Let him die and you'll never have what's in that photograph."

"Who are you?" Wlodek had kept his eyes on the photograph instead of looking up to ask his question.

"You can call me Love," she'd snapped. "And a greater amount of irony surrounds that name than you can possibly imagine."

Wlodek had looked up, then, blinking as the woman disappeared.

"Dude, how did you get here?" Sali asked.

"I got my misting talent back an hour ago." Ashe and Sali walked down the sidewalk toward the Evans' home. It was Wednesday afternoon, after school and the Grand Master and Mr. Winkler were at Marcus DeLuca's home, questioning Dawn Smith. Ashe had informed Trajan that he wanted to visit Star Cove and Trajan had given his permission.

"Coming back, one piece at a time?" Sali asked.

"Seems that way. At least I can mist, now. I felt naked without it. Still feel like I'm in my underwear," Ashe nodded.

"Don't know what you have until you don't have it."

"Yep."

"I'd feel naked if I couldn't turn to wolf," Sali said. "It's a part of me. Can hardly remember not having it."

"Yeah. I remember you in Transformational Arts, dude."

"Too bad you never turned to the bat in class. That would have been epic."

"Nah, people would have made fun of me."

"I don't think they'd make fun of you, now. If they know what you can do." Sali hunched his shoulders. "Jeremy—that was—I don't know."

"Yeah. I didn't do it for him."

"I know."

"Randy's coming," Sali looked up. His sensitive nose, even in human form, had picked up Randy's scent.

"This may not be pretty," Ashe mumbled. "Sal, you may not want to stay for this." Ashe watched as Randy strode purposely in his direction.

"I'll stay. He's human. I'm werewolf, remember?"

"Ashe, did you have something to do with this? With putting my mother through this?" Randy flung out an arm as he swiftly approached Ashe and Sali.

"Randy, do you know what she was doing when she was sent back here?" Ashe asked, stopping so Randy could approach.

"She said she stopped to visit Sara on her way to Canada. Couldn't you just let her go?" Randy sounded close to tears.

"Randy, she had a gun. She was about to kill Sara. Have you talked to Sara?"

"She won't return my calls."

"No surprise," Ashe sighed. "If the prospective mother-in-law waves a gun in your face and tells you you're about to be dinner, it's usually a deal-breaker on the relationship front."

"I want to hit you," Randy snapped.

"Hey," Sali held up a hand.

"Something going on?" Marco had driven up with Cori in the passenger seat.

"Randy talked to his mom. Got her version of the incident in Chicago," Ashe said.

"I hear she was about to kill your girlfriend, Randy. You should be grateful Sara's not dead," Cori pointed out. "Daddy questioned her for Marcus last night."

"You're all liars," Randy shouted. "Liars." He turned and stalked away.

"He's had one parent killed already. Now the last one is about to go down," Ashe shook his head.

"Want to get something to drink?" Marco asked. "Cori doesn't have to be home for dinner for another hour."

"Sure." Sali and Ashe climbed into Marco's back seat and settled there. Marco drove them toward Dandee Burgers.

"Did you want to be there—you know," Sali asked as they drank sodas in a corner booth at Dandee Burgers.

"No."

"I wouldn't, either," Cori shivered. Marco placed an arm around her shoulders.

"I think your dad may go," Sali slurped his soda.

"Yeah. She did try to kill Mom. Would have killed Mom, if something hadn't prevented it."

"Daddy says he saw a woman."

"I heard," Ashe toyed with his straw. "I'm still not sure what that means."

"I don't think anybody knows what it means," Marco said. "Maybe your mom's death wasn't meant to be."

"Or somebody changed what was." Ashe sipped his drink.

"Can somebody do that?" Cori blinked curious green eyes at Ashe.

"I hear that they can. Maybe we've seen proof of it."

"Doesn't make any sense," Sali said.

"But lots of things don't make sense, Sal. To humans, we don't make sense." Marco tapped his chest.

"It doesn't make sense that Dawn would sell herself to the people hunting her son," Ashe drew a pattern on the wood tabletop. "Or that she'd involve herself in the murder of her son's best friend. Or that she'd take money to sell the kids in Star Cove to Zeke Tanner."

"Jackson's dead because of her," Marco growled. "He was family. Our cousin." Ashe looked up at Marco's words and blinked.

"Something wrong, Ashe?" Cori watched Ashe carefully.

"Just another piece of the puzzle falling into place."

"That's weird, Ashe." Sali pointed his straw at Ashe. He'd already finished his large soda and was now playing with the straw.

"Weirder than you know. Things are slowly coming around. Sort of."

~

"Can you be in Corpus Christi by Friday?" Zeke Tanner offered a backpack to Craig.

"Sure. No problem."

"Then hand that backpack to the werewolf waiting outside the Funky Panda Chinese Restaurant. Minus the gun."

"I'll keep the gun," Craig agreed.

"Just tell Winkler you have information for him. That ought to get you to him, quick enough."

"I'll take care of it."

"We'll have a boat on the shore to take you across the river."

"Thanks." Craig shouldered the backpack and climbed inside the vehicle Zeke provided. Hutch would drive him to the river, where another werewolf waited to get him across by boat. Craig figured he should have done this years ago. With the payday promised by Tanner if Winkler died, he'd never have to work again.

~

"Trajan? Can I talk to you?" Ashe knocked on Trajan's bedroom door. Trajan was reading reports on his cell regarding Pack business in Dallas.

"Sure, kid, I was about to fall asleep, reading this boring junk." Trajan set his cell phone aside and looked at Ashe expectantly.

"Trajan, I don't think things are gonna be the same in Star Cove after tonight."

"What do you mean?" Trajan was concerned immediately.

"Well," Ashe perched on the edge of Trajan's bed, "Dawn hasn't always been a member of the community, but she managed to get sensitive information anyway, during that time."

"True," Trajan nodded. "Information on you and a bunch of other stuff."

"Yeah. What if I told you that the Grand Master and Mr. Winkler are about to find out who she got that information from? That somebody who knew better was handing out information anyway?"

"Kid, this is starting to sound scary."

"Yeah."

⁓

Ashe stared at the gun cabinet he'd misted inside the hidden basement room days earlier. At least he could mist inside the room again. He knew the dart gun and poison darts were safely inside the cabinet, and Winkler held the key. Only one other person could easily reach what was locked inside. Holding out a hand, Ashe *Pulled* another dart to him and misted it inside the cabinet before withdrawing.

"We may need you," Ashe whispered to the contents of the safe.

⁓

"Mr. Thompson, are you a good shot?" Ashe asked as the Thompsons filled two plates with food to take home with them. Flossie had finished dinner and left plates in the oven for Winkler and the Grand Master when they finished in Star Cove.

Amos Thompson studied Ashe for a moment before grinning. "Sure am, kid. I was a sharpshooter in the army."

"Good. If I asked you sometime soon if you'd like to avenge your brother's death, would you be willing to do that?"

"Son," Amos dropped a hand on Ashe's shoulder, "I would be more than willing to avenge his death. I'm not sure how you know about Alex, but he's been missing for a while."

"I'll remember you said that," Ashe nodded. "Thanks for dinner, Mrs. Thompson. That was really good."

"No problem," Flossie offered Ashe a smile. "We'll be back in the morning."

Ashe shut the front door of Winkler's beach house behind the Thompsons with a sigh. And then he cursed. So many things needed his attention, and without his full talents available, it was difficult to know which one to handle first.

~

"Cori, I was planning to give this to you for your birthday, but I can't wait for that."

"What? Marco, my birthday is only three weeks away."

"I know. But this—I can't wait three weeks." Marco stared down at Cori, her pretty, blonde hair lifting in a breeze that swept the beach east of Star Cove. He'd asked her to take a walk with him, and she'd readily agreed.

"What is it, then?" Cori looked up expectantly at Marco, and then dropped her eyes as Marco went to his knees before her.

"Cori," Marco pulled a small, velvet box from a pocket and opened it, revealing the diamond ring inside, "will you marry me? Please?"

"Oh, my gosh, Marco." Cori dropped to her knees in the sand and flung her arms around Marco's neck. "I want to. Yes. Yes, yes, yes!"

~

"Mr. Montegue, I know you're sleeping now, but when you get this message, will you consider tailing Curtis Roberts? I think he's up to no good," Ashe left the message on Gavin's cell, along with the address of Curtis' office. "He'll be working late tonight. If you can't do it yourself, will you ask somebody else who's trustworthy to do it and keep you advised? Thanks." Ashe ended the voicemail with a sigh.

~

"Are you sure that was wise? Letting Roberts know that vampires, werewolves and shapeshifters exist?" Hutch asked, leaning an elbow on the white buffalo's head.

"You know I don't care if the whole world finds out," Zeke growled. "Haven't cared for a while. What does it matter if the humans panic? Just makes it easier to pick them off, don't you think?"

"Haven't killed a human in at least a week," Hutch chuckled. "Sounds like fun."

~

"I can't believe this. You knew? And didn't tell me?" Curtis Roberts flipped the folder shut and glared at Arthur Vaine.

"I'm on other committees, remember?" Arthur snapped. "Of course I know. As does the President."

Curtis cursed and threw the folder at Arthur, scattering papers everywhere and making Arthur duck.

"Curtis, it's time you left my office," Arthur said. "Get out."

"So you can call the President and have him can me? Is that what you're planning to do?"

"I can't—you can ruin me, remember?"

"Yeah, that's right. Keep that in mind, Congressman. Keep that in mind." Curtis stalked out of Arthur's office, slamming the door behind him.

~

"Radomir, I feel this is important. Will you discreetly follow Curtis Roberts?"

"I will. I have the night off before traveling to Belfast tomorrow evening."

"Just keep an eye on him and use your best judgment if you see him doing anything improper."

"Of course. Shall I keep you and the Honored One apprised?"

"Yes."

Radomir, Wlodek's youngest vampire child at more than eleven hundred years old, waited discreetly outside the building in Silver Spring, Maryland, which housed Curtis Roberts' office. Gavin had forwarded a photograph of the government employee who, according to several sources, had overstepped his authority on many occasions.

As Wlodek's child, Radomir had access to vampires and werewolves who worked for the U.S. government, and had contacted three highly placed sources. Each had given him identical information, causing Radomir to growl softly.

Curtis walked past the security guard with barely a nod as he dropped his briefcase to the marble floor and adjusted the cuffs of his suit coat. He'd arranged to meet with a well-known journalist and Curtis was prepared to hand over important information—information revealing that werewolves and vampires were not a myth.

In less than twenty-four hours, everyone on the planet would know. Curtis wanted to laugh—he imagined that vigilantes, religious groups and thrill seekers might be hunting vampires and werewolves by the weekend.

A cab pulled up outside the building, and Radomir watched as Curtis Roberts exited the building and opened the back door to climb inside the vehicle.

"I'll be joining you," Radomir seated himself beside Curtis before Curtis could blink or reach for the door to close it.

"Who are you?" Curtis stared at the tall, handsome man now sitting beside him. For some reason, a tingle of fear crept up Curtis' spine.

"You should not be concerned," Radomir placed compulsion. "Inform the driver where you wish to go."

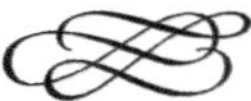

CHAPTER 17

"Traje said he thought you knew," Winkler settled on a barstool beside Ashe at breakfast.

Ashe looked up from his eggs and ham. Flossie Thompson had been unusually quiet since her arrival. Ashe figured he knew why.

"It happened last night, after Paul Johnson took the execution. The Grand Master called a meeting with all of Star Cove's werewolves. He announced what he'd learned after Aedan placed compulsion on Dawn Smith and asked her who she'd gotten information from inside the community. Turns out that Marcus has been giving Denise sensitive information when he shouldn't have, asking her to keep it to herself. She's been gossiping with Dawn all along, and all Dawn had to do was ask the right questions."

"What did the Pack do?" Ashe wanted to shiver. He figured he knew the answer but wanted to ask anyway.

"You know there's only one way to remove a Packmaster, if there's no challenge made. The Pack declared Marcus and Denise outcast last night, by a majority vote. Marco isn't a part of the Star Cove Pack any longer, so he couldn't vote. Sali abstained."

"Who's in charge, now?" Ashe didn't express his concern for Sali right then; he'd wait to see what Winkler had to say, first.

"Micah Rocklin. Frank Dodd is acting Second at the moment. We learned that Denise has been feeding information to Dawn about you that she and Marcus had gotten from Sali and a few others. Information that should have been kept confidential. The Grand Master warned Marcus about releasing information on you to anyone else."

"Damn," Ashe cursed softly. "That's why Dawn chickened out on Josiah, then. Denise told her, after I told Marcus not to say anything and the Grand Master agreed."

"Sounds like it."

"What about Randy?"

"Randy is going through his mother's things. I have no idea if he plans to stay or will leave the minute he can get away."

"Too bad," Ashe shook his head and cut another chunk of ham before stuffing it in his mouth. "Randy needs to think this through before making important, life-changing decisions."

"He's emotional, right now. Shirley refused to allow Dawn's burial in her groves, so the remains were hauled to the gulf afterward."

"What did James' parents say? Anything?"

"They called Dawn out before the execution. Pointed out that James had been Randy's best friend, and she'd watched him die without helping. Dawn just growled at them."

"Crazy."

"Yeah."

"What do you think Marcus will do?"

"He and Denise are packing, but haven't told anyone where they plan to go."

"Do you think they'll leave Texas?"

"Yes. The Grand Master told Sali that at sixteen, a werewolf has the right to petition to stay, as long as someone agrees to take him in if his parents have been outcast by the Pack. I heard from Sali this morning." Winkler cut into his slice of ham, which had gone cold while he and Ashe talked.

"What did he say?" Ashe wanted to hold his breath. Forcing himself to breathe normally, Ashe turned back to his breakfast.

"He asked to stay. Said he wanted to be with his brothers. Asked if I'd take him in."

"Brothers?"

"You and Marco."

"What did you tell him?" Ashe wiped moisture from his face with a napkin.

"That I'd be happy to act as his guardian, and pay for his education if he wanted one. After he graduates from high school."

"Thank you, Mr. Winkler," Ashe slumped in relief at Winkler's words and wiped his face again.

"I didn't do it just for him and Marco, Ashe. I did it for you, too. Felt like that's what you'd want."

"It is." Ashe agreed, cutting another bite of ham. His appetite, which had threatened to desert him, had returned quickly. "Will Sali live in Star Cove, or will he live here?"

"I told him to pack his things. I figure you can get him moved in, and then get him to school every morning," Winkler grinned.

"Yeah. I can do that. I just want to wait until," Ashe sighed. Things were so weird, suddenly. He'd never known a life where Marcus DeLuca hadn't been Packmaster.

"Until he can say good-bye to his parents? Ashe, they're welcome to keep in touch. That won't change, as long as they don't go rogue."

"I'll probably bring him home tonight, then. He can come to dinner with me at my parents' house."

"Sounds good. There's an empty bedroom next to Marco's on the second floor."

"Thanks, Mr. Winkler."

~

Ashe? Sali's text came through while Ashe was running on the beach with Trace.

Sali? Everything okay? Ashe texted as he ran beside Trace. Trace just shook his head and kept running.

As good as can be expected. Mom and Dad are only packing clothes. Said they'd send a moving van for their other stuff when they decided where they were going.

I'm sorry things turned out this way.

Me, too. I had no idea this was happening. It hurt a lot of people, Ashe. I don't know what to do or say. Nobody is blaming me, looks like, but it's still awkward.

Yeah. Awkward. A good word to use, Sal.

Two syllables, Sali returned. *Dad isn't saying anything. Mom, well, things aren't so good on that front. The Grand Master stayed with the Rocklins, last night. I guess to go over protocol. And to make sure of things here, probably.*

Sal, this isn't your fault. None of it. People make their own decisions. We all have to live with the consequences.

I know. Look, I've been given the day off from school, but I have to pack.

I heard. Come to my house for dinner tonight, around seven. I hear there'll be meat loaf. I'll bring you home afterward.

Home. Won't ever be the same, will it?

Welcome to my world, Sal.

Yeah. See you tonight.

K.

~

"Salidar?" Adele gave Sali a hug when he walked into the kitchen with Ashe.

"I heard there'd be meatloaf," Sali mumbled when Adele let him go.

"There is. Plenty of meatloaf. Hungry?"

"Yeah." Sali hunched his shoulders.

Ashe watched as Sali moved uncomfortably. Marcus and Denise had left two hours earlier, taking only one vehicle. Denise's small import remained in the garage. The plan was to send for furniture and the car later. Ashe had no idea where they might go and hadn't bothered to consult the medallions on his arm. Sali's parents had moved outside his sphere.

"It's almost ready, I just have to mash the potatoes," Adele offered brightly before hugging Ashe and standing on tiptoe to kiss him on the cheek.

"I'll set the table," Ashe offered. He and Sali set three plates around the table as Adele mashed potatoes for dinner.

"It is and isn't like old times, huh?" Sali said quietly.

"Yeah."

~

"Son," Aedan's hand dropped on Ashe's shoulder as Ashe and Sali loaded the dishwasher and cleaned cabinets after dinner.

Ashe's body stiffened as visions crowded his mind. Visions of his father, sitting atop a broad, flat-topped rock as fingers of sunlight crept across Aedan's body. Ashe shuddered as Aedan's skin began to smoke and burn in his visions, the top layers turning to ash as Aedan jerked his head back and howled.

"Daddy?" Ashe turned swiftly and buried himself in Aedan's arms as he wept.

~

"I don't know why Wlodek appeared when he did," Aedan shook his head. He'd lifted Ashe in his arms and carried him to the back deck, leaving a gaping Sali behind in the kitchen.

Aedan had eventually convinced Ashe that things were fine and he'd never consider giving himself to the sun again. "He only said that someone paid him a visit, and pointed out the error of his ways. I'm not about to argue. He said that he wouldn't recall me until after your mother was gone."

"Maybe that will be a very long time." Ashe stared at the night sky. A few stars twinkled overhead and the moon was beginning to make its presence known. "Dad?"

"What, son?"

"Have you ever wondered what's out there?"

"In the stars?"

"Yeah."

"Upon occasion. Not in a while, I guess."

"There has to be something. The Elemaiya aren't native to Earth."

"You're right. I suppose I've never thought about that before."

"I'm glad Wlodek made it in time."

"I'm glad he got a visit from somebody."

"Yeah. Me, too, Dad."

"Ready to go, Sal?" Ashe appeared inside Sali's bedroom later. Sali was playing a game on his laptop, but he shut it when Ashe became corporeal.

"Yeah. Can we take this stuff like this?" Sali had emptied his closet, laying clothes across his bed for the move, since he only had two boxes and a suitcase to carry his belongings.

"No problem," Ashe nodded. "I think I could take the whole house, if you wanted."

"Nah. Leave the house, dude. I only need my stuff."

"Mr. Winkler says you can have the bedroom next to Marco's on the second floor. Trajan says your ass is his in the weight room tomorrow morning before school, and Trace says I can wait to run with you tomorrow, when school is out."

"Tomorrow's Friday, man. The weekend is here," Sali stood and grinned.

"Gonna be a busy weekend," Ashe nodded. "Let's go."

"Principal Wright has shifters coming in this weekend. Around three hundred," Sali informed Winkler as he passed the bag of microwave popcorn to Ashe.

"I heard that," Winkler nodded, shoving a second bag of popcorn in the microwave. "It's one of the things the Grand Master discussed with Micah."

"Micah will be okay," Sali sighed. Ashe handed him a fresh can of soda from the fridge and settled on a barstool to grab a handful of popcorn from the bag.

"I know. He's been a Second for a long time. He knows what to do."

"Mrs. Rocklin has always been sympathetic to shifters," Ashe pointed out. "She's been teaching Transformational Arts for a long time."

"Very true," Winkler agreed. "Perhaps Bear should invite her to the meetings. As soon as you're done eating popcorn, brush your teeth and go to bed. We'll get you up at six for breakfast and then it's a workout for both of you."

~

"Dude, that's two-fifty." Sali struggled to lift one-seventy-five while Trajan watched both boys work with weights.

"Yeah. Maybe I'll grow muscles after all," Ashe huffed, lowering the weights.

"You're a lot better off than you were when we started," Trajan pointed out. "You've got muscles. You'll get more. So will Sali. He's got werewolf mojo working for him. Come on, two more and it's off to the shower."

~

"Hey, it's Ashe and Sali." Wynn and Dori trotted to the sidewalk the moment Ashe appeared, dropping Sali in front of the school.

"That is the awesomest way to show up," Jeff and Larry walked up to Ashe.

"And it saved a half-hour drive," Sali grinned. Nobody was treating him different. He was grateful for that.

"Ashe?" Bear Wright walked through the double doors of the school building and approached Ashe.

"Hey, Mr. Wright," Ashe nodded to Star Cove's Principal.

"Ashe, we'll be taking the vote on whether we should form a

shifter council on Monday night. I want anyone over the age of sixteen there, so that means you can vote, too. I'd like for you to come, if you can."

"I think I can be here, Mr. Wright," Ashe nodded. "I'd like to be here, actually."

"We got invited last night," Wynn said, offering a smile to the Principal. "My parents and I are coming."

"Mom, Cori and I will be there," Dori said. "Dad said he'd drop by after nightfall, if that's all right."

"He's welcome to come, as a spouse and father of shapeshifters," Bear Wright confirmed. "Ashe, your mother is coming as well. I think your father may come by at some point."

"Good. I'll let Mr. Winkler know. I should go; I have homework and a lot of other things to do," Ashe waved at his friends and turned to mist.

"It really is the awesomest way to get around," Sali sighed.

❧

"I don't know why I couldn't say anything to that reporter," Curtis Roberts grumped as Calhoun laid papers on his desk.

"About what, Director Roberts?" Calhoun asked.

"I can't say," Curtis found himself saying before he could consciously decide otherwise. "I really don't know why."

"If you change your mind, I'll be right outside at my desk."

"I know. Thanks, Calhoun."

❧

"Mr. Thompson?" Ashe found Amos Thompson in buffalo form, standing guard behind Winkler's beach house when he came back from dropping Sali off at school. The early morning light was bright as it reflected off the water of the gulf, making Mr. Thompson's white buffalo glow as he stood amid the dunes and creepers at the back of Winkler's property. "Look, if you want to do what we talked about, meet me here in ten minutes, dressed and ready to go. I'll bring a weapon with me. Okay?" Ashe said.

Amos Thompson's buffalo snorted and nodded to Ashe.

~

"You have one shot, Mr. Thompson," Ashe said softly as Amos Thompson reached out and lovingly touched the top of his brother's head. Zeke Tanner, the homicidal werewolf, had not only killed Alex, he'd dishonored him by treating his body like this.

Ashe and Amos Thompson stood in Zeke Tanner's private study, waiting for the werewolf to walk inside. Amos was mourning for his brother as they waited.

~

"Craig, what do you have?" Winkler spoke on his cell.

"I got information on Zeke Tanner, that's what I have," Craig claimed. "Can I come to the house? I have photographs, too, of his new compound."

"You know, I'm not even going to ask how you got that," Winkler growled. "Come on, I have an hour I can give you this morning. That's it."

"Thanks. It won't take longer than that, I promise."

~

"What's that?" Zeke Tanner walked inside his office, talking on his cell. "He took the bait? That was easy. Put a bullet through his brain. That's all I ask." Zeke tapped end call on his cell and tossed it on his desk before sitting down.

"Hello, you murdering bastard." Amos Thompson stepped around his brother's body, revealing himself to Zeke Tanner. The dart rifle he carried was aimed at Zeke's heart.

"My werewolves are all over the place," Zeke growled. "All I have to do is yell and they come running. Want to die, you stupid shifter? Yeah, I can tell by your scent what you are."

"I have the place shielded, scream your lungs out," Ashe stepped from behind Amos Thompson.

"What the hell? Wildrif said you'd be disabled. For a long time," Zeke sputtered.

"Wildrif only thinks he knows what I am. He miscalculated. Badly. Ready, Mr. Thompson?" Ashe asked. "If you don't get him, I will."

"Oh, I'm ready, all right." Amos pulled the trigger. Zeke Tanner jerked as the dart pierced his chest. Amos watched in satisfaction as Tanner jerked once more as a large dose of lion snake poison entered his system. Zeke Tanner died, his last vision one of his killer, the boy and the white buffalo disappearing from his study.

∽

"Craig, Winkler is waiting in his office for you." Trajan answered the door and allowed Craig to walk inside. "You remember where that is, don't you?"

"Sure." Craig nodded. "On the third floor."

"Yeah. Have fun." Trajan waved Craig through the foyer and the stairs leading to the second and third floors.

∽

"Boss, he's not carrying anything except his cell phone and a gun," Trajan spoke softly in his cell.

"Figured as much," Winkler replied. "Thanks."

∽

"Hello, Craig, have a seat," Winkler offered Craig one of the chairs in his office.

"That's all right," Craig waved away the offer. "I just came to give you this." He reached inside his pocket briefly, before a fearful expression crossed his face.

"Looking for this?" Ashe became corporeal, holding up the gun that had disappeared from Craig's pocket.

"What the hell?" Craig sputtered, backing away from Ashe.

"Your new boss is dead. Mr. Thompson shot him with a poison dart a few minutes ago," Ashe went on. "Mr. Winkler told you to sit. Sit!" Compulsion thundered from Ashe's voice on the last word. Craig sat down immediately.

"But how?" Craig's eyes darted from Winkler, whose arms were crossed furiously over his chest, to Ashe, who merely looked angry.

"I took Mr. Thompson and brought him back, that's how," Ashe snapped. "That white buffalo in Zeke's study? You remember that, don't you?"

"Y-yeah?" Craig nodded unwillingly.

"Mr. Thompson's brother, Alex. Mr. Thompson was understandably upset that Zeke killed his brother and then had him stuffed."

"B-but," Craig quavered.

"I made a promise to myself and a couple other people, Craig. I promised I'd go hunting as soon as I was able. You got added to that list this morning, when you came here to kill Mr. Winkler. Now, you can either die fighting Mr. Winkler, or I can take you down. Your choice."

"A shapeshifter taking me down? Faugh," Craig's voice held ridicule.

"See, that's where you miscalculated," Ashe pointed a finger at Craig. "Mr. Winkler, what do you want?"

"Kid, do your thing. I think I'd like to watch while Craig becomes one with the universe."

"Good enough," Ashe nodded. "Watch your feet, Craig. They'll go first."

Craig's shriek could be heard inside Winkler's beach house, from top floor to basement.

~

"I can make arrangements for a suitable carved box, Amos." Winkler knelt beside the sofa, where Amos and Flossie Thompson sat, staring at Alex's white buffalo.

"Where can we put it?" Amos turned reddened eyes to Winkler. "I'd like to bury him in a safe place, but I want Bear to see him before we do that."

"I know. Call and invite him over tonight, after he gets away from the school."

"I will."

~

"I'm not a hundred percent, yet," Ashe shrugged when Trajan asked. "Zeke Tanner's dead."

"I heard. Good job, kid." Trajan pulled Ashe into a hug.

"Mr. Thompson took him down. Perfect shot, too."

"Wish I could have seen it."

"Want to? See it, that is?" Ashe asked. "I warn you, it may be disorienting at first."

"You can do that?" Trajan sounded surprised.

"Yeah. I just have to do this," Ashe pressed fingers against Trajan's forehead. Images from earlier in the day played out in Trajan's mind.

~

"Tanner got it," Trajan settled on one of Winkler's guest chairs. "I guess the good thing about the kid handing out justice is there's no mess to clean up."

"Matt's got some of his flying to Tanner's compound—the kid gave me the location," Winkler sighed. "That place will be history after tonight. Matt plans to bomb the place."

"I don't blame him. Does he plan to use the excuse that a rival cartel attacked?"

"Yep. Who's gonna argue with that logic?"

"Nobody. Marco asked Cori to marry him. A few weeks early."

"The fact that she's wearing a big diamond was no giveaway, I'm sure."

"The kid gave me the images from Tanner's takedown. Amos plugged him, center of the chest. I have a feeling we have one less poison dart in the cabinet downstairs."

"You think I care?" Winkler snorted. "The Grand Master almost laughed his ass off when I told him."

"Any word on Wildrif?"

"Not yet. I got communication from Wlodek, through the Grand Master, too. Remember Radomir?"

"Yeah," Trajan nodded.

"He tailed Curtis Roberts. Roberts was going straight to the media, to let them know that werewolves and vampires were real. Radomir disabused him of that notion."

"That vampire is badass," Trajan grinned.

"Almost as badass as Montegue."

"No argument, there. Seemed to develop a soft spot for the kid, though."

"Both of 'em did."

~

"One of your informants is dead," Calhoun laid a folder on Curtis Roberts' desk.

"Who?"

"Zeke Tanner, in Mexico."

"What? That can't be right," Curtis stood quickly, staring in disbelief at his assistant.

"I hear through channels that Matt Michaels has the location of Tanner's compound. It'll be bombed to the ground before daybreak tomorrow morning."

Curtis cursed and tossed his chair across the room. He'd gotten the best information from Tanner. Now, Tanner was dead and Wildrif, Tanner's informant, had disappeared.

"It's that kid," Curtis snarled. "Somebody miscalculated. What the hell is he, Calhoun?"

"I'm not sure, sir."

"Well, I'm no longer interested in forcing him to work for me. In fact, maybe we ought to do a little bombing of our own. See what excuse we might use to attack two locations in South Texas, come Monday night."

"I will, sir. Right away."

~

"How do I look?" Friesianna smoothed the skirts of an embroidered silk gown.

"Like the Queen you are," Parlethis flattered Friesianna. "We are to meet outside the gate in Kansas City. If things become untenable, it merely requires the opening of the gate so we might pass through. Easy enough to get away, if we must."

"Good. Who is going with me? I wish to leave Rabis here. He keeps prattling about that wretched H'Morr and I can get nothing coherent from him."

"I have five more waiting to travel, my Queen."

"Very well. Let us go." Friesianna placed her hand on Parlethis' arm.

~

"I am ready, Laridael," Baltis announced. "Do you have my Destroyers ready to accompany us?"

"I do, my King," Laridael bowed.

"Then let us go."

"As you say."

CHAPTER 18

"That's Alex, all right. What did they do to you, buddy?" Bear knelt beside the buffalo and leaned his forehead against Alex's jaw.

"Tanner's dead," Amos Thompson muttered. "Kid helped me get him."

"Good. Amos, where were you thinking about putting Alex? I got an offer from the Grand Master. He says we can bury him on his property, in North Dakota. He'll be the only shifter laid to rest, there."

"I think that's a good idea. How are we going to ship the body?"

"I can do it," Ashe walked in. "If you don't mind."

"Kid, you can do anything you want. You gave us closure, today," Mr. Thompson said. "Bear and I will dig his grave. It's fitting."

"Mr. Winkler?" Ashe turned to Winkler, who'd followed him inside the media room.

"Kid, we'll all go. I'll leave Ace behind, to watch the house."

"Okay."

"Give me ten minutes to warn the Grand Master, and we'll be ready."

"Sara, please pick up. Please. Mom's dead, and I need you to talk to me." Randy couldn't keep the sob from his voice.

"Randall, your mother tried to kill me," Sara said, reluctantly answering the call. Randy had phoned her landline when she refused to answer her cell.

"What?" Randy whispered.

"You heard. She was here, telling me she was either going to shoot me or let her werewolf tear me to pieces. I'm sorry, Randall, but we have no future."

"No, baby. Please. The werewolves took her down. I don't have anybody, now."

"Did you know she was on the run? That she might be headed this way?"

"I knew she was running, but I didn't know she'd—do this." Randy sounded defeated.

"If that man hadn't shown up, I'd be dead, now. Is that what you wanted?"

"No. Baby, that's the last thing I'd ever want. I love you. I mean it. Please don't shut me out."

"I'll consider it," Sara snapped. "I'm leaving for the airport in a few minutes. Mr. Wright invited me to attend the shapeshifter meeting in Star Cove. It's up to you, Randall, whether we have a future or not." Sara hung up.

～

"That's it—six feet," Bear lifted himself out of the large hole he, Amos Thompson and the Grand Master had dug on Weldon's property. "How are we going to lower him into the grave?"

"I can do it, if you'll allow it," Ashe offered. He, Winkler, Trace, Trajan, Sali, Florence Thompson and Marco had stood by while a werewolf and two shapeshifters dug Alex Thompson's grave.

"I'll allow it," Amos Thompson nodded to Ashe.

"All right." Alex Thompson's white buffalo was levitated gently upward and then floated through the air before turning on its side while being lowered into the ground.

"Ready?" Bear asked Amos, once Alex's body was laid gently at the bottom of the grave.

"Yes. Alex, we've missed you. I'll miss you as long as I live." Amos Thompson lifted a handful of dirt and let it fall in the grave.

"Alex, we did fine work together. You always had my back and were the best friend I could ever ask for." Bear let a handful of dirt fall.

"I only met you a couple of times. You, Bear and I got pretty drunk at a bar in San Diego. Happy trails, friend." Weldon dropped his handful of soil.

"I'll get the rest," Ashe said quietly. The pile of dirt from the excavation disappeared and reappeared, covering the grave. "Mr. Thompson," Ashe held out his hands and a folded American flag appeared. "This is for your brother's service."

"Ashe, does this mean you're back to normal?" Winkler asked.

"Mr. Winkler, there'll be no normal for me. If you're asking if the drug is out of my system, it's pretty close to being gone."

"Why do I get the feeling you're not telling me something?" Winkler accepted a drink from Trajan, who settled on the other end of the sofa inside the media room. Ashe had already dropped Bear Wright and Amos and Flossie Thompson off in Star Cove before bringing the others back to Winkler's beach house.

"Mr. Winkler, do you remember the old Ashe—before I got the drug?"

"Yeah. Pretty much."

"There's a new Ashe coming. I don't know how to explain it."

"Like Ashe, two-point-oh?" Winkler lifted an eyebrow.

"More like Ashe, nine-point-oh," Ashe muttered, staring at his hands. "Get ready."

"Ready for what?" Winkler asked, just as the beach house suffered a jolt.

"What the hell was that?" Trajan was on his feet, followed quickly by Winkler.

"Armageddon just started," Ashe's eyes were dark and filled with stars.

∽

"What's happening?" Friesianna screamed, although her words sounded garbled and drawn out. Light bent and flickered about her crown, rendering her helpless.

Baltis shouted for Laridael as light and power flowed from his crown, crashing into that formed by Friesianna's coronet. Neither could move; they were held immobile, as were the ones surrounding them as each crown fought for supremacy.

"Open the gate," Friesianna shouted at Parlethis.

"I cannot move my hands," he wailed.

∽

"Hurricane-force storms are forming across the Eastern Seaboard," the meteorologist announced on the ten o'clock news. "Earthquakes are occurring in the Pacific northwest, South America, and Japan. Tsunami warnings are going out across the globe. Six storms have formed off the coast of Africa in the past two hours, moving at incredible speeds into the Atlantic. Rain is falling in record amounts in Great Britain. Tornadoes are crossing the Midwest, leaving destruction and death in their wake. This is unprecedented, folks. Take emergency precautions if you live in the path of any of these storms or earthquakes."

"Jeez, kid, it's pouring outside." Winkler stood at the wide windows overlooking the deck, just as a rumble of thunder shook the beach house.

"Can you do anything about that?" Trajan, who sat near Ashe, asked.

"Not right now. Ashe nine-point-oh is still not ready."

"How much time is left? You can't do anything about this before that?" Winkler settled on the sofa again.

"I need power I don't have, yet. Things will get worse before I can do anything about this."

"That doesn't sound good," Trace sighed, flopping onto the sofa beside his brother. Sali, who'd settled on the floor to watch the news with the others, turned to Ashe in surprise.

Child?

Grandfather? Ashe sat upright, waking from a sound sleep when the mindspeech came from Rabis.

The crowns are locked in battle, child, fighting for supremacy. Is there nothing you can do?

Not now. Wildrif managed to get somebody to give me a drug, and I'm still disabled. It'll take two days before I can do anything.

This is more than unfortunate. Wildrif deserves death for this.

Wildrif managed to convince a vampire to make him vampire. I think I can do something about that, at least.

He is making the turn? I will point my thought in that direction.

Grandfather, I've pointed my thought in that direction. Do you want me to come for you?

No, child, although I appreciate the offer. My father told me before his death that I must see this thing through. He said that you would come for me when I finally left the Bright race of my own accord.

Then I'll see you when that happens.

Yes, that is my sincerest wish. To see you then.

"We can drive or you can take us. Your choice," Winkler told Ashe while he, Sali, Trace, Trajan and Marco waited for toaster waffles to pop up.

"It's still raining," Ashe sighed. "I'll take us."

"Good. We need to be in Star Cove around ten."

"I can do that." Ashe nodded

"Why don't we have a second toaster?" Trace moaned.

"I'll go get two. Give me a minute." Ashe disappeared, returning a few minutes later with two new toasters in boxes. "There. Now we can make six waffles at a time."

"Why didn't we think of this before?" Winkler pulled more boxes of toaster waffles out of the freezer. "Do we have enough syrup?"

~

"Hi, Mom." Ashe hugged his mother when she answered the doorbell.

"Come in," she waved all her visitors inside; the front porch wasn't large enough to hold everybody. "It's so wet out. Is this weather usual for late August?" she asked as Winkler stepped inside.

"No, Adele. It's extremely unusual."

"Well, it came this morning, and thank goodness it arrived in a covered carrier," Adele had hands on her hips. "You didn't tell him, did you?"

"We didn't say a word," Winkler grinned.

"About what?" Ashe and Sali said together.

"Come on, it's in the third stall in the garage."

~

Two Elemaiya, who'd thought to pull the Bright Queen and Dark King away were now dead. Friesianna and Baltis had stopped speaking; both were gripped in a paralysis created by their crowns. While they'd been yards apart in the beginning, their bodies were inching closer together while their subjects watched in horror.

Mindspeech had been sent to both camps, and Bright and Dark Elemaiya were appearing in a panic. They were aware that the Earth was in trouble and desired to leave it behind by going through the only gate they might use.

All were dismayed to learn the gate wouldn't open, and then

were terrified to see that the crowns were engaged in a terrible battle, the Bright Queen and Dark King helpless to stop it. While the weather, earthquakes and other natural disasters across the Earth increased, Kansas City had become the eye of the storm. All Elemaiya seemed caught in the vortex, with no way to escape its impending wrath.

~

"This is causing the problems." Curtis Roberts tossed a photograph on the President's desk. "Go ahead, ask Mr. Michaels over there, if the boy didn't create that earthquake in Canada."

Curtis had finally gotten what he'd been asking for—a meeting with the President. The circumstances couldn't have been less ideal.

"Matthew, is this true?" The President lifted the photograph—a close-up of Ashe from the British Embassy raid, and turned questioning eyes on Matt.

"He didn't do it to harm anyone. He did that to help. Something else is creating chaos out there." Matt angrily flung out an arm.

"The boy is an alien. You know that. He's out to destroy the world if we don't stop him," Curtis pressed his point. "He's one of the creatures who slaughtered those children and anyone else who got in their way. We have to stop this now, if we expect to survive."

"And just what do you propose we do?" The President asked.

"Kill him," Curtis snapped. "The only way we can."

"Are you crazy?" Matt shouted at Curtis.

~

"Wow," Sali breathed, running a hand along the fins of the red, vintage Cadillac. "Ashe, this is awesome. Just like we always wanted." The top had been folded back, revealing the cream interior of the vehicle. The leather was in pristine condition.

"Yeah." Ashe's arms were crossed over his chest as he examined the car. "This is exactly what I wanted."

"I'd say take it for a drive, but you don't want to go out in that storm," Winkler said. "Save it for a sunny day."

"At least sit in the driver's seat, just to see what it feels like," Sali coaxed.

"Yeah." Ashe opened the door and slid into the driver's seat. Sighing, he placed both hands on the wheel and everything shifted.

～

"What am I doing here?" Ashe studied himself in the dim, metallic reflection of a hotel's elevator doors.

What you are supposed to do, while I Change What Was, filtered into his mind. It was a woman's voice.

Where are you? Ashe returned, looking around. He was alone in the plush, carpeted space outside the elevators.

You cannot see me now. You cannot recognize me in the future, when we meet for the first time.

Why?

Some things must happen as they will.

But, why am I here?

A better question would be when are you.

When am I?

You'll see.

The elevator doors opened, and Ashe blinked in surprise. Lissa—Winkler's Lissa—stood inside. Ashe boarded the elevator, determined to follow her.

"Going to the soda machine, too?" Lissa asked, as Ashe got off on the second floor of the hotel and walked with her.

"Yeah," Ashe nodded. He wanted to ask her about Winkler. Ask if she loved him. Tell her that Winkler still grieved for her. He didn't.

"This dollar isn't working," Lissa sighed after trying it for the fourth time. Each time, the soft drink machine spit out the crumpled bill in an electronic snit.

"Try this." Ashe dug in his pocket and pulled out another dollar—one that wasn't quite as crumpled or ragged around the edges.

"Thanks." Lissa smiled and traded her dollar for his. "Technology makes it impossible to buy orange soda," she quipped. "Film at eleven."

Ashe grinned. He and Lissa watched as the soda machine accepted Ashe's dollar and dropped a bottle of orange soda in the bin.

"Success," Lissa pulled the bottle out and unscrewed the cap. "Thanks again," she smiled and turned to walk away.

~

"Ashe, buddy, where did you go?" Trajan knelt beside the open car door as Ashe drew in a painful breath. He was back in the present, his hands gripping the wheel of Donald Workman's Cadillac.

"Winkler," Ashe turned to the Dallas Packmaster, whose face bore a worried frown, "This car belonged to Lissa's husband. Before he died."

"You're not kidding, are you?"

"Nope. She was funny, wasn't she?"

"And really smart."

"Mr. Winkler, take this." Ashe handed the crumpled bill he held to Winkler.

"What's this?" Winkler smoothed out the bill.

Something Lissa touched, Ashe replied mentally.

"Kid," Winkler almost unraveled.

"Mr. Winkler, I need to talk to you. In private," Ashe said, climbing out of the car.

~

"Matt, I'm sorry. Even you admit this child is powerful, and that he created the earthquake in Canada. There's no reason to believe that he isn't causing this mess, too. We don't have enough resources globally to handle the difficulties we're facing. We've got to stop this, and if one death will do it, then so be it." The President wasn't mincing words.

"It won't be just his death, it'll be ours," Matt hissed.

"I've already got cooperation from the Secretaries and Joint

Chiefs," the President ignored Matt's warning. "We're going in—today."

~

"Mr. Winkler, things are about to get worse," Ashe rubbed his forehead.

"What do you mean, worse?" Ashe had pulled Winkler, Trajan and Trace into his father's study.

"The nutcase in Washington—that Curtis Roberts guy?"

"Yeah, but how did you know—never mind," Winkler waved away the question.

"He's convinced the President to kill us all."

"What?" Winkler exploded from his seat. "I'm calling Matt. Right now," Winkler hauled out his cell phone.

"He won't answer. He can't. Roberts has convinced the President that Matt's helping to put all of us in jeopardy, so he's under house arrest."

"This is crazy," Winkler raked fingers through his hair.

"Crazy doesn't begin to describe all this," Ashe replied. "We'll be attacked later today, when they can get everything in position."

"What are they sending against us?" Trajan asked.

"Everything. They have no idea that if they manage to kill us, what's causing all this will only get worse, until the Earth disintegrates."

"Kid, you're scaring me."

"You think I don't feel scared? Mr. Winkler, I have decisions to make, and some people aren't going to understand them. You have decisions to make, and some of them I won't understand."

"Ashe, you're talking in riddles," Trace said softly.

"It's what my kind do. A lot."

"Your kind?"

"Yeah."

~

Six bodies surrounded Wildrif as he slept. He'd enjoyed killing after he'd wakened the night before, although the first human he'd taken had slaked his thirst. The last five; he'd merely enjoyed their screams as he ripped their bodies apart with long, sharp claws.

He'd been forced to sleep in his basement the moment sunrise came, although there was little light—New York was flooding under black clouds and heavy rains. The earthquake that came later in the day couldn't wake him—he was deep in the rejuvenating slumber any vampire experienced while the sun was overhead.

~

"What the hell?" Winkler stepped around body parts that were already turning rancid.

"Boss, this is insane." Trajan couldn't walk anywhere inside the darkened basement without stepping in blood.

"You'll have to remove his head," Trace muttered.

"No, I have another solution," Ashe said.

"Ashe, what are you gonna do, man?" Sali stared at Ashe. Somehow, in the past hour, Ashe had changed. Sali could almost feel the power pulsing from his best friend.

"There's one place where the sun is shining," Ashe muttered, his voice stern. "I have to go there, anyway."

"What do you need?" Trajan asked.

"Will you carry Wildrif's body for me?"

"Sure."

Trajan stepped through blood and gore to reach the newly turned vampire, who slept the sleep of his new race, curled up in a corner.

~

"What the hell is that?" Winkler stared at the dome of light in the meadow where Ashe had taken him and the others.

"Armageddon," Ashe replied, his eyes going dark. "The crowns have gone to war. Place Wildrif's body here," he gestured with his hands at the grassy clearing surrounding him. "I have Wildrif shielded for the moment."

"I've never seen a vampire die in sunlight," Trajan said, dropping Wildrif's body on the grass.

"You'll see it now. Back away, I'm about to remove the shield."

"Ashe?" Sali reached out to touch Ashe's arm.

"Back away, Sal."

Trace pulled Sali backward, until he stood twenty feet away from Wildrif's body. Ashe raised his arm. Wildrif's body jerked in the bright sunlight and he screamed.

~

"Ace, I'm afraid." Wynn buried herself in Ace's arms.

"I know, baby. I don't know what to do about any of this."

~

"Do you think it's the end of the world?" Dori asked. She cringed as the hailstones falling on the roof became louder, hammering the shingles and denting any vehicles left outside. The wind had picked up as well, blowing lawn furniture, trash carts and debris down the flooded street.

"I don't know," Lavonna said. "I wish your father were awake. Right now, I want to crawl into his shelter with him."

"Mom, we can't take any chances with Daddy. We can't expose him to any sunlight," Cori said.

"Mrs. Anderson, we'll ride this out," Marco said, pulling Cori against him and wrapping his arms around her waist.

"I know."

~

"That's it? That's all there is? Man." Sali shook his head. Wildrif's screaming had been brief, thankfully, and only a dusting of ash remained.

"Responsible for many deaths," Ashe said, his voice a rumble. His eyes were still dark as stars shot through their depths. "I must deal with the rest of it now." He began walking purposely toward the dome of light.

"Ashe?" Winkler called softly, knowing he would hear.

Stay where you are, Ashe's mental voice carried a command.

"Stay here," Winkler directed as Trace and Trajan attempted to follow Ashe.

"What's he doing?" Sali asked softly. Ashe's image became smaller as he walked farther away from them.

"Winkler?" Trajan turned to his Packmaster. "I could have sworn we were only half a mile away from that," Trajan pointed to the dome of light. It now appeared to be more than a mile from where he stood.

"What's happening?" Trace rasped, as the distance seemed even further than it had seconds earlier.

"I don't know," Winkler said. "Wait—where's Ashe?"

"I can't see him," Sali howled.

Baltis couldn't blink. Couldn't move. He had no care for Friesianna, although he vaguely realized that the same must be true for her. Light bathed them, covered them, pulsed through them. He was barely aware that the members of both races, Bright and Dark, now surrounded them.

All of them, willingly or not, had come. The gate, lying tantalizingly nearby, stayed shut. In some way, the crowns had seized it, just as they'd seized him and the Bright Queen. Inexorably, the crowns drew closer together, bringing Friesianna nearer and a terrible doom with her.

Rabis wanted to weep, but like the others surrounding him, he was held spellbound. Had he imagined that it might be this frightening? Struggling against the pull of the crowns, he attempted mindspeech. It echoed back to him, unsent.

Not only were the crowns pulling Baltis and Friesianna closer together, the Elemaiya, Bright and Dark, were now being drawn in, too. Rabis took a step against his will. And then another. His moan was plucked away in a strand of light.

Still furious at the events that had brought her and Baltis together, Friesianna was unwillingly pulled forward. Only a few feet separated her from the Dark King, and that space was shrinking rapidly.

The H'Morr hadn't described this—still she had no understanding of the crowns and why they seemed to be locked together. Wanting to curse, the force that held her prevented it. She wanted to blink at the blinding light gathered about her like a shroud and couldn't. Would she die? She cursed mentally at that thought and was forced forward another step.

A tear coursed down Rabis' cheek as Ashe brushed past him. He was getting a first glimpse of his grandchild, and grieved for the circumstances that brought them together. Another tear fell, and another.

Ashe, somehow, had neutralized some of the effects of the crowns, but that was fleeting. When the boy disappeared outside Rabis' vision, he could no longer blink, weep or call out. The power of the crowns pulled him forward again.

Ashe felt as he were buffeted by the winds of a hurricane, which became stronger the closer he strode toward the Bright Queen and Dark King, and threatened to knock him down.

There was no power to siphon away and add to his own; here, all of it was dangerous and tainted. The ones who separated the crowns had used a forbidden energy, and it affected everything around it. Loss of life had fed it in the beginning, and it had turned darker and more evil through the years.

Ashe only had the power he carried and that of the medallions circling his arm to combat the strength of the dark god and those who'd died to force one crown to become two.

"Boss, what's going on?" Trajan felt his words fall flat, as if they were suddenly too heavy to travel the short distance between him and Winkler. Everything had gone silent and still. Trajan was afraid to speak again.

Winkler blinked in confusion at his Second before shaking his head. The small gesture took a mighty effort and left Winkler nearly exhausted afterward.

Power and fury radiated from the crowns, as Ashe slowly made his way forward. Could he open the gates and get the Elemaiya away before dealing with the crowns? It would take a toll on the power he held, he realized. If he didn't, it was possible that all might die—the crowns wanted no part of him, and even now drew Baltis and Friesianna closer together. Once the crowns touched, everything would explode in a cataclysmic event he couldn't stop.

"The Vice President is safe, Mr. President. It's time to come to the bunker."

The President, who'd stolen a moment to stare out an Oval Office window, worried at the stillness outside. Rain had stopped abruptly, with no pattering of a few stray drops to mark a storm's passing. No, this was completely unnatural, and the skies had turned a frightening shade of green.

"Mr. President?" His chief of security was calling him away, preparing to take him to safety. *Or at least the illusion of safety*, the president snorted softly. Blinking once more at the strange skies outside, he turned away as Secret Service agents gathered about him.

～

Ashe knew it would cost him, and wondered how long it might be before he recovered. *If* he recovered. Griffin hadn't said it, when he'd given Ashe the story of the Three. Hadn't realized who, exactly, he'd been giving the story to.

It was moot—Ashe knew. He knew that if those of the opposition managed to defeat or turn any of the Three rogue, all would be destroyed and the rogue gods would easily win their victory. Two of the three had no hope of containing all of them—it was the way things were meant to be, all three of them working, not just together, but separately toward a common goal.

He wanted to sigh and knew he couldn't. Wanted to send mindspeech to those who mattered and knew he couldn't. All he could do was try his best, using what he had. Drawing in a painful breath, Ashe turned away from the crowns, forced his power toward the gate and cracked it open.

～

"Daryl, I've never seen anything like this." Weldon pointed his coffee cup toward the green sky overhead.

Daryl, Weldon's son, shook his head. "Me, either, Dad. This is scary as hell. If there was a way to get off the planet right now, I'd sure do it."

"Not an option," Weldon muttered. "Whatever this is, I get the feeling that it could kill us or change everything."

"Yeah."

Go. Through. The. Gate. Ashe grunted with the effort to keep the gate open wide enough to get a few through at a time, although they would have to lean down to struggle through it.

The power required to release the Elemaiya from the pull of the crowns was draining the medallions around his arm, too—and he wondered if he'd have anything left to deal with the crowns after he got the others away.

I am here, on the other side, filtered into his mind. A male voice. One he didn't recognize. Ashe blinked as the gate widened.

The Elemaiya, too, were suddenly moving faster, almost in a panic to get through the gate. Ashe could hear their shouts as they passed through—no sound would come from any throat until the other side was reached.

The crowns, though, saw their prey escaping. If Ashe thought they were expending all their strength, he was very wrong. The blast that emanated from them knocked him to his knees.

Do it now! The voice shouted desperately. *I am prevented from sending much power through. Take them now!*

With great effort, Ashe jerked his body toward Friesianna and Baltis. Reaching out, he *Pulled*.

"What the hell?" The dome of light had gone so bright Winkler had to cover his eyes with an arm before turning his back to it. The others were doing the same; blocking out the blinding light and turning away. The explosion that came immediately after deafened them, rocked the grassy surface beneath their feet and knocked them to the ground.

CHAPTER 19

"Look, I don't know how we got here." Winkler swore and raked a hand through his hair as he spoke with the Grand Master on his cell. "We must have blacked out. The last thing any of us remember is the explosion knocking us into the dirt. When we woke, we were on the floor in my media room."

"Ashe?"

"The kid's gone. That dome of light is gone. Everything is gone."

"Weather seems to be clearing up. Earthquakes have stopped and the sky is blue again," the Grand Master pointed out.

"I can't get any information on the attack, though. You think they're still planning to go through with this? I mean, Bear has more than three hundred extra shifters in that community, right now. At least the weather we had didn't kill anybody here. I already sent Sali, Trajan and Trace to Star Cove to help out—Ace and Marco were doing their best to guard the place, but two werewolves can't do much against Mother Nature."

"That wasn't Mother Nature and you know it," Weldon growled.

"I know."

"I've got a call in to some of mine to see if they can get information for us, but at the moment, we're going into this blind."

"If I get my hands on that Roberts jerk," Winkler's free hand clenched.

"Yeah."

"It doesn't matter that the problems seem to have stopped. We're still going in," Curtis Roberts snapped. "There's nothing to prevent the kid from doing this again. If he can do this to us, what else might he be able to do? Now," Curtis spread a map of the targeted addition in Star Cove across the hood of an armored vehicle, "My sources say this house is currently unoccupied," he tapped the image of the house nearest the gulf on the southern side. "My special agents and I will go over the back fence and see if we can help clear your way. The rest of you are scheduled to go in after the bombing stops. The bombers will arrive in half an hour. Be ready."

Curtis handed the map to the General who'd been reading over his shoulder. "Ready?" Curtis turned to the six he'd brought with him. It had taken some work to gather six known criminals and dress them as Special Ops, but they were now well armed and weren't afraid of killing anyone.

"Ready," one of the six growled.

"Let's go."

"I suppose you're wondering why all this happened?" Griffin sat in Winkler's guest chair the moment Winkler ended the call with the Grand Master.

"I want to kill you," Winkler growled.

"You won't. You can't. You know it." Griffin steepled his fingers.

"Fine. Enlighten me, then, since you seem to know so much."

"It has to do with two crowns and a thumbprint," Griffin sighed.

"Ashe said something about the crowns, but not about a thumbprint."

"There was one crown in the beginning," Griffin explained, his hazel eyes staring past Winkler's shoulder. "The god of the Dark Realm gifted it to the Elemaiyan Queen, who held him in reverence. He placed his thumbprint on the inside of the crown, to lend it power to protect the Elemaiya race."

"You're saying they were one race?"

"In the beginning. A Dark race. Like the vampires, werewolves, shapeshifters and a multitude of others."

"What happened? Why are there two crowns, now? Where is Ashe, now?"

"I don't know where Ashe is. Nobody does."

"Great." Winkler rose and turned his back to Griffin, staring through the window of his study.

"To answer your question on the two crowns, well, the Elemaiyan Queen had a consort. She offered him a crown, made by her craftsmen. He refused it. He wanted a crown with power, like hers. His refusal of her gift hurt her, but he wouldn't bend on what he wanted. Eventually, she gave in and had her crown divided, to make two crowns, hoping that each would wield equal power. The ones who accomplished this task for her employed forbidden spells and power. It corrupted the gold and tainted the god's power."

"Did they wield equal power after they were made?" Winkler asked.

"Yes and no. The god's thumbprint was divided as well, and as its purpose in the beginning was to protect the race from encroaching power, and with the taint affecting them afterward, each crown saw the other as a threat. They'd become individuals in their purpose, instead of working together as originally hoped. They destroyed the Queen and her consort, as well as the world given to them by Kifirin, the Dark god. The race barely managed to get away before everything was destroyed, but they were split—half defended the consort's actions, half sided with the Queen."

"How did they get the crowns back?"

"Each half of the race chose their own planets. One was called Morningsun, the other, Evensun. A crown appeared sometime later to one Elemaiya on each world, who named themselves Queen and King after that. The rest is a long story and is lost in time."

"That's why Ashe called it a chain reaction. Why he stopped them from killing each other in Canada. The crowns couldn't be close together."

"Not without destroying everything around them. Somehow, Ashe managed to stop it this time. I worry that it has cost him."

"Cost him? How? Is he dead?" Winkler stared at Griffin.

"I don't know. Nobody does."

"Look, I've got things to do. I may have to move an entire community in the space of—I don't know how much time we have," Winkler raked through his hair in frustration.

"You have fifteen minutes," Griffin's eyes unfocused.

Winkler shouted a curse as Griffin disappeared.

"Most of them are in a meeting inside that large building on the other side of the canal," Curtis hissed after one of the criminals asked where the targets were. "I was told we'd have protection—that we'd be able to get into the community easily and the ones here won't see, scent or hear us, but I don't know how reliable that might be. I'm not taking any chances. We'll go from house to house so we won't be seen, and take out the guard in that little shack up front, first."

"Not a problem. This'll be like old times." Curtis watched as the man's hands, encased in black leather gloves, clenched around the assault rifle he held. "Legal killing. I hope you'll let me know if I can do this again, sometime."

"Do this for me and I'll hire you and pay you more than you're making now."

"Good. Let's go."

Curtis smiled as this one took the lead.

Frank Dodd, Star Cove's werewolf History teacher, had volunteered to staff the guard shack while the shapeshifter meetings were held in the school auditorium. He'd spoken with Greta Rocklin twice already; she'd given him updates on how the meetings were going.

So far, most agreed that the shifters needed to band together, but not many could agree on how that might be accomplished or who might serve on the first council. He was still on the phone with Greta when he noticed a leaf, blowing in the wind, stop in midair for several seconds before flying away again.

"Greta, I have to go. Something doesn't look right."

"Let me know if you need help, Frank. We don't need problems when there are this many shifters with us."

"Agreed." Frank ended the call and stepped out of the small building. The werewolf history teacher's eyes widened as six invisible assault rifles fired and multiple bullets pierced his body. His attempt to shout a warning to the community died with him.

"Bombing strikes, Grand Master. In less than ten minutes." A government-employed werewolf informed Weldon Harper over the phone. "I just found out about this. There isn't any time and probably no way to get anyone out of there—I hear there are tanks, armored vehicles and police cruisers surrounding the community."

The Grand Master cursed. He wanted to destroy his study, too, but that would accomplish nothing. Every werewolf, shifter and vampire in Star Cove would be obliterated by bombers within minutes, and there was nothing he could do about it.

"Randy, a part of me is sorry your mother is dead. Another part of me is glad she's gone. You weren't there. You didn't see her." Sara held the cell phone to her ear as she spoke with Randy. "Why don't you meet me here for dinner? We can talk about this."

"Sara, I can't believe you said that—that you're glad she's dead."

"Randy, I see this is going nowhere. Look, the break in the meeting is over. I have to get back."

"You're just like the rest of them. I'm only an insignificant human. I won't ever be a werewolf or a shapeshifter and belong to that special clique."

"Randy, being either of those things carries its own stigma. You know that. I have to go." Sara hung up.

Randy cursed. Cursed the werewolves, shifters and finally, himself.

~

"Traje, I know you can't get them out in five minutes. Hell, I can't get you out in five minutes," Winkler moaned into his cell. "The Grand Master says that all the streets outside Star Cove are blocked by police and armored vehicles. Nobody can get out."

"They're aiming for the kid, and he's not even here. Are we expendable?" Trajan growled.

"I guess. Traje, you've been the best Second any Packmaster could ask for. Tell Trace, Marco and Ace they were the best. I'll go see your parents and try to explain."

"Thanks." Trajan ended the call and brushed tears away.

~

Sali sat on the concrete floor of the Evans' garage, staring at the Cadillac. As yet, he had no idea that his death was flying swiftly toward him. "Ashe, you were supposed to drive me down the highway in this," Sali wiped tears away. "We were supposed to be together, dude."

~

"Kill all of them," Curtis Roberts hissed as he and five of his six disguised criminals followed him into the school. The sixth had been sent to the back, to kill anyone escaping through the back door. "Auditorium is on the east side. Just stay with me. Once we're inside, open fire."

"With pleasure."

~

"I know you don't feel safe," Bear Wright agreed. He, Kerry Slater, Thurmon Novak and Opal Tadewi stood on the stage and spoke before the shapeshifter crowd as they discussed the future of their race. "I'm hoping that with a joint council, we can improve relations with the werewolves and the vampires."

"They have nothing but contempt for us," someone in the crowd stood and baldly stated. "I'll never trust them."

"I'm sorry for the interruption, Mr. Wright," Trajan strode inside the school auditorium, Trace, Ace and Marco close behind him. "The government has sent bombers to Star Cove, and they have tanks, police cars and who knows what else surrounding the community. They intend to kill all of us."

"What are you saying, son?" Bear jumped off the stage and strode toward Trajan. He, Trajan, Trace and Marco were the first to fall as bullets sprayed through the crowd.

~

"Gunshots?" Sali stood as the sound of assault rifles firing rapidly reached his ears, followed by panicked screams. "What the hell?" He hit the button to open the garage door and raced outside.

Only a few shapeshifters had managed to escape, and they were running through the streets in panic as an invisible force fired rifles. Sali turned to werewolf, ripping his clothing as he raced toward the sound of weapons firing. He died in the street, his werewolf's paws jerking after a bullet pierced his brain.

~

"Oh, no." Ashe appeared inside the school auditorium, and then slid down the wall, his fingers gripping his hair in grief and dismay. Trajan lay dead beside his brother. Cori and her mother were nearby, blood sluggishly leaking from a multitude of bullet wounds. Marco had died not far away, reaching for Cori. Dori had managed to get a little farther before falling and dying.

Ace died while attempting to shield Wynn and her mother. Then, Ashe's eyes settled on his mother's body. She'd died near Cori and Lavonna Anderson, her body crumpled and bloody.

He wanted to weep. Hundreds of shifters and werewolves, some Ashe knew, many he didn't, lay amid thick pools of blood. All of them dead. What had kept him from arriving sooner? He was too grief-stricken to sort it out. Ashe moaned as the hum of jet engines reached his sensitive ears. He rose, his eyes going as dark as midnight while stars burst in their depths. Ashe misted away.

~

"Did that boy turn to this?" One of Curtis' hired criminals kicked Sali's wolf.

"He did," Curtis smiled gleefully. "That was easy. We wiped out the whole community."

"Easy except for that one guy, who had a gun," a second criminal spoke up. He frowned while examining the bullet hole in his left arm. "Took him down, though, after he hit me. Good thing he couldn't see us. He might have done more damage. The woman who was with him turned into a swan and hissed in my direction. Do you believe that? Shot her, too." He laughed.

"You shot Mrs. Thompson. And my mother and Sali," Ashe appeared before Curtis and his thugs, his arms crossed angrily over his chest. Power vibrated from his body in dangerous waves, clouding and turning a purplish-black once it escaped his personal shields.

"He can see us," one of Curtis' gunmen pointed out.

"I can see you." Ashe's eyes were turning red.

"Well, well, well. Our target finally shows up," Curtis chuckled. "Get out of this, if you can." Six criminals fired their guns at Ashe.

~

"We only have one target, now? I thought there were two," the lead pilot sounded confused.

"I only show one target—that new addition in Star Cove. The rest of the community has been evacuated."

"This is so confusing," the pilot replied.

"One target. Bomb the hell out of it." The command came.

~

"We can't get through whatever is around him," Curtis snapped, after telling his thugs to stand down. A shield lay about their target, who continued to stare at all of them angrily, his eyes completely strange, the air about him vibrating dangerously.

"You won't get through to me, either," Ashe rumbled. The ground shook beneath Curtis' feet; Ashe's voice had gone as deep as any ocean.

"What's going on?" The lead gunman struggled to keep his feet when the ground shook harder.

"You're hopeless," Ashe roared. "All of you. Do you think you're going to get away with this? I can destroy everything!" He flung out his hands while lightning crackled and flew from his fingers.

"Those bombers are coming," one of the gunmen shouted, pointing eastward. "I can see them. We need to get out of here. Now!"

"You're not going anywhere. Go ahead and try," Ashe's words had become soft and deadly.

"I can't move," one of the gunmen wailed. His feet were stuck to the pavement beneath him.

"What are you doing?" Curtis only then thought to be afraid. He couldn't move his feet or legs, and the bombers were almost upon them. Star Cove was about to be obliterated, and him with it.

"Trying to decide how to torture you, so you'll suffer the most," Ashe growled. "I can keep you alive forever. Torture you forever," he added. "Is that what you wanted, when you did this?" Ashe swept an arm out, encompassing all of Star Cove's dead. "But before I do that," Ashe continued, "the Earth will fly apart. It will give me a great deal of pleasure to kill the planet that spawned you."

Winkler couldn't help himself; he stared at the television screen. News crews couldn't get close to Star Cove, but they stood behind barriers while tanks, armored vehicles and military personnel crowded the distance. What frightened him the most, however, was that the ground was shaking and thunder rumbled overhead. The sky outside the beach house was turning purple.

"Trajan, I'm so sorry," Winkler muttered, as bombs dropped on Star Cove in the distance.

CHAPTER 20

"I can't help you if you go rogue," her voice came. "Get yourself in hand and get rid of that trash quick, so I can do this."

Ashe turned and stared. The power he'd expended had been drawn back inside his body and his thoughts cleared, whereas only moments before, his anger had taken over and he'd been prepared to destroy everything.

Now, he was blinking in shock as the realization came that he'd almost destroyed something that wasn't meant to be destroyed. The shining woman had given him respite and clarity, before he could take a step that could never be reversed. The woman—the one who'd stood at a gate in his past—was standing at his side and shining brighter than he remembered.

"Who are you?" he stammered, suddenly feeling sixteen again. He hadn't been sixteen for a very long while.

"Somebody from the future. Put a shield over this place and get with it. All seven of these need to die."

"Yeah. They need to die, all right." Ashe turned back to Curtis Roberts, who was quaking where he stood. Ashe lifted his hands and all seven turned to sparks, beginning with Curtis Roberts.

~

"The bombs aren't hitting the streets. Something is stopping them," a microphone-wielding journalist reported as the ground shook beneath his feet. "Unfortunately, the repercussions of this seem to be affecting everything else around the target."

"What the hell?" Winkler stood and stared. The television camera showed bombs bursting in mid-air—as if a huge, transparent dome had been placed over that section of Star Cove.

~

"What now?" Ashe stared at the woman, who continued to shine brightly, preventing him from seeing her features.

"Now, I *Change What Was*." Ashe held an arm over his eyes as a sun seemed to burst around him.

~

Sali sat on the concrete floor of the Evans' garage, staring at the Cadillac. "Ashe, you were supposed to drive me down the highway in this," Sali wiped tears away. "We were supposed to be together, dude."

"Sal, get up." Ashe deposited Aedan's sleeping body on the back seat of the Cadillac. "I have to get Nathan and Casimir, and then we'll get out of here."

"What the?" Sali stared at Ashe. Ashe was older, that was easy enough to see. The short sleeve of Ashe's shirt pulled back, revealing a gold crown resting over the gold medallions circling his left arm. "Dude, what the hell is happening?"

"It was the only way, Sal." Ashe placed his father in an upright position as he spoke. "I had to take the crowns and send the Elemaiya away. I closed the gate in Kansas City against them. They'll never be able to come back here. If they don't have these, they can't do this shit again." Ashe pulled back his right sleeve, showing Sali the second crown. "As long as my body is between the crowns, they can't destroy anything."

Sali lifted himself off the garage floor as Ashe disappeared and the first bombs hit.

~

Trajan, followed by Trace, Ace and Marco, rushed inside the school auditorium and stopped in front of the stage. The tall werewolf was about to inform the school Principal that the community was under attack when the first bombs could be heard hitting the gulf water on the community's eastern edge.

"Star Cove is under attack," Ashe appeared beside Trajan and patted Trajan's shoulder affectionately. "Mr. Wright, I'm offering a way to escape and a safe place to live, but it means that nobody who goes with me can come back to Earth."

"What?" Bear breathed as more bombs exploded overhead.

"I have Star Cove shielded, but the shield goes when I go. Anybody left behind will die." Ashe's eyes had darkened.

"Son, somebody has to carry the message to the other shifters across the globe—that the shapeshifters need to unite and form their own council." Kerry Slater's voice held wonder as he stared at Ashe's eyes. Somehow, he wanted to trust that. To believe in it.

"I will allow one to go through my shield," Ashe's voice had turned deeper, his eyes darker while stars filled their depths.

"I'll go. Tell me how to get out." Bear nodded to Kerry and squared his shoulders.

"No." Opal touched Bear's hand with her own. "I can get past the others. My last name means wind, remember." She offered a trembling smile to Bear.

"Opal," Bear breathed a troubled sigh.

"I will go," Opal turned to Ashe.

"Ashe?" Cori had come to stand beside Marco, who'd gripped her hand and squeezed it. The bombing increased overhead, and the strafing of bullets joined the muted noise, making the crowd of shapeshifters gasp and stand in alarm.

"Cori, I'm taking the vampires, since they're asleep and can't make a decision for themselves," Ashe nodded at Cori's unspoken question. "I have a safe place for all of you, if you'll trust me and go to the street."

"Son, what are you planning?" Bear asked.

"I'll open a gate," Ashe replied softly. "Opal Tadewi, are you ready?" he turned to Opal.

"Yes."

"I will set you down outside my shield. Once you are on firm ground, run."

"I will," Opal promised.

Ashe's body glowed with power and Opal disappeared.

Go to the street and pass through the gate when it opens, Ashe spoke into every mind.

~

"Mom, Dad, we love you," Trace wiped tears away as he spoke to his parents on his cell. At least the call had gone through—the signal hadn't been lost.

"You think I'd forget your parents?" Ashe appeared and lifted the cell from Trace's hand. Trajan stood beside his brother—he'd heard his mother weeping when Trace made the call. "Mrs. Gibson, Mr. Gibson, *come*." An undeniable command lay in Ashe's voice, and Titus and Patricia Gibson appeared beside their sons.

"Mom," Trace embraced his weeping mother while Trajan hugged his father.

"Trajan, I'll need a Second where we're going," Ashe said softly. "And a Third. I want you and Trace to do that for me, if you're willing."

"Kid, for this, I'll do anything you want." Trajan let his father go and nodded to Ashe.

"It won't be a hardship, man," Ashe grinned.

"I guess you *can* fit three vampires in the back seat of a Cadillac," Sali muttered as Casimir's sleeping body was placed between Aedan and Nathan's. "Dang, how many bombs do they have?" More muted bomb blasts sounded overhead, making Sali duck instinctively. Ashe had appeared again, just as suddenly as he'd disappeared earlier, only this time he'd brought Casimir with him.

"Sal, get in the passenger seat. I told Mom to meet us out front."

"Where are we going, dude?"

"A long way from here." Ashe gripped the steering wheel, blew out the garage door with power and backed out quickly.

"Randy, this may be the last conversation we have," Sara said over her cell. "I get the idea we're going somewhere. Too bad you didn't pick up." Sara ended the call.

She and every shapeshifter and werewolf in Star Cove stood in the streets as bombs hit an invisible shield over their heads and rocked the ground beneath their feet. Many gasped and cried out as the bombing increased. A few screamed in terror as the end of the world seemed imminent.

"Flossie, I'm trusting the boy," Amos pulled Florence Thompson against his side. "He's never done anything to make me believe he'll hurt us. Those folks who sent those bombers," he lifted his eyes, "well, they're the ones who want to hurt us."

"I know." Flossie stood on her toes and kissed her husband's cheek. Amos reached out and wiped tears from his wife's face.

"Mom, Ashe says he's taking Daddy, Mr. Evans and Mr. Casimir," Cori's smile trembled as she gazed at her mother. "He can shield them, so they'll be safe."

"I hope so," Lavonna hugged her oldest daughter. "Did he say where he's taking us?"

"He only said we'll be safe. If we stay behind, we'll die." Cori had to raise her voice; the noise of the bombs was getting louder.

"Then we'll go," Lavonna nodded determinedly, although her eyes were filled with tears.

~

"Well, Lewis, I hope you're not leaving anything important behind," Bear clapped Lewis Sharpe on the back.

"No. I'm glad I came," Lewis said. "The kid saved my life. I'm willing to trust him, now."

"Me, too," Bear agreed. "I wish they'd stop dropping those blasted bombs." Heavier bombing was taking place as Bear and Lewis walked out of the Star Cove auditorium together.

~

"Ace?" Wynn touched Ace's face. He grasped her fingers and kissed the palm of her hand.

"Baby, we have to trust Ashe."

"I know."

Turn and go through the gate quickly when it opens, the voice commanded inside their heads.

Wynn gasped. She, Ace and her parents stood at the rear of a large crowd of werewolves and shapeshifters, who became their animals in a tremendous ripple.

"Baby, it'll be the first time we've run together," Ace offered Wynn a lopsided smile.

"Yeah. Let's go." In seconds, a white werewolf stood beside the only unicorn shapeshifter on Earth.

Run, the voice commanded. They ran.

~

"Honey?" Adele said as she was squeezed between Ashe and Sali in the Cadillac's front seat.

"We'll be okay, Mom," Ashe said. "Ready, Sal?" Ashe leaned forward to give Sali a curious glance.

"Yeah. Ready."

"All right, then." Ashe let the Cadillac idle while he lifted his hands over his head and then let them down slowly. Light appeared before the crowd of shapeshifters and werewolves running in the street, before spreading out to reveal a gate.

Run! You'll find safety on the other side, Ashe's voice filtered into every mind.

"Man, what is that? Through that opening?" Sali craned to see over the crowd of animals before them.

"You'll see." Ashe placed the car in gear and drove forward.

~

Opal ran. As a velociraptor, she could move almost as fast as her name implied. She needn't have worried—somehow, she was protected. She felt it. Knew it in some way. Racing past police cruisers and armored vehicles, she picked up their communications. Many had guns or more deadly weapons trained on Star Cove. Some were firing. Their bullets were bouncing off the invisible shield and exploding in bright flashes of light.

He was right—they really do want to kill all of us, Opal thought as she ran.

When the time is right, filtered into her thoughts, *someone will come for you.*

Thank you. Opal did her best to reply mentally to the message.

You're welcome, came the response.

"Well, look at you, you little rogue godling, you."

Calhoun quailed in her presence. She shone like the sun as she approached his desk. "Who—are you?" he quavered.

"Don't play dumb with me." Her voice had turned deadly. "You thought you'd get away with this. Pretended to be human, to escape notice. Attempted to destroy Earth by using that idiot Curtis Roberts and your evil little snipe, Wildrif. You have to answer for that, you know."

"But I am human," Calhoun claimed, taking a step backward.

"Huh. Too bad for you. You think I'd settle for killing your human body while your spirit flies free to cause trouble somewhere else? Think again."

"Wait, don't you want to know who helped me?"

"And take the chance that they'll show up to help you again while you do the usual blithering that every criminal does at the end? No, thanks."

Calhoun wailed as he was transported elsewhere.

The dome shield disappeared slowly behind the Cadillac as it drove forward. The Last of Star Cove's shifters and werewolves, permanent and temporary, ran or flew through the shining gate ahead of Ashe.

"Ready, Sal?" Ashe gunned the engine.

"Ready."

Ashe left tire marks as he sped forward.

"What do you mean, no bombs hit the community until everybody disappeared?" The President stared at the Air Force General, who stood before his desk.

"Just what I said. Our bombers report that the bombs were hitting an invisible shield overhead and exploding. They also report sightings of several hundred people gathering on the streets below, before weird things happened. We didn't hit anything, Mr. President, until they were gone. I'm telling you the truth—some kind of light appeared and they were just—gone."

"Gone where? I had no idea so many were in that community. Where was the intel on this?"

"We were given bad information, sir. Curtis Roberts, the one who provided the intel, has also disappeared."

"Keep looking for him. Let Matt Michaels go. Maybe he can help us with this."

"Of course, sir."

Sali gaped about him as the brightest light shone and then suddenly disappeared. Ashe allowed the car to roll to a gentle stop.

"Welcome back." Sali gaped at the tall, blue man who greeted them as the Cadillac idled in a grove of trees planted neatly in rows.

"Ashe?" Adele gasped as she stared at the tall, blue-skinned male.

"Don't be afraid," Ashe said. "Mom, Sali, this is Renegar," Ashe grinned. "He's Larentii."

"How did it go?" A man stepped around Renegar and smiled at Ashe.

"Went fine, Edward," Ashe replied.

"Edward?" Sali hadn't recognized him at first—he, like Ashe, seemed older.

"Hey, Sali." Edward's face split in a wide grin.

"Officials report that millions were funneled through Curtis Roberts' office, as payments were made to known criminals for trivial amounts of information," The journalist announced on the late news, while photographs of Star Cove, showing that the community had been completely destroyed, were displayed on the television screen.

"Rumors are running wild across the Internet and all social networks, and most indicate that innocent people were targeted in this bombing raid, because of faulty intelligence. No bodies have been found, but anonymous sources report that the community was occupied when the bombing began. Word from the Oval Office is that this is a tragedy and an embarrassment to the nation, as few thought to question Roberts' methods of gathering intelligence, his spending habits or those he associated with."

"Old news," Winkler growled as he hit the remote button to turn off the television. He'd moved back to his home between Denton and Dallas, making Buck his temporary Second while Wayne's training was accelerated.

Winkler missed Trajan, Trace, Ace and Marco, but as no bodies were found when the bombing was stopped two months earlier, he had hopes that somewhere, they were still alive. He knew, too, that he might never see them again. Inexplicably, Trajan and Trace's parents had also disappeared.

"You were right, kid," Winkler muttered, powering off his computer for the night. "You did have decisions to make that some people aren't going to understand." He reached for the lamp, to turn it off as well when a cream-colored envelope dropped onto his desk.

"What the hell?" Winkler stared at the envelope for several seconds, a worried frown crossing his features. Finally, he reached out to pick it up. Two items dropped out. He studied the photograph, first, as a wounded sigh escaped his lips.

Lissa was richly dressed in an evening gown, while a jeweled tiara graced her head and sparkling diamonds hung from her ears. Two wide-shouldered men who looked to be Asian by birth escorted her. Both wore their hair in long, black braids.

"What the hell?" Winkler repeated as he unfolded the accompanying note. It held only two words.

She lives.

EPILOGUE

AFTERMATH

By
Randall Smith

For twenty years, I have lived with my loss. I go to work every day. I come home every day.

Empty.

It is a derogatory term, employed by werewolves and shapeshifters. I'd been called that word when I was young. I hadn't really known what it meant. I know its meaning all too well, now.

The werewolves and shifters whisper the story of Star Cove to their children. That one day, some were carried away. Nobody knows where or how, only that it happened. The story has become a tale of magic. Of hope. That somewhere, there's a community of werewolves, shapeshifters and vampires, living together in peace and prosperity, watched over by an unassailable strength. At times, I hope the stories are true. That Sara is with them, living a happy existence. Afterward, I curse my shortsightedness. My inability to see past my weaknesses. My willingness to turn blindly away from the truth.

Randy tapped his pen against the pad of paper, considering what to write next. He sat at his desk inside a Chicago apartment—a far cry from the one he'd had when he'd first started working for the Chicago newspaper. Several journalism awards littered a shelf on the wall behind his desk. They meant nothing to him.

"Hello, Randy."

Randy dropped the pen as he gaped at Ashe. A much older Ashe than the one he'd last seen stood before him. A beautiful woman stood at Ashe's side. Her long, black hair hung in waves about her shoulders and her piercing blue eyes offered Randy a smile filled with salvation.

"What—Ashe?" Randy could barely form a coherent thought.

"Randy, this is Kalia," Ashe introduced his companion.

"Uh, hello," Randy scooted his chair back and held out a hand. Kalia took it.

"Call me Kay," She said, her voice and demeanor quite shy.

"Kay," Randy nodded as politely as he could.

"Kay's here to give you what you want," Ashe grinned. "I'm here to take you home."

"But—what?"

"Sweetheart, do you see his lines? See the dormant werewolf lineage?" Ashe placed a protective hand on Kay's shoulder.

"I see it," she nodded. "Don't worry," she assured Randy, her blue eyes studiously examining the air around his head. "I can see past aura colors, to the lines making up those colors. I can change your aura lines. It won't hurt. You'll be werewolf in a few seconds." She nodded, attempting to calm his fears.

Randy gulped as the air around Kay began to glow. He felt heat wash through him. Something was happening. Painless lightning coursed through his body, and he wondered at it.

"There, all done." The light around Kay disappeared. "Don't worry; I can only change things with people. I can't *Change What Was*. That takes more power than I will ever have. Ashe says it saved him, once." She offered Randy a lovely smile.

"Now, Randall Smith, are you ready?" Ashe asked as his eyes darkened and stars filled their depths.

"Uh, I guess. Where are we going?"

"You'll see."

Ashe's Journal

Randy went to his knees in the groves the moment he saw Sara. She hadn't aged a day since he'd last seen her, and he wrapped his arms around her waist and wept while she stroked his hair. I can only imagine that Trajan, Trace and the others will welcome him into their Pack come the full moon.

There was a time, though, when I almost turned rogue. Had been manipulated to do so. That would have been disastrous. If I hadn't had help then, all might have been lost. The shining woman, too, has disappeared. None have seen her since I left Earth behind. She'd said she was from the future, but I have no idea how far that future might be.

Meanwhile, Ren and I have built a small city for the ones taken from Star Cove. No, there is no gulf—no beach here for them. We are on the Southern Continent of the planet known as Avendor, and we are surrounded by gishi fruit groves. I have used my power to keep all inside the boundary of SouthStar Groves safe. As long as they stay here, they will never age. I have decreed it. I have that power.

I am Ashe Evans.
I am Ir'Indicti.
I am the Mighty Hand.

The End.